Tales from

Half Moon Room

Booklocker.com, Inc.
2011

First Edition

Tales from
Half Moon Room

A compilation of short stories and poetry from
writers instructed and inspired by Jordon Pecile at
Manchester Community College, Manchester, CT

By

Fred T. Blish, III
Tracy Blythe
Felix Giordano
Beth Hillson
Esther McCune
Janice McCune
Tom Panaccione
Barbara Passmore
Dave Porteous
Bob Sessions
Joan Sonnanburg
Stacey Stone

Jordon's Twelve

We are a group of writers unleashing our voice to readers wishing to lend an ear. Our teacher and mentor, Jordon Pecile taught creative writing classes at Manchester Community College in Manchester, Connecticut. We learned much from Jordon and it is evident that he helped us grow as writers. Of all his students who came and went twelve of us remained in contact with one another once Jordon retired in 2009. We decided to gather our short stories and publish them as a group. We began working on this project and met as an ongoing writers group naming ourselves *Jordon's Twelve*. In less than a year, we polished off our short stories and submitted them for this collection.

D299, the classroom at Manchester Community College where we attended Jordon's creative writing classes formed the shape of a half moon. A straight wall on the left side of the room complimented by a semi-circle of floor to ceiling windows to the right provided the perfect name for our book.

In *Tales from Half Moon Room*, you will find stories about growing up, romance, relationships, travel, adventure, fantasy, comedy, tragedy, and drama. In short, everything that makes up our human experience. These are stories written from the heart in ways that demonstrate how we as individuals interact with one another in all the many inspiring, heartbreaking, and fascinating ways that people do and how we mature because of our experiences.

Table of Contents

Frederic Thomas Blish, III

July 10, 1933 – October 25, 2010

In September 2010 at a luncheon in honor of Jordon Pecile, our writing teacher and mentor in Manchester Community College's Continuing Education program in Manchester, Connecticut, fellow classmate Fred Blish challenged us. Fred, a prolific writer as well as an actor, stage designer, director, founder, and generous contributor in all aspects of the Little Theatre of Manchester, suggested that we as a group compile our best short stories into a book format and have it published.

We accepted Fred's challenge and targeted a completion date of early 2011. Sadly, Fred Blish passed away before he saw this project to its conclusion. We regrouped, set our priorities, and with Fred's life-long zeal for the arts as our motivation, it is now complete.

Fred, we dedicate this book to you.

Books by Fred T. Blish, III

Five Minutes to Curtain – a summer theatre in 1955 through a Broadway debut

The Second Season – running a summer theatre in 1956

ACT III – renovating an old movie theatre in Boston in the 1950's

What We Did For Love – the 50-year history of the Little Theatre of Manchester told through the eyes and soul of one of its founders

Untitled
by Fred T. Blish, III

My mom is the most incredible lady! I mean, like she is awesome! Do you know what she did? Last Monday night, she goes to the Board of Education meeting – you know like – when they are going over the budget for the next school year. She waits until they open it up for public comment and then she makes a couple of suggestions how they could save some money. Hey, she had done her homework, so it's not like these ideas came right off the top of her head. She had studied the budget before the meeting.

Anyway, what happens is that her ideas get shot down. The superintendent of schools tells her they couldn't do what Mom suggested and my Mom says, "Why not?" And the superintendent says because of the teacher's union. Well, my Mom asks her to explain and then the Chairman of the Board says, "You obviously don't understand." "You're right," my Mom says. "That's why I'm asking her to explain what she meant about the teacher's union. "You're thinking like a housewife," the Chairman says. "Let's move on to the next item."

Kapow! He says it just like that. See, he doesn't know my Mom and before he can bring up the next items, my Mom gives a little speech. She says, "I *am* a housewife and I run my house on a budget and I have to look for ways to save money all the time and that's what I'm doing right now – looking for ways to save money. The article in the newspaper said this was an open budget meeting so you could hear what the public thinks. That's why I came – to tell you my ideas for saving money and cutting the budget without taking away critical classroom programs."

Then he says, "Well, thank you for expressing your opinion, but what you've suggested is impossible, so we're going to go on to the next item."

I'm up in my room, working on my homework when Mom gets home. Dad is watching TV. I hear the door slam as Mom comes in and then I hear her telling my father how she was never so insulted in her life and she tells him what happened. See, one thing you should know

1

is that before she went to the meeting, she and Dad had discussed her ideas and Dad thought they were good ways to save some big money.

Anyway, Dad tries to calm her down. He tells her to sleep on it because it may look different in the morning. And Mom says, "I'll show them what a housewife can do. I'm going to run for the Board of Education."

Dad says, "Honey, I don't think that's such a good idea." I agree with Dad. Can you imagine the crap I'm gonna take from my teachers if my Mom is on the Board of Education, especially if she's going after the teacher's union?

Dad tells her that neither one of them is even registered with a political party and there's no way she could possibly run as an independent and ever hope to win and Mom asks him why not. Dad says, "You need an organization to back you. You need money to run a campaign and I don't care how hard you work, you won't be able to do it on your own."

"Okay," Mom says and then she asks Dad what party the Chairman belongs to and Dad says he's a Democrat.

"I figured as much," Mom says. "He's a liberal snob and the teacher's union has probably got him right in their back pocket." When she says that, I know I'm in trouble if she gets on the Board!

At breakfast the next morning we're all reading the newspaper – Dad has the funnies, I'm reading the sports page, and Mom has the local news. Suddenly, Mom explodes! "Listen to this," she says. "There was a reporter at the meeting last night and this is what he wrote, and I quote, 'One local housewife was put in her place by the Chairman of the Board when she suggested cuts in the school budget that would be impossible to implement because of the union contract.' How do you like that?"

Calmly, Dad says, "You know that paper leans so far to the left it's in danger of tipping over."

"Fine," Mom says, "But that belongs in the editorials, not in a news story. Then she tells Dad that as soon as she gets the dishes done she's going down to Town Hall and register as a Republican. You know what? She did too. She finds out who is the head of the Republican Party in town, she meets with him, and he says they are looking for candidates and since Mom is so well known in town, she would be a person they would consider as a possible candidate.

That night at dinner, Mom is all excited about running for office. She tells us she spent the afternoon lining up her friends, which means the two groups of ladies she plays bridge with, all of whom have said they would support her. Mom says they were just as angry and upset as she was about the way she was treated.

She must have been on the phone for hours, because by the end of the week she had contacted everybody on the Republican nominating committee and had received enough endorsements to be sure she would be nominated. Then she began to lobby the other members of the organization to make sure they voted for her at the meeting on Wednesday night.

By now, you can see that when my Mom makes up her mind that she is going to do something she is like a whirlwind of wild horses. Nothing is going to stop her.

On Wednesday, dinner is ready and on the table when Dad comes in the door from work. Beside each placemat on the table is a brochure with Mom's picture. She is wearing a nice, neat dress. It's not fancy at all and she has on an apron over the dress. Printed on the front of the apron are Mom's name and the words *The Housewife Candidate*. I look up at Mom as she brings the salads to the table. She has the same dress on that's in the picture.

After we say grace, Dad asks if she is going to change before the meeting.

"Nope. I'm wearing this dress. All I have to do is put on my apron and I'll be ready," Mom says. "I didn't put it on because I was afraid I might spill something on it."

Dad smiles. "You're really going to do this, aren't you?"

"You bet I am and I'm going to win too."

Now I am really worried because if Mom wins, I know what's going to happen to me, especially if Mom takes on the teachers union. I'm gonna take it from my teachers and also from my friends. This is turning into a personal disaster!

Mom says, "I want you and Dad to come to the meeting tonight with me."

"We're not on the Republican Town Committee," Dad says. "I'm not even a party member."

"You will be after tonight," Mom says. "The Chairman told me it would be a good thing if my family supported me and I told him that you would."

"What about me?" I ask. "I'm not even old enough to vote."

"That's okay. I just want you there to show them that I have the full support of my whole family."

Dad looks at me and shrugs his shoulder. "Come on, son," he says. "We better go up and change. It looks like we're going to get our initiation into town politics tonight."

I thought I'd be bored to death, and for a while, I was. They nominate four people for the Board of Directors first. It looks like a set-up to me. They all gets one-hundred percent of the votes, like they knew before they even got to the meeting that that would happen.

Then it's Mom's turn. After she's nominated, there are all kinds of speeches saying what a good person she is. Mom is all smiles. Then it gets exciting. The Vice Chairman stands up and says he's not sure she's right for the job. Suddenly, the whole atmosphere in the room changes. Mom is not smiling anymore. Then a couple of more people challenge her nomination. Now it's getting exciting.

Mom stands up and asks to be recognized and the Chairman calls her to the front of the room. Mom explains how she thinks the members of the Board of Education have lost their perspective. She says they are acting like there is a bottomless pit of money and it is their duty to spend as much of it as they can. "Times are tough," she says. "I intend to make them understand that they have to be more inventive and find ways to do more with less."

There is some applause when she says this.

Mom ends by saying that if she is nominated she will work hard to win the election and she says, "I will win a seat on the Board."

Someone calls for a vote and someone else says, "I'll second that." The Chairman asks everybody who supports Mom to stand. It looks to me like about half the people on the committee stand up. It's gonna be a squeaker. He counts the people standing. Then he asks those opposed to stand and he counts them. It's a tie vote.

4

Then he asks for any abstentions and three people stand.

Editor's Note: this work by Fred Blish is untitled and unfinished. Fred was working on this piece when his untimely departure for dressing rooms, stage sets, and theatre box offices of a higher calling was requested of him. Knowing Fred, one can expect that he planned plot twists, surprises, and humor for this family.

Ode to an Oak by Fred T. Blish, III, June 6, 2009 on Green Hill

O grand and stately oak, standing tall against the sky,
What histories you must have seen in your long life!
Did you spring from an acorn stepped upon
By some Pequot as he strode across the land,
Long before our forefathers discovered this verdant hill?

I like to think that's the way you began.

First, no more than a single twig with tiny leaves,
Fighting with others just to stay alive
And ultimately winning the victory.
Your roots spreading outward and down deep into the soil
While your trunk grew strong,
Boldly thrusting branches like arms,
As you grew in majesty.

Each autumn your leaves turned
From green to yellow to brown
Before dropping to the ground,
Leaving your branches bare
To hold the winter snows.

And then each April you come alive
With tiny buds and lace-like leaves
That burst into full growth
With the first warm days of spring,
Announcing that summer will soon begin.

Year after year, after year, after year, you grow,
Until now you tower over all else,
Blocking the sun's rays,
Demanding that all pay homage.
You are indeed a grand and stately oak!

My Friend Fred
by Bob Sessions

Recently I attended a memorial for Fred Blish. I really listened to all the stories about Fred. At the end, I realized what a unique bond Fred and I had. I would like to share it with you.

Fred and I developed our friendship during the first several years of going to Jordon's classes. Then one tragic event changed everything.

My adult son died. He died alone, in his apartment, during a drug overdose.

When Fred heard about that, he was on the phone to me like a flash. He shared with me the story of how he lost a son in the same way.

That one kindness wasn't the end by any stretch. Fred continued to guide me and support me for months to come.

During that time, I found out how wonderful it was to have a big brother. Long after the surface pain had passed Fred and I still met weekly just for fun and talked frequently.

Fred's greatest attribute was he really listened. He made me feel that I was the only thing that mattered. He never tried to change the subject, glance at his watch, or mention something else he had to do.

From all this I have made a conscious effort to treat my younger brother like Fred treated me.

Thanks Fred!

Remembering Fred Blish
with Deep Affection and Appreciation
by Esther McCune

Fred was our Concert Master. Before each "performance", he sounded his A, turning up the players, urging us to begin. He was a proficient performer managing the intricacies of Vivaldi's concerti with their dramatic contrasts of color, harmonies, and dynamics. This we heard as Fred took us behind the scenes of theatrical productions to meet manipulative and heartless divas, aspiring young actors, and callous power brokers.

We all fell under the hypnotic glow of the "ghost light," and grew to understand why so many are passionately in love with the theater.

As Fred composed his themes and variations his "scoring" was vigorous and clear. Melodies were as warm and winning as those of Fritz Kreisler. Because Fred's work was tightly focused and beautifully tuned, he was able to achieve an artistic whole.

That we are following his lead would have brought him naught but pleasure. How lucky we were to have Fred in our midst.

For Fred T. Blish
From Janice McCune

I first met Fred in 2005 in writing class. He was writing vignettes about a young actor, Jack Crawford. I saw Fred again in 2010 at a writing class reunion. By that time, Fred had chronicled Jack Crawford's adventures in three printed novels: *Five Minutes to Curtain, The Second Season, and Act III*. Three novels in five years – that was inspiring! And Fred not only inspired his fellow writers with his actions, but also with his words. He was full of encouragement for each of our writing projects and during that reunion lunch is when Fred suggested we organize and put together this book you are reading right now.

I always learned something new from Fred. I benefited so much from his wealth of knowledge and experience and his joyful and enthusiastic personality. I left the writing class reunion with a task list he gave me. We were talking about great films and he wrote down three must-sees on a napkin: *The Third Man, Bert Rigby You're a Fool* and *Red Shoes.*

As of June 2011, I still need to watch those films, but I have read all three novels about Jack Crawford. There's an openness and enthusiasm for life Jack possesses that always makes me think of Fred. Fred played a glorious role on the stage of life – pursuing his dreams full-tilt and being present in each simple moment.

"He knew his role was only a tiny part of the whole, but it was each speech, each gesture and movement – each actor – that brought the playwright's story to life…" *Five Minutes to Curtain*

Tribute to Fred
by Barbara Passmore

Fred Blish had a voice. Fred had stories he wanted to tell and no one was going to change them. I liked the way he was true to himself. The thing I admired most about Fred was his persistence. He worked at his writing and saw to it that his stories were published. Fred encouraged other writers to finish their stories, so when I procrastinate, putting writing off to another day, I try to remember Fred's example.

Fred Blish as Inspiration and Leader
By Dave Porteous

One of the most powerful and passionate forces in our evolution as a writing group was Fred Blish. A leader in the Little Theater of Manchester since its beginning and a man who could take, use, and give critical commentary on all of our writing, Fred was an inspiration. His heartfelt greetings whenever we gathered in class at Manchester Community College, or when we met in his home for informal writing groups, was always uplifting.

Fred's spirit and example with his prolific and skillful books live on in my life, my writing, and our work together as writers. I am thankful for all that he, and Mary, his wife and our supporter as a group in their home, gave to us over the years. We were blessed to have Fred in our writing lives.

Thank you for always being there for all of us, Fred.

Dedication to Fred Blish
By Joan Sonnanburg

Fred exuded energy, passion, focus, good will and a desire to get things done. His presence in a writing class was positive and palpable. He had an encouraging word for everyone and was a model of hard work and perseverance, publishing four novels while the rest of us struggled to produce a short story or two. This book was his idea and the force of his personality has propelled it to fruition.

A Tribute to Fred Blish
by Felix Giordano

I met Fred Blish in one of Jordon Pecile's creative writing classes. As I grew to know Fred, I learned that he was involved in many interests. Fred's writing centered on the theater but his real passion was the Little Theatre of Manchester of which he was a founding member.

Fred would offer brutally honest critiques of my work and I of his. He once posed a challenge to me of trying to finish our novels together. I was able to keep up with him for a few weeks but then I was amazed at how prolific his writing became. Fred far out surpassed me both in quantity and quality of work. I thought to myself, I'm still employed while Fred's retired so how could I expect to keep up with him. Little did I know that his involvement with the theater equated to more than a full-time job in and of itself. He designed and constructed sets, wrote plays, acted, directed, and offered support and expertise to others involved with the Little Theatre of Manchester. Through all this, Fred was very humble and an example for us all.

Fred, even though you have made your final encore on this Earthly stage and passed on to greater places your suggested revisions are still in my writings and your creative talents live on in your novels.

Godspeed my friend.

Jordon Pecile
by Tracy Blythe

In mid-March 2007, I moved from England to Connecticut. Two weeks later, I found myself sat in a Creative Writing Class at Manchester Community College with Jordon as my tutor. He scared me to start with. He told us all off for not making notes. We all scribbled furiously from then on! At the time, I didn't realise what I was learning but looking back I realise how lucky I was to have met Jordon when I did. He made everyone feel interesting, like they had a real story to tell. I clearly remember one woman bemoaning her boring life, which Jordon immediately dismissed as ridiculous. Within minutes, with his encouragement, she was recounting a fascinating tale of the group dynamic on a recent trip to Maine. He treated all subject matters as valid and equal from my happy-go-lucky romantic comedies to a fellow student's tales of prostitutes who castrated their pimps. He pushed as all to comment on each other's work forcing us to recognise what worked and what didn't, forcing us to realise how our own styles differed making us strive to maximise our uniqueness.

But most of all he made us write. He made us write week in week out. I started Jordon's class having never written fiction before. He made me think I could. He made me write. He made me think I was good. Now I am a published author. A dream come true. Thank you Jordon.

Why I Write
by Tracy Blythe

Prior to having children, I was lucky enough to enjoy a career in marketing which provided me with a diverse range of experiences from trying to convince Russia to wear Hush Puppies to testing roller coasters on behalf of the UK's leading theme parks. When my husband relocated us to Connecticut, I decided to seize my chance and try my hand at writing that book I always said I wanted to. With a four-month-old baby under my arm and a blind eye to a mountain of housework, that's exactly what I did. I soon found that I loved the escape it provided. To have my mind totally immersed in a different world for a couple of hours a day kept me sane quite frankly. I love the problem solving challenge as you try and piece together the right characters in the right places at the right times to make a story that you hope eventually will slot together as one and pull you along with its own force. But most of all I love the rare occasions when you feel like you have nailed it. When a sentence appears that so clearly communicates what you are trying to say that you can't help but stare at it for some time knowing that you have just put together a string of words that are totally unique to you, that wouldn't exist without you, that you are proud to call your own.

What was my escape is now my job. The book I wrote will be published in four countries this year and so I am hard at work on the next one. This has made me realise that the other reason why I like to write is to entertain. I have been lucky enough to have watched people read my words and laugh out loud. What a feeling that is.

A Costume Drama
by Tracy Blythe

"So did they tell you what happened to the last one?"

"Last what?"

"Last Wonder Bear."

"No."

"Killed himself."

"He didn't."

"He did."

Short silence

"How?"

"Stabbed himself with Pirate Sam's Magic Dagger."

Slightly longer silence

"Where?"

"In the Enchanted Forest just behind the talking toadstools."

"Actually I meant where on his body?"

"Oh I see. In the chest. Just here look. See that patch there. Took me two bottles of bleach to get all the blood out."

Very long silence.

Clare finally took a deep breath and dared to look down at the Wonder Bear suit that Elsie from the costume department was fitting on her. She immediately noticed a section of sunshine yellow fake fur that looked somewhat flatter and more worn than the rest, on the left side of the chest. And when she looked really hard she could see a row of perfect tiny white stitches deep in the fur, done as precisely as a surgeon closing a wound.

She glanced back at Elsie wondering if she was being wound up as part of some sort of new employee initiation but Elsie was probably in her sixties and surely past such juvenile antics.

"Do you know why he did it?" she asked.

"He saw something," replied Elsie. "Something he shouldn't have seen that tipped him over the edge, you mark my words. You'll see. The minute you put on this costume you become invisible and it's unbelievable what you see when you're invisible."

Being invisible had in fact proved to be perfect for Clare. Starting a new job after recovering from her illness had been daunting and being able to just disappear amidst The Wonderland Theme Park and pretend she was a different person (or bear) was her ideal job. On top of that, she got to make every kid's day that ran through the gates in hot pursuit of a hug from the one and only Wonder Bear. All day she was surrounded by over sugared children pulling her, mauling her, jumping on her and sometimes even biting her in their hyped up excitement. But she didn't care. She loved it. Unable to have children of her own she craved the unfettered affection reserved for family members and costume characters. Every kiss on her furry yellow cheek, every tiny hand in her off white paw, every bear hug around an under three foot high frame was like balm to her wasted heart.

And Elsie had been right about another thing. It was unbelievable what you see when you are invisible. Clare found the goings on of people who believed they were unseen both shocking and surprising. Some of the personal hygiene habits she witnessed made her want to retch inside her bear head cocoon. And hormone pumped teenagers really should be banned from manhandling each other in ways that lead to hands disappearing into clothing. But what really shocked Clare were her observations of parent child relationships when they believed they were not being watched. On more than one occasion, she looked on horrified at slapping, hitting, and repeated threats. And that was the parents, not the children. For the recipients of such childish behavior she reserved her extra special Wonder Bear hug. She would sit down on a bench, not an easy task with a nearly three-foot wide bottom, and take the child on her knee and surround them with her bear arms like a protective shield. Then she would rock them gently until the smile returned to their face. The joy would be short lived, as inevitably an ungrateful, impatient father would drag them off to go to ride coasters that terrified them but thrilled their selfish parents. Clare would fight the desperate urge to chase after them and offer to take home their unwanted children and care for them how they deserved to be cared for.

By a childless woman with enough love for all the unwanted children of the world.

Not all parents were like this of course Clare observed. Some were models of good parenting and Clare found herself making mental notes of any particular techniques or phrases that were impressive. For in her heart of hearts Clare knew that one day she would care for a child. She didn't know how but she would. It was her reason for being. On this particular day she watched in awe as a mother pulled out a pink, princess band-aid that miraculously dried up tears as well as patched over bloody scratches sustained by an overzealous three year old who'd hurled herself at Wonder Bear and missed. The woman's calming voice was pitch perfect for soothing a bawling toddler and Clare smiled at her from within her bear head knowing that that was the type of mother she wanted to be.

As she watched a panicked male voice came from Clare's blind spot, somewhere west of her ear.

"What happened?" he cried. The blind spot was irrelevant. She knew immediately who he was. She gasped and stared down at the child as the voice bearer moved into her eye line.

"Is she okay?" his voice cut into her head again like a blunt knife.

"She's fine," came that soft soothing voice from the perfect mom. "She was just too excited to see Wonder Bear and tripped that's all."

"Baby," he cried and took the child in his arms, enveloping her in his own protective shield.

"Daddy's baby," he murmured rocking his daughter backwards and forwards.

Clare had to get away. She was horrified at the scene before her. She was hot, sweat pouring down her back.

"Would you like a hug with Wonder Bear now honey?" she heard him ask. She watched as the girl nodded and jumped out of his arms into hers before she could turn and run for her sanity. She felt her plump arms envelop her and head rest against her fluffy, ample belly.

"I love you," she said looking up and staring into the black holes that lead into Clare's eyes. She looked back and saw his eyes. She looked away unable to breathe, tears pouring down her cheeks and soaking the lining of her costume.

"She really does you know," she heard him say, his eyes twinkling at her like they had all those moons ago. She'd married him because of his eyes. His eyes, his body, and his mind. She'd known he had excellent genes. Excellent genes for making perfect babies with her. Only her genes turned out to be not quite so perfect didn't they. She had pointless genes. Gene's incapable of pro-creating with this perfect man that stood before her with his perfect wife and perfect child. She held onto the girl even harder and stared into his eyes. This should have been her daughter. This should have been her family.

"Let me take a picture," came the soothing voice again and before she knew it he had his arm draped around her padded shoulder whilst the girl jumped up and down, squeezing her paw for all it was worth.

"Say cheese Wonder Bear," she shouted as the flash blinded them whilst Clare wondered if she was about to collapse.

"Brilliant" he said as the three of them crowded round the camera to view the perfect family portrait minus perfect mom but with perfect *should be* mom.

"No come on," he laughed as the girl came in for a final hug. "We'll see Wonder Bear later. In the parade perhaps?"

Wonder Bear nodded mutely and held on even harder. She felt the girl reciprocate then wriggle away to clutch at her father's hand.

"Say thank you to Wonder Bear," he learnt down and told her.

"Thank you Wonder Bear," the three of them chimed.

She'd seen something she shouldn't have seen.

Six years it had taken to recover. Six years since he'd left her, their marriage in tatters as she failed to accept the crippling news that she would never bear children. He'd refused to go through any further fertility treatment with her. He said it was pointless after five times. Then he left when she insisted they had to keep trying. Said he couldn't stay with her if she couldn't move on and be happy as a couple without children. She continued her blind pursuit of another way. The other way proved to be countless dead ends that eventually lead to a referral to a psychologist for treatment for depression. Three years in therapy and she'd finally felt confident enough to return to the world of work. Then she'd seen something she shouldn't have seen. Something that she could have only seen whilst dressed as Wonder Bear at Wonderland Theme Park.

She sat in a changing cubicle in her sweat and tear soaked costume gently fingering the tiny white stitches on the left side of the bear's chest. She sat there for four hours. She sat there until the park closed and the lights were turned off. Then she pulled herself up and went to find the props cupboard where she found what she was looking for. She put her Wonder Bear head back on, picked up Pirate Sam's Magic Dagger, and let herself out of the costume department to head for the talking toadstools in the Enchanted Forest.

Jordon Pecile
by Felix Giordano

My wife told me of a creative writing teacher named Jordon Pecile at Manchester Community College and I registered for one of his courses. The first two weeks didn't go well. Then I submitted one of my unfinished science fiction stories involving an autopsy. Jordon liked it and asked me to try to expand the story into a mystery/suspense novel and provide him with a scene-by-scene outline and a list of characters and their backgrounds. I complied with Jordon's request and the following week began the start of *The Jim Buchanan Novels*, a series about a mixed-blood Native American Sheriff from Montana.

I have Jordon to thank not only for helping me find my voice but also in helping me find my spirit. Through these novels, I have discovered what is truly important in life and that we are integrated with everything else on this Earth. Without Jordon's patience, nurturing, and brutally honest advice I would never be the writer or the person that I am today.

Why I Write
by Felix Giordano

Intrigued by 19th century Americans searching for the promise of a new life while battling the elements and coexisting with indigenous tribes, I wrote my first story based upon the novel *The Oregon Trail* by Francis Parkman when I was twelve. Upon college graduation, I attended creative writing classes although my writing resulted in many incomplete rough drafts.

While attending Jordon Pecile's classes I discovered my voice. With Jordon's encouragement and the invaluable help of my classmates, I have written three mystery/suspense novels about the American West albeit in modern times with my protagonist as a mixed blood Native American sheriff.

I performed a live audience reading of one chapter from my novel, *The Killing Zone* at the May 2007 edition of the Mishi-maya-gat Spoken Word & Music Series at Manchester Community College in Manchester, Connecticut. The companion novels, *Montana Harvest* and *Mystery at Little Bitterroot* complete *The Jim Buchanan Series* with more novels on the horizon.

In writing these novels, I've realized my long held beliefs of how we as human beings must interact with the Earth and respect all living creatures. It is the indigenous way of life or as Native Americans refer to it, *Walking the Red Road.*

I routinely attend Native American Pow-wows and support the Red Feather Development Group, an organization providing straw bale housing on Montana Indian Reservations.

I am a member of the Connecticut Authors & Publishers Association (CAPA). I retired after 36 years as a Financial Analyst for Northeast Utilities and am a Second Lieutenant in the Civil Air Patrol. I live in Ashford, Connecticut with my wife and our three companion dogs.

My website: http://thejimbuchanannovels.com/

The Lost Relics of Mount Quarantania
by Felix Giordano

The racing Jeep Wrangler braked hard. The driver jumped out as the arid wind quickly ripped the brown felt fedora from his head. Ignoring his fallen hat, he instead struggled with the odd-shaped burlap bag under his arm. He leaned his body onto the driver's door and closed it with a thud. Righting himself, he stopped to look at his wife in the passenger seat.

"Don't worry Carmela, I'll be safe."

"Oh Aaron," she moaned then dropped her head in her hands.

He sprinted up the museum's marble steps and went inside. A black-haired receptionist with an olive complexion greeted him.

"Welcome to the Jericho Museum of Natural History."

"Where is your curator?" Aaron asked.

"He is busy."

"He must see this." Aaron shouted. "I must see him now!"

The woman picked up her phone and spoke in Arabic. As quickly as she hung up, from a side door, a hefty, bearded man, dressed in tailored gray slacks and a crisp blue polo shirt emerged. He walked up to Aaron. "You are an American, no? I am Juhaym Razam, the museum curator. May I help you?"

"Yes, my name is Aaron Cohen. I'm Assistant Professor of Anthropology at Columbia University in New York. I'm in Jordan visiting with my wife and…"

"Where is your wife?"

"My wife… she's in the car."

Mr. Razam looked through the front door's glass windows. "Please ask her to come inside. A woman should not sit in a hot automobile. It is my responsibility as a host to welcome her."

Aaron first hesitated and then responded. "My wife is not well. She has trouble walking."

Mr. Razam took a step toward the front door. "I will assist her."

"No… she uses a cane. It's very painful for her to move more than necessary."

"I'm sorry for her. Perhaps we can help. My sister is a therapist. She would be pleased to…"

Aaron interrupted him. "No, you don't understand. My wife has an incurable illness. We've been to so many doctors."

"I am truly sorry. Then we must waste no time. What can I do for you?"

"I found an artifact." Aaron handed the curator the burlap bag. "I need its significance verified."

Mr. Razam peeked inside the bag, looked out of the corner of his eye at the receptionist, and waved Aaron into his office. "Let us go here." The curator closed the door behind them and placed the bag on his desk. He carefully removed the rolled up scroll from inside the burlap sack.

Aaron could not control his enthusiasm. "I believe it's from the first century."

A weak, sarcastic belly laugh escaped from Mr. Razam at Aaron's comment. "Where did you find this?"

"The Mount of Temptation."

"Mount Quarantania?"

"Well, yes… in a cave on that mountain. The mountain where Satan tempted Christ."

Mr. Razam partially unraveled the scroll with great care so as not to damage it. He pulled out a magnifying glass, sat in his red leather chair, and with his face up close began to study the artifact. He stared at Aaron. "It is in Aramaic. It is written on papyrus."

Aaron nodded to himself. "I translated the first few words, can you decipher the rest?"

Mr. Razam continued to read the transcript, then stopped and placed the magnifying glass down. "I need someone to help. Someone to… decode it."

"Who?"

"Leave it with me. I will have someone look at it."

Aaron shook his head. "No, I'll go elsewhere."

"I am sorry. It must remain here… in museum."

"What do you mean? It's mine! I found it!"

"No sir. It will remain in the Jericho Museum. All artifacts found in Jordan belong to the government."

"But…"

Mr. Razam interrupted him. "That is all. Go now. I will call tomorrow."

Aaron sighed as he watched Mr. Razam return the scroll to the burlap bag. He stuck the bag in the upper left hand desk drawer and locked the desk. Frustrated and helpless, Aaron gave Mr. Razam his business card. On the back of the card, Aaron inscribed the name of the local hotel and the room number where they were staying. Aaron returned to his Jeep and told Carmela the news.

"Can they do that?" she asked.

"Apparently but I'm going to stay on top of this. If it's what I think it is, and they let us keep it, it will change our lives forever. We'll finally have the money for your operation."

Aaron drove to the hotel, parked the Jeep, and walked to the passenger side to help Carmela. He opened the door and lifted her out of her seat. She put down a wooden cane and limped along, putting her left arm on his shoulder for support. Aaron practically carried her up to their room and gently placed her on the bed. They spent the next few hours talking about their adventure on Mount Quarantania.

"You seemed to be walking better, Carmela."

Carmela lay on the bed with her head propped up on two pillows. Patches of dark skin on her shin, a manifestation of her disease, contrasted with her Mediterranean complexion as her crooked and shortened right leg lay in plain view. "The doctors say they can't cure the fibrous dysplasia so what does it matter."

"It's not those doctors. It's the money that will find you the best doctor who will operate."

"Aaron, there's no cure. Can't you get it thorough your head? They might as well have cut it off. Your life would be so much happier if I went back to Napoli to live with mia Madre." Carmela broke into tears.

Aaron walked over, sat on the bed, and hugged Carmela. "I love you and I'll do anything for you. We'll get help." A few minutes later, a knock at the door got his attention. "Yes… who is it?"

"Chief of the Jericho Police, please open the door."

Aaron complied and asked, "What is it."

A large man in full uniform wearing a sidearm greeted Aaron. His black hair, framed by a mustache that seemed to span from one cheek to the other, was marked by a multitude of curls. "I am Basil Maloof, Chief of the Jericho Police. Are you the American, Mister Aaron Cohen?"

"What is this about?"

"You found the scroll?" Chief Maloof looked past Aaron at Carmela's twisted position on the bed.

"Yes, I'm Professor Cohen. I'm an Assistant Professor of Anthropology at…" A flash of anger flew through Aaron's head and he decided to impress the local man. "I'm also the chief archeologist at the New York Museum of Natural History."

Chief Maloof blinked his eyes slowly. "I'm sorry Mr. Cohen. The scroll has been surrendered to our government. I am here to inform you that your business in Jericho has ended and you must leave at once."

"Leave? But I found that scroll. It belongs to me."

"It belongs to our government. You have until tomorrow morning to leave. If you do not comply, you will be arrested. Good day, Mr. Cohen."

The police chief turned and left. Aaron shut the door and looked at his wife.

"Aaron, forget about it. It's just scribbling."

"I'm going to get it back. It's our ticket to fortune."

"Aaron, don't you dare."

Later that evening, well past midnight, Aaron left a sleeping Carmela. He went downstairs and removed a crow bar from his Jeep. He walked the two-mile distance to the museum careful to stay off the sidewalks and streets, walking between houses and in dark alleyways. A barking dog caused Aaron to panic and he ran. Reaching the museum, he peered in the museum window and saw that no one was inside. Aaron shattered a windowpane and slipped into the museum. He leaned his shoulder onto the door of the curator's office and split the doorframe. He walked up to the desk, opened the drawer, and discovered the prize. Aaron examined the scroll in the burlap bag to ensure it was still intact and escaped the way he entered. He returned to the hotel room just before daybreak and awakened Carmela.

"You did what?"

Aaron was defiant. "It belongs to me. I found it."

"Well, let me see it."

Aaron removed the scroll from the burlap bag and a piece of lined notepaper fell onto the bed. "What's this," he said grabbing the paper.

Aaron helped Carmela sit up in bed. "Let me see it," she said. "It looks Arabic. I still translate for my Lebanese students in New York." Carmela looked at it for a moment, then up at Aaron. "It seems they were converting the Aramaic to Arabic."

"What does it say?"

"There are verses. *My Father hath sent Me. Receive Me for I am the Way, the Truth, and the Light.*" Carmela looked up at Aaron. "I think…"

"Continue."

Carmela searched the scroll and found other verses. She read aloud. "*It will come to pass I will spread the Word of My Father to the ends of the Earth. I will gather disciples one by one to explain to all of humanity what My Father expects of His people.*" Carmela looked up at Aaron and then read on. "*And these disciples, if they so be clean even unto death, shall live for all eternity with Me and I with them. For I seek not worldly riches, nor earthly kingdoms, nor vast armies to rule. My riches will be the souls of men. My Kingdom will be the Heavens above. My armies will be the believers of My Word.*"

Aaron stepped away from the bed. "Oh my God."

Carmela stared at her husband. "Aaron…"

"Carmela, do you know what we have here …"

"It appears to be the lost book of Jesus."

"He wrote it when he spent forty days alone in the desert and buried it in a cave on The Mount of Temptation… where we discovered it."

"People often wondered what Christ did… why there was no direct written record of his life prior to his ministry."

"He wrote it hoping that someday someone would come along, find it, and reveal it to the world."

"Aaron, we can't keep this."

27

"Carmela, this is priceless. Just one day at Sotheby's will garner a value high enough to buy you your operation and then some. Don't let it out of your sight."

"Aaron, there are more important things in life than stealing this religious artifact."

"We're not stealing what we rightfully found. Besides, it will make us rich."

"So tell me Aaron, for what?"

Aaron stared at Carmela. "For the operation you need so that you can walk again... so that you can lead a normal life."

"Aaron, I don't want anything to happen to you. We have a good life now. My love for you is more important than being able to walk again. If you get arrested our life as we know it would end."

Aaron ignored Carmela's last few words. "I need to formulate an escape plan. We're getting out of here before they discover it's missing." Aaron looked outside. The hot Jordanian morning sun was already full over the eastern horizon. "I'll bring our luggage to the Jeep. Keep that scroll hidden. I'll get out of bed and help you dress when I come back to the room."

Carmela shook her head and sighed. She slipped the scroll and the brief translation into the burlap bag and stuck it under her bed sheets. She got comfortable in bed and covered herself with the blanket. Aaron busied himself packing their luggage. He turned to Carmela, told her he'd be right back and carried their two suitcases downstairs. When he reached the lobby, he saw the curator, the Chief of the Jericho Police and another police officer waiting for him.

"Where are you going Professor Cohen?" asked the curator, Juhaym Razam.

Aaron pointed at the Chief of the Jericho Police, Basil Maloof and explained. "He told me that I had to leave today and I'm doing just that right now."

Aaron tried to walk past them but Chief Maloof interjected. "A few questions first, Mr. Cohen. Where were you last night?"

"I was... I was sleeping in my room."

"Who can verify that?"

"My wife. Why, what's wrong?"

Chief Maloof first glanced at Mr. Razam and then at Aaron. "It seems the museum was broken into last night and something was stolen... something that you claim to have found yesterday on Mount Quarantania."

Aaron began to perspire and fumbled with his words. "I... yes I found something but the last time that I saw it was in his office." Aaron pointed at Mr. Razam.

"It is missing now!" Mr. Razam glared at Aaron. "He has it."

Chief Maloof instructed his police officer on duty to take Aaron's luggage back upstairs where they would perform a complete inspection of the room and the couple's belongings. Aaron swallowed hard and complied with Chief Maloof.

Reaching the door to the second floor room, Aaron knocked twice. "Carmela, are you there?"

"Yes, Aaron."

Aaron turned the doorknob. The door forcibly swung open seemingly under its own power and slammed against the wall. The four men took a step back. Carmela stood in the middle of the room, her summer pajama shorts revealing the straightness of her leg and the absence of its discoloration and shortness. She held the scroll in her hand.

"Carmela!" Aaron screamed.

"Aaron something I can't... I can't explain has happened. After you left, the bed grew warm and this feeling entered my leg... stretching it... making me feel like I haven't felt since I was a young girl. My leg slowly straightened all by itself. Then the colors in my leg began to disappear right before my eyes. Then I saw the mattress rise and a light grew in the room until it hovered above my bed. Then a voice beckoned me to get up... to get out of bed." Carmela began to cry. "So I did and I... I walked out of bed... on my own."

Chief Maloof, Mr. Razam, and the other police officer knelt and prayed in Arabic. Aaron heard them, turned, and saw their reaction. He reached for Carmela to hug her and felt a sensation like he had never experienced before. It was as if an electrical impulse surged through his entire body reaching toward and through his extremities. A sense of pure love ebbed and flowed deep within his being while he hung onto Carmela.

Full of tears, Aaron said, "Oh Carmela, I love you so much."

"I love you too Aaron." Carmela hugged Aaron and buried her head on his shoulder.

Aaron turned to the others. "You do realize that this is the actual Book of Jesus. I must take it with me. The significance of this find needs to be articulated to the world."

Mr. Razam ended his prayers and stood up. "The scroll must be honored with respect. It cannot be dispatched to…"

Carmela interrupted him and wiping her tears said, "With all due respect, sir, seeing that this has cured me of my disease; it proves that this scroll belongs to all peoples and must not be hidden away inside a museum."

"The madam is correct," said Chief Maloof. "This is the Almighty's blessing. I have jurisdiction over the relic. It must be shared with all religions and does not belong to any one. This is a gift from Allah… Jehovah. My brother is Mullah of Jericho. I have friends in Jerusalem. One is a Rabbi and the other is the Israeli tourism minister. I will speak with them… I will tell them what I have seen with my own eyes. All religions will have a voice in this matter before anyone decides what should become of it."

"Are you sure that everyone will cooperate?" Aaron asked.

Chief Maloof nodded. "We have witnessed a miracle today. I assure you that I will lay down my life to protect this spiritual relic. It is a direct link with our Creator." He pointed to Carmela. "Her cured affliction is proof of that."

Aaron placed the scroll into the burlap bag and handed it to Chief Maloof. The police chief nodded, thanked Aaron and Carmela, and then left. Mr. Razam apologized to the couple and told them that not only would he not be pressing charges but that he wanted no compensation for the damage to the museum.

Aaron and Carmela decided to leave that same day. After packing their luggage in the Jeep, they sat inside and reflected on everything that had happened.

With his hands on the steering wheel and looking at the front doors of the museum, Aaron laughed. "What an amazing adventure… and to think that we actually touched something that the Lord created."

Carmela smiled. "Aaron, every day we touch something the Lord has made." She leaned over, held his face in her hands, and kissed him.

Aaron touched the moistness on his cheek where Carmela's lips had been. "It's been so long since you've done that."

"Aaron, we'll have a wonderful rest of our life together. It's a true wonder what the Lord has done for us. Letting us find that scroll, driving us toward the healing of my illness. I can't seem to comprehend the magnitude of it all. Are you sorry that you don't have the scroll anymore?"

Aaron glanced at Carmela. "No, I have you and you're well again. I'd trade a rolled up scroll for a miracle any day."

"Are you sure?"

"I'm sure. Besides, the scroll will go where it belongs. To be shared with the world."

"No regrets?"

"None." Aaron reached into his pocket and pulled out a long, thin burlap bag. "We still have this."

"What's that, Aaron?"

"When I found that burlap bag with the scroll inside, I also found this." Aaron unraveled the bag revealing a thin reed pen broken in a half-dozen pieces.

"Aaron what is that?"

"Carmela, I think this is the pen Christ used to write his words on the scroll."

"Aaron, if it is, it belongs with the scroll."

"Carmela, we will deliver this directly to the Israeli Tourism Minister and explain everything to him. This will ensure that they both end up together where they rightfully belong."

"Are you sure that's the right thing to do?"

Aaron gazed into Carmela's eyes. "Last night on my way to the museum I was startled by a dog tied in the backyard of one of the houses. It was dark and in the confusion, I dropped the crowbar. I still ran to the museum but I knew I couldn't get inside. That's when I

31

removed the bag with the reed pen and held it up to my face to look at it. I was outside the museum near one of the windows and the glass pane shattered on its own. I went inside and walked up to the door to the curator's office. With the bag in my hand, I felt around for a place to pry the door open with my fingers. When the bag touched the door, the doorframe broke by itself and the door swung open. When I got to the curator's desk, I placed the bag against the drawer and the drawer popped open."

"Aaron?"

"Carmela, they will find their way… they belong together."

Forever Without End
by Felix Giordano

Patsy was like any other Italian-American kid growing up in the era of flower children. Long hair, tie-dyed clothes, facial hair appearing and disappearing based upon what new musical group appeared on American Bandstand during any particular month. Close to six-feet tall, the girls in school would tell him that he was cute but to Patsy, he didn't understand what that really meant. He lived with his parents and sister in a middle-class home in an industrial town in the northeast where gray and orange smoke from countless factories spewed their particle-laden chemicals into the sky. The Grimaldi's house sat on a hill and every morning, Patsy would wake up, gaze from the third floor parlor window, and watch the sun become obliterated by the haze.

"You'll be late for school Pasquale," his mother warned.

Known to his friends as Patsy, his mother referred to him by his given name. Because she measured success by a person's efforts, Patsy's mother saw her son as a disappointment. Although both his intelligence and potential overshadowed his motivation and accomplishments, he was basically a good kid, a morally correct young man. Drinking and drugs were as foreign to his being as a golf pro trying to hit a baseball with a tennis racquet.

Patsy always had fun and success on the sandlots but achievements eluded him on the organized teams at high school. Not from a lack of desire but from his point of view, endless sessions of practice made no sense at all. What fun was practice? Playing the game was all that mattered to Patsy but those worries were long gone. Patsy had graduated high school two years ago.

"I said, you'll be late for school," she warned him again.

Patsy's gaze left the window. "My first class is at ten. I won't be late."

"Young man, you still have to shower and dress. Did you finish studying last night?" she asked.

Patsy faced his mom and sized-up the middle-aged woman. His aunts and uncles said his mom was pretty but to a twenty-one year old, anyone in their fifties was past pretty. She ran the household with an iron fist and to her, Pasquale was a problem. He wasn't like his sister, Philomena. She was earning straight-A's in high school. The failing grades he had received in high school were made up in summer school. The IQ tests didn't lie. His teachers and even the principal had commented to Mrs. Grimaldi that Pasquale was bordering on genius. He just needed to apply himself. But then again, IQ tests weren't like high school football practice to Patsy. To him, the IQ tests were game day and the league championship was on the line. He didn't have to study for them.

"Well, what are you waiting for?" Patsy's mom now walked up to him and demanded action. "Go get ready, now." Her screams were followed by tapping from the second floor tenants. "See what you've done! Now the Berardi's know what a fresh boy you are."

"Mom, I'm not a boy. I'm in college."

"College, you call that two-year school college? You flunked so many times in high school that two-year school was the only school that would accept you."

Patsy grabbed the clothes from his bedroom and ran to the bathroom. He shut the door and from inside he pleaded, "I'm trying, mom. I'll do better."

"You better do better," she screamed. "All you care about is dinosaurs. Dinosaurs won't put food on the table. Do you want to end up like your father, working in a factory the rest of your life?"

Patsy stared in the mirror as a tear rolled down his cheek. "I wish someone really cared about me," he said to himself.

Pounding on the door accompanied a shout, "Hurry up, your sister has to finish in there. Don't make her late for the bus."

Patsy quickly showered and dressed. He walked outside the bathroom as Philomena pushed her way past him.

Patsy grabbed his books and left the apartment. He ran down the winding stairway to the ground floor. Mr. Testa, the owner of the three-family house was having a cup of coffee on the back porch. It was early June and he was admiring the tomatoes he had just planted. Patsy spotted him and said, "Hi Mr. Testa."

In broken English, Mr. Testa said, "Pasquale, why you no cut your hair?"

Breaking stride for just seconds, Patsy replied, "All the kids are wearing it like this now."

"You not all a kids, you a gooda boy."

"Haven't you heard of the Beatles? They wear their hair long, they even started growing beards," remarked Patsy as he brushed back his curly black hair with his hand.

"You want to look brutto?" replied the elderly man.

"No, I just want to fit in," replied Patsy who then ran down the porch steps toward his car.

Mr. Testa waved his hand and said, "Lei è brutto."

Patsy unlocked the driver's door of his 1964 maroon Chevy Impala and tossed his books on the back seat. He revved the engine and drove away from the house, across town to the community college campus. Tucked in the western hills of the city, it was a sprawling array of temporary trailers and park benches. The one community building that served as a cafeteria was a gathering place for students. Patsy parked his car and walked up to the building. His friend Michael Rizzo was waiting for him.

"Hey, amico, did you study for today's final exam?

"Yeah, I studied," replied Patsy as he sat next to his friend on one of the benches.

The boys leaned back and watched the other students pass by. Patsy stared at a number of the coeds but the only one who returned his glance gave him a sneer.

Michael saw the look from her and jabbed his friend. "She's dating that redhead Irish guy. What's his name, Bobby O'Dwyer I think?"

"O'Brien."

"What?"

"O'Brien is his name," corrected Patsy.

"O'Dwyer, O'Brien, it doesn't matter. He's Irish, right?"

"Yeah."

"So, you still dating that Laura Wilson girl?" asked Michael.

Patsy turned to his friend and stared. "Why? If I say no, are you going to ask her out?"

"Maybe, why?"

"Good luck."

"Why do you say that?"

"It's just that we get into an argument every time we're out on a date."

"That's because she wants it."

"Yeah, right."

"You got to give her what she wants," Michael laughed and nudged Patsy.

"I'm still looking."

"So you're not dating her?"

"I'm going to tell her it's over between us," Patsy said facing Michael.

"Here's your chance, she's coming now."

Patsy turned his head and his face flushed red. Laura walked toward him as the boy tried to regain his composure.

"Hi Laura."

"Hi," she said as she slowed to talk to her boyfriend. "What's going on?"

"Patsy has something to tell you," replied Michael.

"What do you want to tell me?" asked Laura.

"I'll tell you later," Patsy replied.

"Tell me now. I have to meet someone in ten minutes."

"Yeah, tell her now," prodded Michael.

Patsy felt the warmth envelop his whole body as he searched for the courage to confront his girlfriend.

"Well?" asked Laura.

"We're... I mean... I'm not going to see you anymore," blurted Patsy.

"Is that all?" Laura asked.

"Yeah, I guess so."

"All right then. So I guess I'm free on Saturday, right?"

"Yeah."

"Good, Mark Bailey asked me to go with him to the Irish Festival. So I'm going."

"You're going with him?" asked Patsy.

"Yeah, you're going with him?" Michael asked.

"Yes," Laura replied and with that, she left the two boys in her wake.

"Wow, she's a real bitch. I see what you mean," said Michael.

The horn sounded on campus and everyone hurried to their class. Patsy took the test. Unlike high school where he didn't have a sense of urgency for study, he was comfortable with community college. The desire to do well now resided within him.

Patsy spent the remainder of the day taking two more finals. His semester was over and he ran to the community building to look for the posted final grades of the courses he had taken exams for earlier in the week. He searched for his subjects, teachers, and classes. He found them and whispered, "All right." One final grade was a B+ and the other an A-. Patsy drove home with a smile on his face. He parked his car in front of the house and ran up the steps. Patsy opened the door and found his family seated at the dinner table to a meal of ziti and meatballs.

"Where have you been?" asked his mother.

"Two of my grades were a B+ and A-," Patsy boasted.

"Answer your mother," Patsy's father instructed.

"I looked for my posted grades after school."

His sister laughed and his mother slammed her fork on the table. She looked at her daughter and said, "Shut up or I'll send you to right to bed."

"Connie, she didn't do anything wrong," pleaded her husband.

"Shut up Sal or this will be the last cooked meal you'll get this week."

Patsy's father sealed his lips and politely asked his son, "Sit with us."

The boy looked at the food on his table and said, "I'm going to skip dinner. I can't play hoops with that in my stomach."

"If you don't eat with us, you're not going anywhere," replied his mother.

Patsy sat at the table and explained, "But if I don't get to the park soon, the guys will have already decided on teams. I won't get to play."

"Never mind basketball, you eat with us," his mother demanded. Patsy reluctantly spooned some ziti in his dish. "Are you working tonight?"

"I start working days next week," replied Patsy.

"Can you bring home some eggplant from the store for us?" asked his father.

"Yeah, I can."

"I want to make eggplant parmigiana tomorrow," his mother said.

After a few minutes of silence, Patsy spoke up and asked, "Why can't I go to the park and play some basketball with the guys?"

Patsy's mother said, "No, I don't like those…"

"Sure you can go," interrupted his father. He looked at his wife and winked his eye. "After taking those exams and before you start work next week, you need a break. Finish your meal and then you can go."

Patsy's mother at first didn't say a word and then relented, "All right. Be home before it gets dark."

"I promise I will," replied Patsy.

Patsy finished dinner and helped clear the table. He pulled on a pair of cut-off blue jeans and an oversized tee shirt, red with the letters SAINT MICHAEL THE ARCHANGEL written across the front. He grabbed the basketball from his room, said goodbye to his parents and his sister and ran down the stairs to his car.

It was a short drive to the park. Certainly within walking distance but it was a status symbol to drive. Patsy thought, maybe one of the neighborhood girls would want to go to that new McDonalds restaurant near where the Interstate highway ends. It was a good parking spot, dark, and away from home. It was safe from the trouble that always erupted near the downtown shopping plaza.

Patsy parked his car on the outside of the fence that wound its way about the perimeter of the park. He got out of his car, grabbed his basketball, and noticed the guys playing three-on-three on the court. To Patsy, it was always important to scout the people on the court. He could tell how long of a wait it would be before he could play, based upon the teams likely to be eliminated. He sized up the other guys hanging around and projected the team he'd likely be on. He dribbled his basketball and walked up to his friend Bill.

"Are you on a team yet?"

"Yeah, me, Joe, and Mike are all set."

"Who's not on a team?" asked Patsy. Bill pointed to two younger kids standing on the sidelines. "Dave and Chuck? They're high school kids."

"I know but that's all that's left."

"How long of a wait? Maybe someone will leave on the other teams and I can fill in."

"I doubt it. It's about an hour wait. Two teams are ahead of me and the loser of this game plays the winner of the next game."

Patsy looked at his watch and saw that it was already after seven. An hour wait would put any game's end close to darkness and he remembered what his mother said.

"Hey, I'm going to pass on a game tonight. I might run to McDonalds. Want to skip your game and come with me?"

"No way, I'll stay here," replied Bill.

Patsy nodded and left the park. On his way out, he saw two girls and recognized them as high school seniors. He asked one of them, Sara, if she wanted to go to McDonalds with him.

"Drop dead!" she exclaimed as her friend laughed.

Patsy touched the one acne blemish on his cheek, tossed the ball in his car, and drove off. He got onto the Interstate and headed toward the end of the highway. Once past the amber flashing lights and the red and white wooden barriers on the exit ramp, he pulled into the McDonalds parking lot. He drove his car around to the back and shut the engine. A familiar shiny blue Camaro rested under the trees. It belonged to John Miles, the sophomore quarterback from Syracuse who was on Patsy's old high school football team. He was a three-sport athlete and was in the car with someone. It could be his girlfriend Sue, or maybe it was Valerie, or Donna, though he would probably boast that it was all three.

Patsy shook his head and remembered the last game of his senior year against cross-town rival Roosevelt High. Patsy finally got in the game when his team wasn't ahead or behind by three touchdowns. The score was 22-16 with Saint Michael the Archangel ahead and with control of the ball. They were playing a split-T formation, 3rd and five to go on their own 16-yard line in the 4th quarter with 2:45 left to play.

Coach Sorrento sent in a play, power pitch right. It was a play meant to open a lane down the right sideline. Designed to provide the fullback with a chance to break a long run, the quarterback, halfback, tight end, and pulling right guard would provide the blocking. Patsy would carry the ball and he was ready, boy was he ready. Those long, boring days of practice would finally pay off.

Miles was under center and Patsy was drooling in the backfield. But there were college scouts in the stands that day. Rumor had it that they were from Syracuse, exactly where Miles planned to go. When the center hiked the ball, everything seemed to move in slow motion for Patsy. He ran to the right expecting a pitch from Miles but the quarterback never released the ball, instead he kept it. Patsy stopped and stood in the backfield and watched Miles run through a hole that the team bus could have driven through. Eighty-four yards for a touchdown and just like that, the game was out of reach for Roosevelt. Mobbed by the rest of the team, Miles smiled when he saw Patsy and then mockingly laughed at him. His team went on to win 30-16 and Miles got his full scholarship to Syracuse.

Patsy waited in the car for twenty minutes, though it seemed longer to him. A few couples made out in the dark part of the lot and some kids hung around near the front door. Out of the corner of his eye, Patsy saw a blue blur arrive in his field of vision. It was Officer McKenna.

"What are you doing here? You're the Grimaldi boy aren't you?" asked the police officer.

"Yes sir," Patsy replied.

"Did you make a purchase?"

"What?"

"Did you buy anything inside?" Officer McKenna pointed toward the restaurant with his nightstick.

"No sir."

"Then get a move on or your father will be picking you up at the station."

Patsy again looked at the blue Camaro and then said something he should have reconsidered, "Why is John Miles allowed to park over there?"

The officer looked over his shoulder at the parked car under the trees where young girls' laughter seemed to emanate. "Because Johnny just got drafted by the Dodgers," replied Officer McKenna.

"The Los Angeles Dodgers?" asked Patsy.

The police officer grinned and replied, "He's going to pitch for one of their minor league teams." Then his smile evaporated and he said, "Now get the hell out of here."

Patsy started up his car and left the parking lot. He watched Officer McKenna twirling his nightstick in his rear-view mirror as he drove away. Back on the Interstate, he flicked on the radio and after a few short comments from the DJ, the hauntingly beautiful Simon & Garfunkel song, *Bridge Over Troubled Water* began. Patsy listened to the tune and took the words to heart. Tears dripped from his eyes as the song wove its message throughout his thoughts. He longed for someone to give him purpose in life, someone that would bring everything into focus for him, someone for him to love.

Patsy decided to stop at the local Rite-Aid pharmacy and drove into the parking lot, stopping next to a dark green Pontiac. He walked into the store and made a beeline for aisle seven and the acne cream. He reviewed the varieties before selecting one he'd tried before. Just as he was leaving for the register, he heard a giggle from the next aisle. Patsy walked to the front of the store and reached the end of the aisle. A blond girl, a girl that he had never seen in town cut in front of him from the next aisle. Patsy got in line behind the girl and patiently waited while the sales person served the other customers.

He got a good view of the back of the young girl's head. He noticed that her blond hair ran below her shoulders as he snuck glimpses of her shape. All were pleasing to his eye as he spied her every move. When she was next in line, another cashier opened a second register and announced, "I can take whose next."

Patsy instinctively took one-step forward as the girl made a move toward the second register. They bumped slightly and Patsy said, "I'm sorry, go ahead."

"Are you sure?" asked the girl.

"Yes, of course. Go ahead."

"That's sweet,' she said.

Sweet? That's sweet she said, he thought.

Patsy waited and when she was done at the register, she walked away and met a girl with short brown hair waiting at the front door. She was ordinary, not stunning like the blonde. They left while Patsy stared and watched them disappear into the parking lot as the cashier said to him, "I don't have all night!"

He paid for his acne cream and left the store. As Patsy walked to his car, he saw the green Pontiac pull out of the lot and drive away. He climbed into his car and drove off. He hadn't driven more than two miles when he saw a green Pontiac parked in a gas station with its hood up. Two girls, a blonde and a brunette were standing next to the car along with the garage mechanic. Patsy watched the girls as he drove by and the blonde looked up and made eye contact with him. *That's the girl from the drugstore,* thought Patsy. He signaled left, pulled onto a side street, and doubled back. He drove into the gas station and parked behind the Pontiac.

"Do you have car trouble?" he asked sticking his head out of the driver's side window.

The blonde looked up while the brunette said, "There's that guy from the drugstore."

"Can I give you a lift?" asked Patsy.

Before the girls could speak, the mechanic said, "Car's OK. You just had a loose sparkplug wire. It was misfiring." The mechanic closed the hood.

"No that's OK," replied the brunette to Patsy's offer. "We don't need a ride."

"Well how about if I follow you home just to make sure you don't get stuck again?" Patsy asked.

"All right," replied the blonde as she smiled at Patsy.

The brunette rolled her eyes and got in the drivers side. The blonde climbed in and they left with Patsy following close behind. It was a short drive to an apartment complex where the girls and Patsy parked their cars. The brunette opened one of the apartment doors and walked in. Just as the blonde was about to do the same, Patsy asked her, "Can I talk to you?"

She stopped and looked at Patsy. "I'll be right out."

Patsy sat on the steps and waited. After about ten minutes, she came out and sat next to Patsy.

"Hi, my name's Patsy," he said and held out his hand.

The girl took his hand and replied, "I'm Inga Keller, and my friend's name is Judy. What's your last name?"

"Grimaldi."

"Patrick Grimaldi?"

"It's not Patrick. It's Patsy, short for Pasquale."

"Pasquale Grimaldi? Wow, that's a cool name."

"Do you live here?"

"No we're just visiting Judy's older sister and her husband. We're from Grand Rapids, Michigan."

"How long will you be here?" Patsy asked.

"About a week." Inga laughed. "But it's going to seem like forever."

"My father has an expression. Forever without end."

"What does that mean?"

"A lot of people say they'll stay with someone forever but my dad always says he'll stay with my mom forever without end."

"That's sweet."

The door to the apartment opened and Judy stuck her head out. "Inga, my sister needs our help."

Inga stood up. "I have to go."

Patsy got up but before Inga went inside he asked, "Can I see you again?"

Inga turned around. "We're going to the beach tomorrow but I'm not doing anything at night."

"Can I call you?" Patsy asked.

"Just a minute," Inga disappeared into the apartment.

Patsy closed his eyes and saw Inga's face. She reminded him of one of the participants he saw in the last Miss America Beauty Pageant; the innocent face, the sculpted body, the golden, silky hair. When Patsy heard the screen door open, he jumped and awakened from his daydream.

He watched her hand over a slip of paper. "What's this?"

"It's the phone number here. Call me about six tomorrow night. I'll be in."

"All right, I'll call you then."

"OK, good night."

"Good night."

Patsy turned toward his car and looked back a few times. Each time he glanced at her, Inga was still looking at him, still smiling. Was this too good to be true? He got in his car and drove away. As he headed back home, a smile grew on his face and he turned on the radio. The Carpenters' song 'Close to You' was playing and Patsy tried to sing along. He couldn't wait for tomorrow night to arrive.

Patsy's day was spent in anticipation of his evening phone call to Inga. When six o'clock arrived, he called and she answered. She told Patsy that she was tired but he could come over and listen to music with her. Patsy was overjoyed. A quick explanation to his parents that he was going to visit a friend was met with skepticism from his mother but his father vouched for him and Patsy was home free.

When he got to the apartment Inga, dressed in low-cut, bell-bottom jeans and a midriff top, greeted him at the door. Patsy soon learned that Judy was at a neighborhood party with her sister and brother-in-law. Inga invited Patsy in the living room and she put Led Zeppelin's first album on the stereo. As the songs played, Patsy asked Inga all about herself. She explained that after graduating high school she had hitchhiked to Connecticut with her friend from Michigan. Her admission of having tried nearly every recreational drug shocked Patsy but by then her beauty mesmerized him. As the evening progressed, the conversation dwindled and indiscriminate touches turned into caresses, then hugs and kisses. By nine o'clock, they were embracing and passionately French kissing. The front door opened at ten and Judy, a bit inebriated, laughed and went upstairs to bed. A half-hour later, the couple in residence returned, introduced themselves and went upstairs. By midnight, when Patsy began to explore and massage the bare skin between Inga's midriff top and low-cut bell-bottom jeans, Inga told Patsy that it was time for him to go.

"Can I see you again tomorrow?"

"Yes, just drop by the same time."

"All right."

Pasty received a goodnight kiss at the door.

"Hey Patsy." Patsy looked back at Inga. "Forever without end," she said with a smile, which Patsy returned in kind.

Another day spent in anticipation of another evening with Inga left Patsy wishing the time would fly by. When it was nearly six, he left for the apartment. He rang the bell, the door opened, and Judy's sister appeared.

"They're not here."

"What do you mean? Inga said to stop by," said Patsy.

"All I know is my sister said they were going out."

"When they come back please tell her to call me," Patsy said handing Inga's friend's sister a piece of paper with his phone number.

Patsy had driven a couple of miles from the apartment when he spotted a green Pontiac headed toward him. He recognized Inga in the passenger seat and her friend was driving. Patsy turned his car around and followed them. It appeared to Patsy that the driver knew she was being followed because it sped up and turned down a side road in an apparent attempt to elude Patsy's car. Nevertheless, he followed and pushed his car to the limit. Bare-knuckle driving, squealing tires, burnt rubber, up to fifty miles an hour on curves and residential roads but the Pontiac would not slow down. Patsy's eyes moistened as he thought of Inga inside the car and how these actions were a mystery to him. When the Pontiac pulled into a driveway to turn around, Patsy parked his Chevy and blocked the car.

"Move your car!" Judy said.

Pasty got out. "Let me see Inga."

"Move your damn car!"

"Not until I see Inga."

"She never wants to see you again. How'd you like my driving?"

"What?" Pasty stared at Judy confused at the sudden shift in her mood.

"Barely kept up with me," Judy said laughing.

Patsy shook his head. "Yeah, right. Let me see Inga."

"She's in the front seat but I doubt she'll be able to talk to you."

Patsy walked over to the passenger door and looked inside. The sight he saw made him shudder. Inga was seated with her head hung low. When he tapped on the window, Inga looked up. Amid her golden hair tossed in disarray and from her mouth, laced drool hanging onto her shirt and arms, Patsy stared at her glassy eyes with their five-hundred mile look.

"Inga!" Patsy turned to Judy and with both concern and hatred in his voice demanded, "What did you do to her?"

"We went to that downtown shopping plaza."

"You what?"

"We met this guy there named John Miles and he sold us some horse."

"Horse?"

"We snorted heroin."

"Drugs? Why?"

"Why not?"

Patsy and Judy looked up when they heard a screen door open.

"Get the hell out of my yard before I call the police!" A woman screamed as she ran down her front steps.

Patsy reassured the homeowner. "Don't worry lady I was just trying to help the girl in the car."

"Is everything all right? Does someone need a doctor?"

"No, everything is all right. We're leaving now," said Judy.

"Do you want me to follow you home?" asked Patsy.

Judy shook her head. "No, let me take care of her. She just needs to sleep it off."

Pasty got in his car and turned around. He followed the Pontiac until they reached a stop sign. Left was the apartment and right was Patsy's home. The Pontiac turned left and after a long moment and with tears in his eyes Patsy turned right.

The next day, Patsy showed up at the apartment late in the afternoon. A knock on the front door summoned Judy's sister.

"Yes?"

"Hi, I'm the guy who was here last night looking for Inga. Can I see her?"

"She's not here."

"Where is she?"

"She left with my sister this morning."

"Where?"

"They went to Cape Cod."

"But I need to see her. When will they be back?"

"They won't be back."

"What... can you give me her address?"

"I don't know it."

"Can you give me Judy's address so I can send her a letter for Inga?"

"I'm not giving my sister's address to a stranger."

"I'm not a stranger."

"You are to me," replied Judy's sister as she slammed the door in Patsy's face.

#

That was a long time ago. Now Patsy sat in a room at a nursing home. In the bed was a woman with long silky white hair.

Entering the room a nurse asked, "Are you a friend of the family?"

"Sort of. I just arrived," Patsy said. His long hair was now white and pulled back into a ponytail.

"Did you vote for Obama's second term yesterday?"

"No, I didn't have a chance. I flew in from Connecticut yesterday. A friend of mine told me about her. So I came to visit as soon as I heard she was here."

The nurse looked at the woman in the bed. "Poor woman. Her husband treated her badly and then died some years ago and I hear her kids never come to see her."

"Will she be all right?"

"She's catatonic. She had a nervous breakdown with the things her husband did to her... that and the drugs she took when she was younger. They all took a toll on her. She's now a ward of the state."

"Think she'll snap out of it?"

"I doubt it. Say you look familiar. Do I know you?"

"I don't think so."

"Now I know where I saw you. Weren't you on one of those educational cable channels?"

"Sometimes I'm on the History Channel."

"I know you. Aren't you that paleontologist from Yale who digs for dinosaur bones?"

"Yes."

"I knew it. My son watches your show every time it's on. He even reads your books." She held her hand out. "Nice to meet you, Mr...."

Patsy spoke before she could finish. "Grimaldi, Pasquale Grimaldi."

"I'll have to tell him that I met you. Maybe I'll bring him by if you're still here tomorrow."

The nurse shook Patsy's hand and then left. Patsy glanced at Inga and clutched her hand. It was cold to the touch. He sat on the bed, massaging her hand and whispering to her.

"Inga, where have you been?" He recounted, "Funny, I've been spending most of my adult life digging up dinosaurs that were lost for millions of years. I was searching for the perfect specimen. Although I lost you a long time ago, I've always kept you in my heart." He continued to massage her hand and thought he felt movement. He looked down and saw a finger move. "I'll be here for you Inga, forever without end."

With those last words, Patsy heard a sound from Inga. It was like a rush of air from her lungs and her breath hastened. She exhaled and her eyes partially opened. She looked at Patsy and he sensed that she immediately recognized him.

"Forever without end," she said weakly squeezing his hand. Then Inga smiled. "Where have you been?"

Dogs are People, Too
by Felix Giordano

Did you ever wonder what your dog is thinking about when he or she is watching you? You know, those times when you're walking by and your dog's deep brown eyes follow you while the rest of their body is motionless.

Of course you have! For what other reason do you ask your dog, "What's the matter, are you hungry, do you want to go outside?"

They have us programmed and know the right buttons to push. In fact, they have more control over our lives than we have of theirs.

Believe it, I'm not barking up the wrong tree. Dogs are intelligent, silly, cunning, revealing, methodical, spontaneous, focused, and capricious.

They are all of what we are and more. Have you ever seen a dog when its owners leave the house? They sit by the window and watch their master back out of the driveway. Do you think every dog then lies down in the corner and waits for their owner to come home? Oh no, from that point on its okay, let the fun begin! Where are the treats? What's that noise? Hey, is that a mouse? Where's that damn cat when you need one! I'm hungry! I wish they'd get another dog. I know there's food around here somewhere! I'm bored, when are they coming home?

I sometimes go to shopping centers and see dogs that have driven there. You've seen them too. They sit in the driver's seat and pretend they don't see you. I don't know why they don't go into the store. Then as you walk by the car, they bark with such ferocity that you'd swear they thought you were an animal control officer.

They're just like human beings! We have even given them human names! My dog's name is Brenda, her best dog friend is named Kiera, across the street is a Cocker Spaniel named Cindy and Boomer, the Dalmatian, he lives in the Cape down the street.

In fact, you can walk through your neighborhood and know the houses by the dogs that live there. Well, how often have you ever seen their owners? See, I told you so.

Oh, here's Buster's house. I see they have a new run for him in the back. And here comes Ginger! My, she's loose today. We're lucky she's in a good mood. And let's cross the street now, we don't want to go by Rex' house. He's broken a few chains you know and they've stopped delivering the mail there.

The mail! My dog gets mail. Of course, let's not count the mail-in refunds she's submitted to reach our family quota. My relatives and friends sometimes address cards and letters to Brenda. And when she gets mail, we always show her the card. She usually reacts differently depending upon whose name is on the card. Of course, even we get excited at times telling her who it's from. You might say we have common emotional experiences.

However, she doesn't like to read the mail from the vet and I don't blame her. She's never had to pay any of the bills herself yet. I've considered pet insurance but it seems so expensive. Wouldn't it be easier to just file them as dependents at income tax time? I mean, would the IRS ever question me if Brenda had her own social security number? Why not? Is that so unusual? Some dogs work for a living.

Many dogs are paid for movies, commercials, and advertisements. They are stereotyped into their roles and never complain. There are even some dogs who work for no pay at all, never ask for vacation time and aren't aware of their career path. Now you know there's something wrong with that. Of course there is: no union!

A dog union is what they need! It could be called the Federated International Dog Organization, FIDO for short. Let's give them a break and some compensation protection. They are underpaid, overworked, slighted at every turn and never protest about those promotions that never come!

Think of what this could do for the national economy. Jobs would be created, positions filled and a completely new segment of our population could be recognized for their value to society.

Uncle Sam would benefit greatly. I know. I've spoken to him about this very topic myself. You don't believe me? Ask him yourself! He lives on East Main Street in Wallingford and you can find him staring at passersby as he relaxes on a warm sunny day.

Okay, so he's a Samoyan named Sammy. But he has to be someone's uncle, right?

The Others
by Felix Giordano

Jonathan waited for the door to open as the sound of street taxis masked the mechanical noises of the elevator. Others were waiting too. Men and women, dressed in their business suits and carrying brief cases, appeared to be urban prisoners of choice. The elevator door opened, allowing some inmates to exit as new recruits succeeded in replacing them.

Jonathan held the door open while the elevator filled to its capacity. Inside, Jonathan stood closest to the door. He recognized the established casual distance between him and the others. He pressed button thirty-seven and adjusted the soiled canvas bag slung from his shoulder. A book attempted to make its escape from a tattered corner of the bag but Jonathan covered it with his fingers. A loud yawn begged him to reflect that he should instead be sleeping at home. He scratched at his face, trying to untangle a small curl of his beard that seemed to have a will of its own.

"Stuffy, in here. Isn't it?" he asked the others.

Jonathan received no answer from his audience of well-dressed professionals. The sweatshirt he wore bore the marks of repeated scuffles with a grimy opponent, as did the moccasins whose holes allowed his bare feet to breath in the hot summer air.

"Sir, do you mind?" asked a balding gentleman in a three-piece suit persuading Jonathan to follow his eyes to the bag brushing the gentleman's suit jacket.

"Is there a problem?" Jonathan asked.

The gentleman exclaimed, "This is a brand new Damiani custom-made suit and I have an executive board meeting in a half hour!"

Jonathan laughed. "A Damiani? You should have chosen an Armani. That would have made a better impression. If you had paged me I could have lent you one of mine."

Jonathan adjusted his baseball cap allowing his hair to cascade to his shoulders.

"Do you work here?" demanded the gentleman.

"Nope."

"I'm so sorry. I would like to have seen you get fired."

"That's really funny," said Jonathan. "Is your face always red like that? It doesn't match your brown tie."

The door opened and the man left the elevator cursing and contorting his body to avoid Jonathan. As the elevator climbed the midtown skyscraper, the others left one by one until Jonathan was alone. He leaned against the back wall, closed his eyes, and drifted into creative relaxation. It had been a long time since he was an active member of the corporate world and an even longer time since he was a participant in a committed relationship. He remembered those days when his expectations of others always seemed to fall short and he would walk away a slightly injured young man. No, he couldn't go back to that life. He'd had enough of unscrupulous bosses and unfaithful lovers. He needed to do what was right for him and never try to please others again.

A loud noise rousted him from his thoughts as the elevator stopped at the twenty-ninth floor. He watched the door open as a young blonde in a tank top and tight skirt ran in, turned, and flung herself down against the back wall of the elevator.

"Are you alright?" Jonathan asked.

"Everything's fine. Just fine!"

"Can I help you?"

"No!" she said. "When this damn elevator gets to the ground floor, I'll be rid of him for good."

"This elevator is going up, not down," Jonathan said.

The woman looked up at Jonathan. Tears had left zebra-like, mascara markings on a face frozen in dismay. "It's going up?" she asked in bewilderment.

"I'll hit the button for the next floor," Jonathan said.

"Thanks, at least you're not a jerk." As the words left her mouth, the elevator jolted and the lights dimmed. "What was that all about?" she asked.

"I don't know." The lights flickered and then went out. A second or two of silence passed before the emergency lights offered their dim luminance. "I think we're stuck," he said.

"You mean like, forever? That's just great. I've got a limo waiting downstairs."

"Not forever," Jonathan said. "Someone will figure out what the problem is."

"Thanks. First, my latest movie is cancelled, and then I come to New York for the first time and find my husband cheating on me and now this. I'm having a helluva day!"

The woman began to sob as Jonathan eased himself down until he was sitting beside her. He placed his bag down and lifting her chin with his fingertips, he said, "Don't worry. Everything will be all right. What's your name?"

The woman stared at Jonathan and wiped her tears away. "What the hell happened to you?"

"Nothing… why?"

She stared at his tattered clothes. "You're either homeless or a college professor."

Jonathan laughed. "I did teach at Columbia."

After a thud on the elevator floor behind Jonathan the woman glanced over and then asked, "Is that Branson Silver's?" She reached for the book that had toppled from Jonathan's bag.

Jonathan looked behind him. "Yes… I guess it is."

"Disciplinary Action… where did you get it?" she asked fingering the raised gold letters of the title of the novel. "I've read every one of his fourteen books. I've heard it wouldn't be out until later this year. Do you think this will be made into a movie?"

"I don't know…"

She continued to ramble. "Do you know that seven of his books have been made into movies? I have dreams that I'm the girl in one of them, I fall in love with that Jake Forrest character, and we get married. In the movie, he never gets the girl. He always leaves her behind at the end of each story."

"Maybe he's afraid of falling in love?" asked Jonathan.

She stood up. "That's foolish. Every one of those girls would have been satisfied to fall in love with Jake. He's everything a girl could ask for."

"Well… I don't know about that."

She gazed at him and tilted her head. "You're shy, aren't you?"

"No..."

"I knew it. You are shy."

Jonathan got up and after a short pause confessed, "I get shy when I'm near a beautiful woman."

"That sounds like something Jake would say. Anyway, you didn't answer my question."

"What's that?"

"What are you doing with a Branson Silver book that hasn't been published?"

"I'm a courier and have to deliver it to Mr. Silver's agent."

She moved closer to Jonathan. "Do you know Branson? Can you give me his phone number? I really have some ideas for screen plays for a few of his books and... and I'd like to be in one of those movies," she said. "I've read all his novels."

"I'm sure Mr. Silver would be flattered by your compliments but no, I'm sorry, I don't even know the man. He lives a secluded life in upstate New York. I'm sorry; I don't know your name."

She offered her hand and introduced herself. "My name is Brandi Bermuda." She whispered with her hand cupped to her cheek. "That's the name my agent came up with. My real name is Greta Obermeyer."

"So you're in show business?"

"The movies."

"Well, I can see why he suggested a change."

"Is there something wrong with my real name?"

"No, not at all. I used to have a boxer name Greta."

"A boxer... you mean a dog?"

"Well, yes but she had a beautiful face."

"Look, it wasn't my idea to change my name it's just that my agent said I couldn't break through using my real one."

"What's your body of work?"

"I've only been in three movies. Maybe you've seen them... Heart of the Demon, Blood Sickness, and Death Dreamer. Death Dreamer, that was my best so far. It was creepy but my agent said it would jump-start my career."

"I'm sorry but I haven't seen them."

"Not one?"

"No."

"Then tell me all you know about Branson Silver."

"Look, I have to drop Mr. Silver's book off upstairs."

"Why don't you wait for me and we'll do lunch? We'll take my limo. I know a nice restaurant where we can talk."

"I don't know..."

"What's your name?" Brandi asked.

"Jonathan Parker."

"I'll meet you in the lobby." She wiped away a tear as a smile slowly enveloped her face. "That is, if this elevator ever starts again."

"I'm not sure..."

Just then, the main lights came on and a loud noise heralded the restart of the elevator. They rode up to the thirty-seventh floor. Jonathan stepped out.

"I'll meet you downstairs in what, fifteen minutes? Will that be enough time?" Brandi asked as Jonathan stood in the elevator doorway holding his canvas bag. "Wait!" said Brandi as she stepped toward Jonathan. Brandi stood on her toes holding back the elevator doors with both hands and planted a kiss on Jonathan's cheek just above his beard. "You're a decent man, Jonathan Parker. I'll wait for you."

Jonathan touched his cheek. He felt the tepid moistness of Brandi's kiss as he watched the elevator door close, the warmth of her smile radiated toward him

A man peered out from his office. "Jonathan. What are you doing standing there? Get in here."

Jonathan awoke from his daydream, turned, and stared at the man. "Luke, I'm sorry. That girl..."

"What girl?"

"One of the most attractive women I've ever seen. She kissed me. You didn't see her?"

"No. Get in here."

"I've got the book with me."

"Great. Let's go in my office and review the contract. What do you think of Disciplinary Action?" asked Luke.

"Not bad. Branson is satisfied with the format. When can you start the first printing?"

"They're already set up at the publisher. We can start Wednesday." Jonathan continued to stare at the elevator door. "Jonathan, did someone make a pass at you? I can see the lipstick stain on your cheek."

Jonathan looked at Luke, touched his face, and then glanced at the elevator one last time. "Maybe." He turned back to Luke. "But I think she's in love with Branson. He's the writer, I'm only the courier."

They walked inside Luke's office.

"Jonathan, I feel like I'm talking to a multiple personality. Why don't you consider publishing a book in your own name?"

Jonathan smiled at Luke. "Because who would want to publish a book by Jonathan Parker?"

"Don't worry I can pitch it to publishers."

"Luke, if I could go back in time I would do it all over again exactly the same."

Luke shook his head. "You were once a rising star in this city. You had the business world at your feet and you turned down that CEO promotion."

"Because the board wanted me to lay off ten percent of the workforce." Jonathan's voice grew louder. "Luke, what would you do if you just met a woman for the first time and you were sure that if you couldn't live the rest of your life with her you would at least be willing to try and see what the future holds?"

"Nothing, my wife would kill me."

"No, suppose you weren't married."

"Well, I guess it would depend on who she was, what the situation was, whether I thought anything would come of it, and if I thought it was all worth it in the end."

"Thanks. You've answered my question. Are they still repairing the back stairwell?"

"No they finished last week," said Luke. "Answer me, why don't you publish a book in your own name? And why don't you give yourself a shot with that girl if you think she might mean that much to you?"

"Branson Silver can do anything he wants, get anyone he wants, but he always leaves the girl. I can't trust others. I may be more like Branson than you've ever imagined."

To be continued…

The Continuing Saga of Humpty Dumpty
by Felix Giordano

All the King's horses and all the King's men,
returned Humpty Dumpty to the King once again.

The King knew Humpty needed treatment very soon,
and proclaimed, "Bring him to the hospital emergency room."

The doctors and nurses, they consulted for hours,
while in the lobby were some cards and some flowers.

They ordered a cat scan and some blood work too,
for they did not know if Humpty had the flu.

Sitting and brooding in intensive care all week,
Humpty Dumpty's mood turned to mild and meek.

"I wish I could leave," Humpty spoke to the nurse,
she said, "Let me give you this from deep in my purse."

A master key appeared and was surrendered away,
and Humpty made his escape on that very day.

He was not broken or bruised, cut or impaired,
just in dire need of someone who cared.

You see, Humpty was rushed to the local ER,
since all the King's men did not know CPR.

The doctors were interested in fees and expense,
therefore, Humpty was detained under false pretense.

Mr. Dumpty hired a lawyer, who sought compensation,
and in the King's realm, it caused quite a sensation.

Now the King is penniless, a pauper it's true,
since Humpty, under advisement, decided to sue.

Now Humpty Dumpty is ruler and presides over all,
his law is simple, respect sitters on the wall.

Attila circa 2525
by Felix Giordano

"Attila, Attila, wake up."

Attila opened his eyes. "Why is the sun on my forehead and why am I tied down. Where am I and what is this strange language I speak?"

The doctor lowered his mask. "We've implanted a revolutionary translator/transmitter in your brain and larynx. That way you can understand us and we can understand you. What you see before you is a high intensity lamp and the straps are for your protection. You are in the Griffiss Air Force Base Hospital Research Center in Rome, New York."

"Rome? Give me audience with Pope Leo," Attila screamed. "I have unfinished business with that scoundrel. Though they call me the scourge of God, Attila Etzel only wants to right things for his people. I must destroy the oppression that is the Roman Empire."

"No, no Mr. Attila. You are in Rome, New York, not Rome, Italy and the year is 2525. You must be having a flashback."

"I know not of what you speak. This must be a dream of wild sorts. Give me my weapons and my horse. I will be on my way or you will face certain death at the hands of my people."

"Mr. Attila, don't get excited now, let me explain. We found a relic, an artifact if you will. Part of your remains. From it we were able to extract your DNA and clone you."

"Who are these clowns you speak of?"

"Mr. Attila, you died in 453 AD but we were able to bring you back to life through a procedure called cloning. We took some of your DNA and implanted them into a donor's embryonic cells. One of these cells was allowed to divide and it eventually formed a human being, which became you. Isn't life wonderful?"

"You are a demon! Let me up. Your God shall cast you into hell where you will squirm with the rest of the Romans. I curse your kind and I swear I will kill you."

"Now, now Mr. Attila, you're not going anywhere. There are no Huns to return to, Gaul is now called France, and Europe is in a market economy. We at the hospital have observations to make, studies to complete and lectures to be taught. This will be a very busy time for you."

Attila fiercely rolled his eyes. "I am an important man, far more important than you, or you, or you," he said glaring at the others in the room. "The hour, it is late and Attila Etzel must go. I cannot wait and play your silly games. I must get back to my wedding. My bride awaits. Tomorrow I will move toward Rome and free its people from the Empire's injustice."

"I'm sorry Mr. Attila. Tomorrow you will be meeting with doctors and scientists from around the world who have pre- registered and paid very expensive fees to examine you. In order for you to cooperate we shall be forced to sedate you."

"You speak words I cannot understand, are you people from Mars?"

The doctor picked up a large hypodermic needle and swabbed Attila's arm. "Now this won't hurt a bit... hold still."

"What dagger is this?" asked Attila. "It is of barbaric proportions. It is fiendish in its nature. I would not do such a thing to mine enemies."

Attila gave out a hellish yell as the needle was inserted in his arm. "My God! I swear I shall never defile You again! I will adore You in all your radiance if You will deliver me from these savage beasts."

With a last gasp, Attila fell into unconsciousness as the doctors made way for the preparatory team of scientists.

The doctor waved to his associates. "All right team, on to room 2A. Let's hope Genghis Khan is in a better mood."

Poetry
by Felix Giordano

TRIOLET

I stare at her crossing the room
and long for her when I'm alone
I see her face at the sound of a familiar tune
I stare at her crossing the room
I remember the day we met in June
and the hours we spoke on the telephone
I stare at her crossing the room
and long for her when I'm alone

On sandstone cliffs so high
what secrets do you hold
brave warriors who chose to die
on sandstone cliffs so high
their sacrifice kissed the Creator's sky
with blind ponies now long cold
on sandstone cliffs so high
what secrets do you hold

A **triolet** is a one-stanza poem of eight lines. Originating from medieval French poetry, its rhyme scheme is *ABaAabAB* and often all lines are in iambic tetrameter: the first, fourth and seventh lines are identical, as are the second and final lines, thereby making the initial and final couplets identical as well. [1]

---

[1] Definition of Triolet from Wikipedia

HAIKU

Snow falls
on mountain cliffs
feeding glacial melt

© 2009 Felix F. Giordano

Haiku is a form of Japanese poetry, consisting of 17 moras (or *on*), in three phrases of 5, 7, and 5 moras respectively. Although haiku are often stated to have 17 syllables, this is inaccurate as syllables and moras are not the same. Haiku typically contain a *kigo* (seasonal reference), and a *kireji* (cutting word). In Japanese, haiku are traditionally printed in a single vertical line and tend to take aspects of the natural world as their subject matter, while haiku in English often appear in three lines to parallel the three phrases of Japanese haiku and may deal with any subject matter. Previously called *hokku*, haiku was given its current name by the Japanese writer Masaoka Shiki at the end of the 19th century. [2]

TANKA

The dead of winter
when trees have shed their leaves
branches sway in the wind
reaching up to the sky
in praise of Creator

© 2009 Felix F. Giordano

Waka or **Yamato uta** is a genre of classical Japanese verse and one of the major genres of Japanese literature. The term was coined during the Heian period, and was used to distinguish Japanese-language poetry

---

[2] Definition of Haiku from Wikipedia

from *kanshi* (poetry written in Chinese by Japanese poets), and later from renga.

The term *waka* originally encompassed a number of differing forms, principally **tanka** (short poem) and **chōka** (long poem), but also including bussokusekika, **sedōka** (whirling head poem) and **katauta** (poem fragment). These last three forms, however, fell into disuse at the beginning of the Heian period, and *chōka* vanished soon afterwards. Thus, the term *waka* came in time to refer only to *tanka*.

Japanese poet and critic Masaoka Shiki created the term *tanka* in the early twentieth century for his statement that *waka should be renewed and modernized*. Until then, poems of this nature had been referred to as *waka* or simply *uta* ("song, poem"). *Haiku* is also a term of his invention, used for his revision of standalone hokku, with the same idea.

Traditionally *waka* in general has had no concept of rhyme (indeed, certain arrangements of rhymes, even accidental, were considered dire faults in a poem), or even of line. Instead of lines, waka has the *unit* and the *phrase*. (Units or phrases are often turned into lines when poetry is translated or transliterated into Western languages, however.)
[3]

---

[3] Definition of Tanka from Wikipedia

In My Life
by Felix Giordano

"They shot John Lennon."

"What did you say?" Jimmy asked the restaurant manager who had wandered on stage and interrupted his acoustic set.

"I said John Lennon got shot."

Jimmy took a step back and sat on his stool. His roaming eyes stared at the tables, chairs, and then at the blank faces of the audience.

"Is he all right?"

The restaurant manager continued barely above a whisper. "Howard Cosell just announced on Monday Night Football that he's dead."

Jimmy looked at his watch, it was almost midnight. "I can't continue, not now."

The manager placed his hand on Jimmy's shoulder. "Let me announce this… take a break."

Jimmy threw back his long black hair and got up from his stool. Carrying his orange Gretsch 6120 hollow body guitar, he nodded to the patrons and said, "I'll be right back."

After he walked off stage and the manager announced the tragic news to the audience, Jimmy noticed a woman crying. She stood next to a group of people, some covering their mouths with their hands. Near the restrooms, a gaggle of twenty-year olds rushed into the ladies room, their faces swathed in handkerchiefs.

The restaurant owner walked up to Jimmy. "Did you hear the news?"

Jimmy nodded, stroking his full beard. "What happened?"

"All I know is that some nut shot him in front of Lennon's building in the City." The restaurant owner continued, "What a shame. He seemed like he was a good person. You know… give peace a chance, all you need is love."

"Yeah, his message was all about treating people right."

"Hey, yesterday you said that you actually met him once."

"Yeah… I did."

"Tell me about it."

Jimmy set his guitar on the cushioned back of a chair in the rear lounge area. "Earlier this year I was heading back to Connecticut and saw him in Penn Station."

"Penn Station... what was he doing there?"

"Having a sandwich at one of the underground shops... I sat on a stool next to him and we had lunch together."

"Was he alone? I'm surprised he'd be out in public."

"He was alone, in disguise. His hair was pulled back. He wore sneakers, jeans, a tan overcoat, a fedora, and sunglasses. I knew it was him. I have all his records. My room back home is covered with Beatles posters and pictures of him. That disguise didn't fool me, and he knew it."

"But why was he there... alone?"

"In his own words he said he sometimes liked to get away from the minted knob heads and get all chuffed with the pikeys."

The owner sported a smile. "I don't know what you said but I have an idea. So what did you two talk about?"

Jimmy pointed to his guitar. "I had just bought this at a friend's store in the City and Lennon asked if he could try it out. We went to a deserted concourse at the station and in a couple of hours he taught me how to play a bunch of his songs." Jimmy shook his head. "I just can't believe he's dead."

The owner was silent for a moment and then asked, "Can you stay a few extra days? I'd like you to play some of his music... and speak to the audience about your meeting him."

"I..." Jimmy hesitated. "I'm not sure. That snowstorm is going to slow me down. I have unfinished business here. I want to hop a train back to Connecticut before the weekend."

"What unfinished business do you have in Syracuse?"

"I was hoping to meet someone."

"Who?"

"A girl."

"Hey, who isn't... any girl in particular?"

"A few years ago I met a girl in Connecticut. She told me she was from Syracuse. She was gorgeous. She loved the color red. She always made sure she wore something red."

"Red?"

"Yeah, we had a couple of dates and things seemed to be getting serious but she left before I could say goodbye." Jimmy shook his head, his long straight hair bouncing back and forth. "I swore I wouldn't shave or cut my hair until I saw her again."

"I can help you. I've lived here my whole life. Do you know her address... her name?

"She promised that she'd give me her phone number and address before she left, but she never kept our next date. The girl's name is Heidi Becker."

The owner nodded and then put his head down. "Yeah I know her... and you're right, she's beautiful but her boyfriend's bad news. Forget about her."

"Why... you have to help me. I never got to tell her how I really feel about her."

The restaurant manager walked up to Jimmy and the owner. "Hey, the audience is ready to hear music again. They want Jimmy to play a John Lennon song. Can you?" he asked.

"Yeah... I guess I can."

The owner smiled and slapped Jimmy on his shoulder. "Good. Think about my proposal. I'll pay you double if you stay another week."

Jimmy shrugged. "I can use the money. All right... if you'll help me find Heidi."

"I'll see what I can do."

Jimmy walked onto the stage, sat on the stool, and related a few kind words of his recollection of John Lennon. He then spoke to the audience. "Here's a song that I want to dedicate to someone I knew and I hope someday she'll hear it."

He proceeded to play 'No Reply' and near the end of the song, a couple walked into the restaurant looking for a seat. Jimmy didn't recognize the man but the girl seemed familiar. Her face with its soft and gentle features complimented by shoulder length blond hair had every man and even some of the women turning their heads. Brushing the snow from her coat, she then removed it revealing a bright red sweater.

When Jimmy saw the sweater and took a second look at the girl's face, he knew who she was. He started playing another John Lennon song, 'Yes It Is'.

#

"Sit down!"

The girl rolled her eyes and reluctantly took her seat at her boyfriend's command.

A waitress walked up to their table. "What can I get for you?"

"I'll have a Bud... and keep 'em coming. What do you want?" the man stared at his date.

She glanced at the waitress. "I'll just have a ginger ale. It won't be long before I'm out of here."

The man laughed. "Bring her a large soda... she ain't going nowhere."

The waitress nodded and walked away.

Feeling a pain in the pit of her stomach, the girl said, "Maxwell, don't do this... I want to go home. I told you we're done."

"Why... what's the matter?"

"What's the matter? Let's see... pick Anna, Michelle, or Sadie for starters."

"Hey, they don't mean anything to me."

"You cheated on me and I heard that you're still seeing Sadie."

Maxwell pounded his fist on the table. "Hey... get this straight. You and I are not married."

"But we're... we're engaged."

Maxwell rolled his eyes. "Well thank you, girl. Hey, isn't it better I get this out of my system before we get hitched?"

"Hey, can you keep it down? We're trying to listen to the music," explained a patron from the next table.

"Mind your own damn business," replied Maxwell.

The patron got up but the glint from a silver handled knife in a leather scabbard on Maxwell's belt was in plain view. He backed down as Maxwell smiled and then turned to his fiancée.

"Tell me why you feel this way."

"Maxwell, I just want out of this."

He glared at her. "Out of what? You're not going anywhere. We can work it out. We've been together too long to end it now."

"A little too long… I wish I were back in Connecticut. There was someone there who cared about me."

Maxwell's voice became louder. "Oh, so now you cheated on me… when? That little cross-country backpack trip you took with Julia a few years ago?"

"I didn't cheat on you… we weren't engaged then. It was just a couple of dates but the boy I met seemed to really care about me. Not like you. He even played a Beatles song on his guitar… just like this guy on stage."

Maxwell cocked his head at Jimmy who had just finished 'Yes It Is'. "So why'd you come back to me?"

"I didn't want to break his heart. He was so nice to me."

Maxwell mocked her. "Don't make me puke. So go ahead… find some freaking longhaired hippie like that one up on stage. See how long they keep you around." Maxwell pointed to Jimmy and then shouted while staring straight at him, "Hey hippy freak… yeah you. Why don't you play that Lennon song 'Run For Your Life'? You know, the one that starts off 'I'd rather see you dead, little girl than to be with another man'."

Instead, Jimmy dove into the chords of John Lennon's song, 'You're Gonna Lose That Girl' and stepped up the volume on his acoustic/electric.

Maxwell's face turned a bright crimson and he looked across the table at a smiling face. "Heidi, what the hell do you want from me?"

Heidi leaned forward. "I want you to leave me alone once and for all."

Maxwell stared at the ceiling and then back at Heidi. "Fine… you want a life without me, you got it." He stood up just as the waitress brought them their drinks and handed her a ten-dollar bill. "Have the beer on me." Maxwell stormed from the table and toward the street slamming the restaurant door behind him.

Heidi gaped at the stage with glazed over eyes and began to cry.

Jimmy started singing a new song. "It's been a long time, now I'm coming back home." It was Lennon's song 'Wait' and Jimmy looked intently at Heidi the entire time he sang it. She returned Jimmy's stare and realized that he looked familiar.

#

When the song ended, Jimmy knew he had been singing to his true love. He introduced another song to his audience.

"If there is one fitting John Lennon song then it is this one that I would like to end this set with." Jimmy looked at Heidi. "I especially want to dedicate it to the lovely young lady sitting alone over there." Jimmy began singing, "There are places I remember, all my life…"

It was the Lennon song 'In My Life' and Jimmy sang it with such passion that a tear rolled down his cheek as he sang the ending coda, "In my… life I love you more."

After the song, Jimmy initiated a short prayer for the soul of John Lennon. Amid applause, he announced that he would return to play tomorrow evening. He received a standing ovation and disappeared off stage. As he walked in the back with guitar in hand, Heidi ran up to him.

"Please… wait. I need to speak with you."

Jimmy gazed deeply into her eyes. "Hello, Heidi."

A smile broadened across her face. "So it is you… Jimmy?"

"Yes."

"What are you doing here?"

"I was hoping to find you but didn't know how to reach you."

Heidi kissed Jimmy on the cheek. "Thank you for being so kind. I'm so sorry for what I did to you."

Jimmy put his guitar down. After a moment of silence he said, "All you had to do was tell me the truth. I would have understood. Maybe we could have worked something out."

"I didn't want to break your heart. Are you willing to give it another try?"

Jimmy smiled. "I would like that more than anything in the world."

Heidi looked around and then asked, "What else do you have to do tonight?"

"I'm done here."

The restaurant owner overhead their conversation and joined in. "Hello Heidi."

"Mister Westcott, how are you?"

"I'm fine... I see you two have finally reconciled."

Jimmy noticed Heidi's puzzled look and explained. "I told him that I came here looking for you."

Heidi wrapped her arm around Jimmy's. "That's right and he found me... and this time I won't let him go."

Mister Westcott smiled. "Jimmy, spend some time with Heidi. You are taking my offer of staying another week, aren't you? "

Jimmy glanced at Heidi, smiled, and then as Heidi tightened her grip on his arm he replied, "Yes, I'll stay."

"Good. Are you leaving now?"

Jimmy faced Heidi. "It's snowing pretty bad. Instead of trying to get home in this mess, I can offer you my room at the Hotel Jefferson-Clinton. I'll sleep in the lobby."

"It's bad out there... all right," Heidi said.

"How about we sit and talk in the lobby until you're ready to go to the room. The night clerk makes a great pot of coffee."

Heidi smiled. "Sure. Let's go."

"I'll escort you two outside... it's just a few blocks to the hotel." Mister Westcott walked ahead of them and then through the rear door of the restaurant.

As the trio approached the street via the alley alongside the building, Jimmy noticed the shape of a man with his coat pulled over his head and leaning against the brick façade of the structure. As they approached, Jimmy realized it was Heidi's date. He saw the man pull a shiny knife from inside his coat and lunge toward Heidi.

"If I can't have you... then no one can."

Jimmy stepped in front of Heidi and felt the sharp sting of a steel knife blade cut into his back. Mister Westcott grabbed Maxwell, wrestled him to the ground, and tore the knife from his grip. Heidi screamed as Jimmy fell backward onto the snow. An ever-growing pool of blood colored nature's white carpet. Restaurant customers leaving the front entrance saw what had happened and immediately flagged down a passing police cruiser.

Heidi cried, "No... Jimmy, no."

Jimmy lay face up on the ground in pain. His lips moved but no words left his mouth. He saw the blood below him, then Mister Westcott twisting Maxwell's hand behind his back while the police officer pulled out a pair of handcuffs. He noticed the onlookers, the concern on their faces and then he saw himself on the ground. Jimmy realized that he was viewing the entire scene from above. A loud noise startled him and he sensed that he was in a long corridor moving ever so slowly toward a bright light. Nearing the end of the tunnel, he felt a hand reach out and grab him.

"Bout time you got off yer plates. Welcome laddie."

Jimmy did a double take as John Lennon, wearing his white suit from the Abbey Road album greeted him with a smile.

"Where am I?" asked Jimmy looking down and seeing that he was still wearing his clothes from the restaurant.

"Are you daftie? Better ya ask where yer not."

"Is this heaven?"

Lennon laughed at Jimmy. "You ought to see the kipper yer sportin'."

"I died?"

"Are you going to stand there and talk the hind leg off a donkey? Yes you died and so did I... earlier than you."

Jimmy shook his head. "No this is wrong... this is so wrong."

John placed his hand on Jimmy's shoulder. "No this is cool. I already met Buddy Holly and Louie Armstrong. And, me mum... I'll see her too."

"No, this can't be. I've got to get back."

"Hold on mate, don't talk rubbish. I'm not allowed to throw a benny here. Remember those songs I taught ya? I heard you play some tonight. You done a fine job too. We've got so much time I can teach you more of them."

Jimmy felt a slight tug from behind. Then it grew stronger until he felt himself moving backward. He looked at Lennon. "I think I'm leaving."

Lennon stared at him. "So ya are... so ya are. So it's not your cards yet, mate. Go back to that girl of yours. I know she loves ya. Be good to her. I'll look ya up the next time you're up here."

Jimmy hurtled back and felt a crushing blow when he reentered his body. He felt the pain inflicted from the stab wound but the coldness of the snow and the darkness of the night were gone. Jimmy sensed the warmth of a blanket around him, the sound of a siren, and jostling as if he were being transported somewhere in a hurry. Slowly opening his eyes, he saw Heidi sitting beside him along with an EMT in the back of an ambulance. Heidi was crying while the EMT compressed his hand against Jimmy's back.

"Heidi?" Jimmy painfully tried to communicate with her. He called again and this time she heard him.

"Jimmy, you're alive."

"His vitals are stabilizing," said the EMT. "I think he'll be all right."

"Heidi, I..."

Heidi placed her fingers on Jimmy's lips. "Don't talk. You saved my life... I'll never leave you again."

Jimmy smiled as Heidi began to sing to him.

"In my... life I love you more."

Union Station Angel
by Felix Giordano

They say you know exactly when an angel touches you. It may be when we face danger and someone or something not of this world influences the outcome. It may be as subtle as a twisted ankle, a red traffic light, or a squirrel crossing the road causing us to delay our activity for a few seconds or it may be as profound as a missed taxi, train, or plane. Whatever it is we can explain the 'what happened' but the 'why it happened' is lost in our orderly rationalization of events.

It was a windy, overcast mid-January morning. The type of weather inherent with winter's bone-chilling influence. Less than six year's after the 911 attacks terrorism was a fading concern. Any sense of our personal vulnerability was more than matched by an 'it could never happen to us' fallacy.

That Saturday morning, the drive into Hartford was uneventful. My wife planned her trip to Maine by long-haul bus and had not forgotten a thing. She's like that, always prepared, never a wasted thought or action. I admire her purpose.

"Think the house will be all right?" I asked.

"I'm sure the girls will protect it," she answered.

In our case, 'the girls' were two German shorthaired pointers and one boxer. Unflinchingly loyal, they would bark whenever anything appeared out of the ordinary. As large as they are, their intimidation level rises along with their exuberance. They are excellent watchdogs as well as wonderful companions.

"Oh, I missed the road," I said looking at the left turn that would have allowed us to navigate into a large parking lot inside the train station footprint.

"That's okay. Pull onto the next road and turn around."

I slowed our Toyota 4-runner to a crawl and took a left onto Union Place, a one-way street. Unable to turn around, I looked for another left to loop back to the parking lot. Then I noticed a number of metered spots on the left sidewalk right in front of the large brownstone building that was Union Station.

"Think this will be all right?" I asked.

She looked at her watch. "The bus leaves in an hour. I'm sure this is fine."

I pulled into a parking spot and we got out. After throwing a half-dozen quarters into the parking meter, I then went to the back of the car. Grabbing her Spartan sum of luggage was a breeze. A one-week's visit with her aunt in Old Town wouldn't require much. Most of their time would be spent sitting and reminiscing, maybe an evening bite to eat at one of the many family restaurants in the area. It was a small-town, blue-collar community. No fancy night spots, no hobnobbing with celebrities or people of influence although we did hear that Stephen King's wife was originally from Old Town.

#

My wife's aunt was recovering from the loss of her husband just a month earlier in December. A heroic figure, he carved out an extraordinary career in law enforcement. First, as a patrolman with the Maine State Police, then promoted to detective with the department, his specialty was homicide investigation. Trained at the Harvard Associates in Police Science at Harvard University, the United States Narcotics Bureau in Washington, D.C., and at the U.S. Department of Treasury and Organized Crime Investigation in Rhode Island helped prepare him to become the senior intelligence officer with the New England Crime Intelligence System in Wellesley, Massachusetts.

When he retired from the state police in 1975, he began a thirty-year career as a premier private investigator in Bangor, Maine. Although standing six-feet four inches tall and being the spitting image of actor James Arness, he had a soft heart for those he loved and cherished, and fiercely defended them. Both criminals and despicable characters everywhere would never see that side of him. His scowl alone, his gruff, deep voice, or even the sight of his meat hook hands could force an adversary into compliance.

When I first met him years earlier, I knew he was special. An intimidating man, he was really a jokester, a kidder. He liked to pull the wool over people's eyes and have a laugh over the most mundane and common things. Perhaps it was his way of lightening the air. Letting others know not to take life so seriously especially when with friends and to be happy with what you have and with those around you. All I knew was that I respected him and felt comfortable in his presence. I believe that he truly loved his niece, my wife and was happy that we had each found one another. I remember the jokes they shared especially about moose sightings.

"Come on up to Maine and I'll show you a real live moose," he often boasted to her.

So she did. He drove her out into the backwoods of Millinocket one year looking for moose but nary was one to be found. Then as if to counter his infectious humor, my wife would mail him anything resembling a moose. Greeting cards, stuffed animals, buttons, just anything with the face or body of a moose would be mailed to him for a laugh.

#

Looking at the station's gallery of front windows with the clouds reflected in their glare, we climbed the steps, walked inside, and crossed the expansive lobby. My mind photocopied the marbled walls and maroon-tiled, uncluttered shiny floor. Down a few steps to the bus terminal, we approached the desk and ordered the round-trip ticket. Then we waited. The crowd of travelers ebbed and flowed with the arrival and departure of busses associated with various destinations.

When the bus to Bangor, Maine finally pulled into one of the dozen or so parking spots outside the bus terminal, I led the way carrying my wife's lone piece of luggage.

"I wish you a safe trip," I said.

My wife laughed. "My angels will take care of that."

She believed wholeheartedly in angels and although I also believed in spiritual forces, the fact that they can interact with us on an ongoing, daily basis seemed like a stretch to me. I always felt that if we placed ourselves into situations then it was up to us to get ourselves out. Nothing else would or could do our bidding. We controlled our own destiny.

We walked up to the bus but the driver closed the door. Not ready for new passengers. More waiting. There were dozens of people lined up against the outside wall, all presumably waiting for busses. Then, later the door to the bus opened once again and the driver stood outside. Passengers approached and one by one were admitted onboard. My wife took the carryon luggage from me, hugged and kissed me goodbye, walked onto the bus, and found a seat by a window.

Some people waiting along with me left when their friends or relatives boarded. I stayed some more, until the bus was ready to leave. Close to thirty minutes must have elapsed. I stood alone against the wall of the building. When the bus left, I breathed a sigh and made my way back into the terminal.

I remember passing the front desk and then up the steps toward the lobby. My peripheral vision caught a glimpse of someone to my right. I dared not look, not in the city. As I crossed the lobby, I caught sight of the person following alongside me in stride as we both headed for the glass front doors. Opening one of those doors, I entered a tiny vestibule. Noticing a young man who appeared to be in his late twenties leaning with his back against the wall, I reached for the doorknob to exit the station.

"Excuse me sir, can you give me a ride to my car. It's stuck on the Interstate."

I surveyed him more closely. Scruffy, sandy hair, a blemished face, a worn gray sweatshirt, and beat-up blue jeans telegraphed more than I needed to know.

An emphatic 'no' was all I said and then bounded down the stairs. As I headed for the parked Toyota, I looked back. The sandy-haired youngster had left the station and was making his way down the steps. Another young person, just a bit older with a dark complexion exited the front doors and joined his companion. I realized what was happening. Reaching the car, I pulled the keys from my pocket and tried to unlock the car door. I fumbled with the lock and dropped the keys into the gutter. Bending to pick them up, I heard the older youth shout to me.

"Give me your wallet and your keys."

I stuck the keys into my pocket and backed away. "What do you want?"

"Just give me your wallet and keys."

"I can't."

The younger one spoke up. "Just do what he says."

I began to shake. Terrified, I said, "Let me go home... here, I'll give you some money." I reached for my wallet.

The older man produced a knife with a six-inch blade from under his jacket. Waving it in a threatening manner he again demanded, "Give me that wallet and the keys."

The word 'no' barely escaped my lips above a whisper. I flinched as the man's arm thrust forward and the blade drove deep into my midsection. The pain doubled me over and then increased in intensity when he quickly ripped the knife out of the wound. I dropped to my knees and then fell to one side. The blood saturated first my clothing and then the sidewalk. I felt someone rifle through my pockets. First my wallet was removed, then my keys. I saw them being lifted away. I distinctly remember a laugh, a clap, then a car door open, then another, and our Toyota being driven away. I lay there bleeding, my last everythings slowly leaving this world.

But is that what really happened that Saturday morning or is it what could have happened? What could have happened if it weren't for angels... for my wife's special angel.

Oh, everything I explained is true from arriving in Hartford up until meeting that sandy-haired youngster in the vestibule of Union Station. What really happened from that time on is subject to conjecture. The physical aspects are easy to explain. My eyes saw what happened and I can describe them most vividly. But does the physical always explain the why things happen? Why did it happen is the mystery that we can never explain.

#

"Excuse me sir, can you give me a ride to my car. It's stuck on the Interstate."

I surveyed him more closely. Scruffy, sandy hair, a blemished face, a worn gray sweatshirt, and beat-up blue jeans telegraphed more than I needed to know.

An emphatic 'no' was all I said and then bounded down the stairs. As I headed for the parked Toyota, I looked back. The sandy-haired youngster had left the station and was making his way down the steps. Another young person, just a bit older with a dark complexion exited the front doors and joined his companion. I realized what was

79

happening. Reaching the car, I pulled the keys from my pocket and tried to unlock the car door. I fumbled with the lock and looked back. The two men had taken a few steps toward my car but then stopped, turned back, and stood at the bottom of the station steps. One pulled out two cigarettes, lit them, and they shared a smoke.

When I heard the squawk of a two-way radio, I glanced up and caught sight of two EMT officers sitting in a parked emergency van across the street within a stone's throw of my car. Their windows were partially rolled down and the red flashing lights on their roof reflected on the windows of nearby buildings. The officers seemed to be reviewing a clipboard and speaking via radio with their command center.

I opened my car door, got in, turned on the ignition, and pulled out of the parking spot. As I drove away, I looked through my rear-view mirror and noticed the two young men, eyes peeled watching me leave.

Why did it happen, you ask. Why didn't the first version of this event, which I described most, clearly become reality? You see, that windy day in mid-January, on a mostly barren street in Hartford, my wife's special angel was watching over me. An angel that stood six-feet four inches tall, resembled James Arness, and had a soft heart for those he loved, cherished, and fiercely defended.

My Journey as a Writer
by Beth Hillson

I waved good-bye to Old Town, Maine and left for college in 1966. I'd like to say I never looked back, never gave a moment's thought to the scruffy little mill town just north of Bangor that I had called home for eighteen years. I'd like to say I severed all ties with my emotionally spent family and did not return to the rickety foundation of my childhood.

But as I moved farther from the place of my birth and made my own life, a recurring question haunted me. Why did my family, a family of Orthodox Russian Jews, settle in a Catholic town in the middle of nowhere? I had no answers.

By the time curiosity consumed me; few family members were still alive. I returned to Old Town to find the mills and stores closed and boarded up and our former synagogue transformed into a storage facility. Nowhere could I find evidence that a Jewish community had thrived and became the cornerstone of this town for nearly a century.

I uncovered synagogue bulletins redolent with history and tradition, and interviewed the few remaining members of the generation before me. But, I had raced so swiftly out of Old Town that my own memories were having a hard time finding me. And when they did, the memories rushed at me from all directions, so fiercely, in fact, that I could not pick through the recollections, could not quell the commotion in my mind.

*****

The noise stopped the day my mother died, the day I stopped trying to patch up her life and protect her from my father who had died eighteen months earlier. The instinct to make her life better lingered until that last moment.

When she died, I uncovered a cache of rarely worn, expensive jewelry that my mother had hidden. A topaz ring the size of Texas and the color of the Aegean Ocean was in a makeup bag in her vanity. A 3-carat diamond that had been my grandmother's was hidden in the bottom of a vitamin bottle, the original cotton fluff covering the opening to conceal its valuable treasure. The flawless diamond had been acquired during a contentious division of my grandmother's estate. Mom rarely wore it, said she couldn't afford the insurance.

A double strand of pearls, in the original black quilted case, was set in the bottom of a shoebox under the silver slippers she danced in at my wedding. Mine was the only wedding of her three children at which she danced.

I uncovered diamond bracelets, a coral ring, pearl and diamond pendants, and pins.

A garish 6-carat diamond cocktail ring was tucked under a pile of sweaters in the false side panel of an old mahogany dresser. It might have been a twenty-fifth anniversary gift if Dad hadn't walked out on Mom the week before they were due to celebrate. He disappeared for two weeks and came home with a small box - - silver paper and silver bow. The diamonds were piled awkwardly in three layers as if they were pieces from other broken marriages. Like so many of the jewels Dad bought her following so many disappointments, this one was not her taste.

I was dazzled by the jewels. But I had also inherited the memories that came with them.

When I buried my parents, I hoped to put my memories in order and write my story, something I could not do when they were buzzing around my life.

And here was the difficulty. I was unable to make sense of the chaos, my childhood. I could not separate minute details from significant facts.

There was my "Coming of Age" story set in the fifties and sixties; the story of a young Jewish girl, a second generation American who lived in a place between Orthodox Jewish traditions and adolescent dreams in a small town that was predominantly Catholic. There were the parents who, by succumbing to family pressure, endured a marriage that should never have lasted.

How could I sort through the many themes and assemble a story that would be meaningful, interesting to read, and a tribute to my family and the others in the Old Town Jewish community?

I examined other authors who had written memoirs. I read *Girls of Tender Age: A Memoir* by Mary-Ann Tirone Smith and Angela's *Ashes* by Frank McCourt. As I read, I adopted the voice of the book of the moment. From Frank McCourt, I learned to write in the voice of a child, first person, and present tense. I didn't use quotation marks. I thought I was being experimental. My writing group thought I was crazy. I wrote about my father and my mother as Mary Karr had done in *Liar's Club*, but I neglected to put myself into the story. The voice was stilted and forced. My parents were gone; their bickering had ended. In its place, I was cataloging fractured images of my childhood. A new commotion was buzzing in my head.

And so, I attended creative writing classes and I wrote. At first, I wrote about the trivialities of life, examining dandelions and bicycle tires. But as I shared my chapters each week, the feedback and encouragement of my colleagues and my mentor, Jordon Pecile, bolstered my spirits, my craft.

Writing memoir has become cathartic. It has brought my childhood into focus in a place that preserves those memories through time. And the words - - those luscious words, the exercise of finding the exact term and abandoning paragraphs that send the story adrift - - these are the tools that I've come to love. These are the mechanisms that permit me to sort through trivia and tell my story.

How gratifying to preserve memory and put it in an articulate space.

Book Worms
By Beth Hillson

What do you do all day, Harriet? My father grills my mother.

It's not the kind of question offered by way of interest, like, *How was your day, dear?* It's more like an antagonistic detective demanding that the suspect account for her whereabouts. Mom stammers as she tries to defend herself against the cross-examination for which no defense (will be) is acceptable. She lists all the chores she's performed, the errands she's run with three little kids in tow,(and)walking everywhere since Dad takes the car to work. She says she has talked to one grandmother or the other on the phone, six times today - a chore by any stretch. Her voice rings with frustration.

You're never home. She continues. *You have no idea what it's like - all the distractions that take me away from what I should be doing. It takes me all morning to sweep the kitchen floor. Today my father walked in just as I was cleaning up from breakfast. I gave him coffee and he stayed and stayed. I didn't get into the shower until noon.*

My father is yelling now. *For Christ's sake, Harriet. I didn't ask for a blow-by-blow description. I just want clean socks to wear when I get dressed. Is that too much to ask?* He picks up the *Bangor Daily News* and goes upstairs to the bathroom where he slams the door and stays until dinner is ready.

Mom mumbles. *Impossible* is the only thing I hear as she propels herself into the family room and plops onto the green and yellow plaid sofa, sending her legs to nest at the end of the bolstered armrest, her head pushed into the pillow at the other end, and a half-read novel propped up in the middle of her chest.

I know that sign. It means I'll have to finish making dinner if we are going to eat tonight. I wait for the instructions that I know will come, the orders she will transmit over the top of her book, the words crackling just like the plastic edge of the book jacket.

*****

Mom relishes the moments when she can read a book or work in her wild flower garden. Taking care of three young children wears her out and she needs these times to put her feet up with a book or dig in the

84

rich soil of the flowerbeds, away from the phone, the kids, and Dad. When I come home from school, I find her on the couch or in the garden, pruning rose bushes.

I don't like weeding the garden, but I like to read. I am hooked on anything by Edgar Allen Poe. But I am not allowed to read. *If that's all you're doing, then you can help me,* says Mom if she catches me with a book. Sometimes she sends my little sister, Jennifer, to see what I'm doing. Jen is five years younger and can't help much around the house. But she's a good spy. She tells Mom everything I do. She tells when I'm reading.

"Well, tell her I need her to iron," says Mom from her couch when she hears the news. She doesn't understand that I can't put down a thriller like *The Pit and the Pendulum* right in the middle of the story. But five interruptions later - - "Mom says you better start the laundry right now... Right now... Come on, she's getting mad" - - I close my book.

*****

Mom can't garden when the weather is cold and three feet of snow cover her flowerbeds. She can't grow indoor plants. They don't like her, turn black or yellow or both and shrivel up, she says. She's not like Grandma Frances, Mom's mother, who has a house full of African Violets. They are difficult to grow, she tells us, but the perfect little blue and lavender flowers nestled among velvet yellow green leaves are everywhere - - the kitchen windowsill, the dining room credenza, even the bathrooms.

There's a lot about Grandma that Mom wishes she had inherited. Not only can Grandma grow violets, she also grows lovely, long fingernails that she has manicured and painted every week and she has silver gray hair that is set in a bun at the same salon. She's stunningly beautiful from her nails to her shiny, stiffly sprayed hair to deep periwinkle blue eyes to the evenly spaced white teeth she flashes when she smiles.

Mom's teeth are brown from tobacco and decay and metal shows on the lower teeth when she smiles. Those are the bridges Dr. Savage made when he had to pull several teeth, she tells me. She has soft teeth, she says. As a child, she spent countless hours in Dr. Savage's dentist

85

chair, him drilling and her sitting there with no Novocain. She had 21 cavities on one visit, she says. I wince in pain just imagining his drill in my mouth. But Mom is resigned to having bad teeth. She knows there's nothing that can be done. She didn't get Grandma's beautiful, strong white teeth. She didn't get her silver hair or her deep blue eyes.

Mom's nails are stubby and nearly the same color as her teeth, probably from the nicotine that bleeds out of the unfiltered Chesterfields she smokes. She doesn't mind getting dirt under the nails. As soon as the weather turns warm, she digs in the dirt, moving irises from one end of the garden to the other, pruning peonies so they will produce more flowers; and cutting back Hollyhocks so they won't fall over when they are swollen with blossoms. She putters in the garden every day except when her knees or shoulders bother her too much to dig and stoop or unless it's raining.

The moisture turns her kinky brown hair into a brillo pad, she says. It's another trait of Grandma's that didn't stick to Mom. She hates her hair. She has tiny, tight dark brown curls all over her head. She has it set once a week, but she can't afford the fancy hairdresser Grandma uses in Bangor so she goes to Judy Leblanc on Center Street. Judy has a chair and a sink in her laundry room and she's cheap.

Mom (complains about her hair. She wears a plastic hair bonnet that ties under her neck if there is the tiniest bit of mist or humidity. No matter what she does, it always looks the same to me.

I must have Mom's genes because I have the same hair. She tells me it's no use spending money on it. My curls hang in my face and I have to push them back so they don't cover my black glasses. The glasses, the hair, lead to another affliction - - at school the kids label me *geek and brain child*. They all have straight blond or light brown hair. They don't understand that there is nothing I can do about my frizzy hair.

*****

Mom reads more than anyone I know. She visits the public library three times a week where the librarian, Lulu Brown, holds all the new releases for her. "Lots of people are waiting for the new Michener book, but I know you'll have it back in no time so I'm giving it to you first," she says. Lulu Brown is 4 foot 11 tall with heels. From the side, she zigzags like the letter Z - - bosom out in front and bottom out in back. From the front, she looks like a barrel with legs. My mother and grandmother call her an old maid. I remember you don't want to eat the old maids at the bottom of a bowl of popcorn or take the last piece of food on a plate for fear you'll be one too. I don't want to be an old maid like Miss Brown.

Miss Brown is one of those half-size ladies that my father buys dresses for at H.M. Goldsmith, our family's clothing store. He has a whole section just for half-size women, a shape that describes most of the over-40 population in Old Town. She is not very heavy, but has wide hips, Dad whispers to me when she comes into the store. She's probably a 14, he speculates. He's right.

One day I wait on Miss Brown and convince her to take three dresses home. She lives with her mother and unmarried sister and she shows them everything before she buys it. She keeps all three - - the gray one for church, the blue one for the library, and the fuchsia for special Sunday dinners.

The following day, I go to the library with Mom and there's Lulu wearing the blue dress I sold her. "You're looking very pretty in that dress, Miss Brown," I say. She twirls around so I can see her ample bust and bustle bottom. I stifle a laugh.

"Here you go, Harriet," she says handing my mother a very thick book. I moan. Mom will have to do a lot of reading if she is plans to return that book on time. She picks up the thick volume and gently sandwiches it between both hands like a piece of fine crystal. *"Hawaii"* is written on the cover. The shiny black jacket is covered in clear plastic that reminds me of the furniture in my grandmother's living room. Miss Brown smiles at Mom and then at me. She asks if I have picked a book and if I like school. She asks what I like to read. Would she believe me if I told her my mother doesn't let me read?

Miss Brown is never friendly when I go to the library with my friends. She is very stiff like she is a mannequin in my father's store. Her eyes narrow when she sees me walk in. She follows me from room to room, snapping up each book when I put it down.

She insists on absolute quiet and looks around every few minutes to make sure we are obeying the rules. She clears her throat frequently as if to remind us that she is watching. This not a gentle rumble in the back of her throat. It carries all the way to the reference room at the far end of the building. It starts with a deep wet inhale. The nostrils widen to take in a stream of air and a big gob of phlegm travels into her windpipe with a fine "*SNURP*." A moment later, she starts hacking like a cat with a hairball. She spits into a tissue and returns to sorting the library cards on her desk. My friends and I giggle behind our books and Lulu glares at us (over flesh colored reading glasses that hang from a fake gold chain. Each time she hacks, the glasses fall off her nose and sway like a divining rod over her ample bosom. I ask my mother what's wrong with Miss Brown, why she coughs and hacks and does she know how disgusting she sounds.

"It's just a nervous tic, dear," Mom says. "Pretend not to notice. It's not nice to draw attention to someone's afflictions," she says. "It's not polite to draw attention to someone less fortunate like Lulu Brown who is a spinster, an old maid, with no husband to support her. She will work in the library and live with her sister and her mother forever, I'm afraid," says Mom. I try to understand how coughing and hacking might have something to do with being an old maid and working in the library forever.

I pick a book, *Mr. Bass and the Mushroom Planet* and pull out the dog-eared card. It is nearly full so I sign on the back. Ten lines are filled with names and six of them are mine. My sister, who is six, picks four books. Three are big books with a lot of pictures and one *Charlotte's Web*, has a lot of words. I tell her she is taking too many. She'll want my help to carry them and then I'll have to read them to her.

We say goodbye to Miss Brown and walk the four long blocks back to Bradbury Street. Mom has long legs and walks quickly. Jennifer dawdles. I yell at her to hurry up, but her books keep falling out of her hands. I take them and grab her by the arm. She cries, but I keep pulling. Mom is nearly two blocks away by now and doesn't hear.

By the time we arrive at home, Mom is laying on the sofa, legs stretched out. Her back and head are propped against pillows and a glass of water and bottle of pills are on the tiny snack table near her hand. A half-smoked cigarette nests in an oversized red ashtray, its ashes joining many others in the glass basin and a multi-colored afghan that Grandma crocheted covers her legs. *Hawaii* is open on her lap. She says the walk made her back ache and she is going to rest for a little while. She reminds me that there is a basket of ironing waiting for me. She tells Jennifer to set the table and wash some lettuce for dinner. Then she dives back into her reading and no protest from me will catch her attention.

I go up the stairs, two at a time, and put *Mr. Bass and the Mushroom Planet* under my pillow next to the yellow flashlight where I will read under the covers after I go to bed. Sometimes I read for two hours, especially when I have a Mr. Bass book or an Edgar Allen Poe story. Mom wants to know why I use so many batteries but she never makes the connection, she never catches me reading at night.

I grab the basket of laundry that sits on my mother's bed and carry it into the family room where Mom supervises the ironing from the couch. I iron my father's handkerchiefs, pants and shirts, her blouses and the kids' clothes. These must be ironed and folded exactly as Mom instructs. First the yoke, then the sleeves and then the bodice, she instructs, as I press the wrinkles out **of** her favorite white blouse shirt.

I'd much rather read *Mr. Bass and the Mushroom Planet* or *The Fall of the House of Usher*, but Mom says ironing is good preparation for when I get married. I'm ten and she is already planning for me to be married, to take on a life like hers. But what if I want to be a librarian like Miss Brown? What if I don't want a husband and children? What if I don't want to be like Mom, smoking cigarettes, popping aspirin, and taking to the couch all the time?

I think about Lulu Brown and wonder if her mother makes her do the ironing or if she feels afflicted by being an old maid who makes scary throat sounds. I wonder if her mother makes her do chores and if she would prefer to read a book, too. Sometimes I wonder who is less fortunate.

Maestro Jordon Pecile
by Esther McCune

After meeting with classmates that first month, I felt that I was in the midst of a chamber orchestra. There were so many different tonalities, pitches, volumes, and rhythms. Dark tales from Montana were undergirded by a haunting basso continuo played by cellos and a bass. Slashes of brass accompanied the acts of frenzied fiends while Jordon guided the textural dynamics through passages of hatred and heroism.

Melodic violins sounded beautiful passages then were tinged with darkness as they ran through story lines in Europe fretted by subterfuge. The writing was enriched by ethnic modes and modalities, as the tempo was carefully conducted by our leader. And across the classroom, woodwinds accompanied stories touched by fear and longing. I heard the mournful oboe when characters were bruised or swollen after being pummeled by the past, or beset by prowlers felt but unseen. Yet moments of hope occurred when the flute persevered with lilts of sunshine, as these stories progressed with long, fluid, legato lines.

Romance fiction was a part of the repertoire. This was accompanied by hoe down musicians taping their feet as they energetically fiddled, while percussion was provided by a washboard. We even had a wildly wicked love story from England. Our English friend was allowed to play her piece with short, sharp staccato notes and abundant syncopation. Her story was produced with strings, bass, sexy saxophones, bells and whistles. Our conductor just let it rip. And we all enjoyed the brisk rhythms of Klezmer music with its heartfelt melodies ignited by love, confusion, and loss.

Jordon was much more demanding with the rest of us. He kept careful watch over tempo, dynamics, and articulation working hard to help us in shaping sound and meaning. Jordon waved his baton (pen, actually), urging us to be creative, insightful. Of course, sessions didn't always run smoothly. One classmate wrote about a boyhood as all American as a brass band. In his case, there was mounting dissension and when his frustration was released, the class was treated to the sound of 76 trombones buzzing raspberries.

One night Jordon tapped his baton at me declaring, "Basta, basta," (enough). Put aside your Holocaust novella, and go back to your travel memoirs. You write best when you have lived what you write."

And this I have done, writing over a dozen travel memoirs all the way from Acadia to Zagreb.

As we pursued our writing, Jordon carefully watched over timbre and coloration, knowing best how to bring forth our work. He wanted us to not only articulate but to also invigorate our stories. He worked hard to assist us all in finding our sounding point, and for that, I shall be forever grateful.

Bravo, Maestro!

On Writing
by Esther McCune

That we are able to create is an incomprehensible wonder. It is remarkable that words can spin from the psyche stirred by images, sounds, and sensations. Writers want to reveal all of these wonders with others, and that is why we share our stories.

Actually, my first creative attempts flowed from the art of storytelling. This came to pass during the dog days of summer, eons before air-conditioning or television. Each afternoon my brother, Ray, and I sat with my mother in the cool of the basement under our small cape in Rhode Island. After lunch, we would participate in a story exchange.

Ray and I were keen on the word, *suddenly,* based on our wide knowledge of Saturday flicks at the Hollywood Theater on Taunton Avenue. This is why our stories were stirring adventures set in jungles or the Wild West. *Suddenly* the hero or heroine would be plunged into insufferable danger; then, *suddenly,* rescue would rush in from the tangled treetops above, or gallop through the high grass of the wide prairie.

Storytelling courses were taken at Wesleyan and during a sabbatical at Leslie College. There, students were taught about the importance of engaging an audience. That was as important as the tale. A tour of Ireland with a group of storytellers expanded my skills. We met in pubs throughout Ireland in both the south and the north sharing tales with those who painted their curbstones in colors to warn and taunt those who didn't share their beliefs. But once our stories began, tension was relieved, and, for a while, we were all just tale spinners.

Writing didn't begin until I retired as an English teacher, and so for a decade I have been putting pen to paper still focusing on images, sounds, and sensations and following where they lead me. For "Once upon a time…," remains a miraculous launching pad.

Easter 2009
by Esther McCune

It was a dark and stormy *morning* as I drove toward Boston to visit my daughter, Karen. The plan was to meet at a drug store parking lot, which was close to her home in Everett, a town just beyond the city. I was rattled by the ride: the harsh sounds of pelting rain, the crash of huge waves of spray from speeding trucks, and the rush of anxiety each time a car zoomed past in the break-down lane.

Her rotary, which I usually don't enjoy, was a pleasure to see, for it meant the drug store was moments away. Parking close to the doorway, I pulled up my rain hood and entered the store to look for bargains and to unwind. I passed three boys, about ten or eleven, standing by the window drawing weird faces in the fog. They noisily responded to the resulting display.

"What are you boys doing?" barked the manager.

"Nothing," said one.

"We're just waiting for someone" said one of the others.

Immediately, I had the strange sensation that they were waiting for *me*, and then quickly dropped the thought realizing that not everything has to do with me. Paying for a few toiletries, I was met by Karen at the cash register. She was laid-back and smiling, as clinical Social Workers tend to be. Her specialty is Crisis Resolution.

"The hotel is just minutes away," she announced. "The kids will love the pool, and you will enjoy a free full breakfast in the morning. Just follow me."

We both dashed through the downpour to our cars; but, as I got in, I was shocked to have grandson, Dylan, and three unknowns join me. And, yes, the boys from the drug store were there. I wound down the window, yelling, "Karen, Karen!"

She came to my car window offering, "They're just friends of Dylan. I told them to tell you about the books they're reading." And she was off.

Karen led the way, dodging in and out of traffic, her car almost obliterated by the rain and autos that intervened. I thought a literary

93

discussion might calm me down. At a traffic signal, I turned to the back and asked a blond boy, "What are you reading?"

His reply was, "We don't read books at my school."

"You don't read books! What kind of school is that?"

"It's anger management school," was his response, leaving me to wonder all sorts of wild scenarios, while grandson Dylan serenely smiled.

At this point, he received a phone call on his cell. "It's my mom. She wants to know how you're doing."

"Fine," I replied.

But the message he relayed to Karen was, "'Fine' she said sarcastically," and that made me laugh and regain a little composure.

I turned to the boy beside me asking, "And what are you reading?"

"*Hatchet Man,*" was the response.

Before I could conjure up a string of gruesome images, Dylan piped up with, "Grandma Tess, it's just a book about a woodchopper."

We were now at the outskirts of town. Traffic stilled and I could see the hotel just ahead. Reaching the parking lot, Karen knocked at my window with orders for the boys. "Go into the hotel, but sit on the couches and chairs. Be as unobtrusive as possible. I'll help Grandma Tess with her baggage. After we check in you can go up to her room and change into your bathing suits.

The rain had stopped so I could ask questions as we took a suitcase and treats out of the trunk, but Karen took the lead. "Mom, I didn't know we'd have extra kids. Dylan must have told his friends at the rec center where we were meeting. We'll just spend thirty minutes at the pool then leave."

Moving into the lobby, we saw all four boys *obtrusively* leaning on the desk eating jellybeans while chatting to the receptionist. "A room for one?" she asked.

"That's right. It's just for me."

Thereafter, action was rapid as Karen gave the boys my card to enter the room and change while she and I looked over the breakfast room and sipped freshly brewed coffee. As soon as the boys noisily burst from the elevator, Karen joined them at the pool while I went up to my room, maneuvered my way around a clump of clothes, dropped my bag by the bed, and plopped on the couch.

After five minutes, I assumed hostess mode. Confronting the ball of tangled clothing, I passed my hands over the mess, invoked Grandmother witchery, then easily determined which top went with which bottom. Clothes were quickly folded and arranged on the bed.

Next, the coffee table was made party ready. I had baked a batch of brownies for my grandsons. Each brownie was decorated with a mound of white frosting embedded with three or four tiny jellybeans. I left them in my large plastic tray, but distributed juice boxes and Easter napkins around the table.

Because a hostess mingles with her guests, unbidden, unsure, or otherwise, I went down to the pool. There the boys had lined up one by one to produce, cannon balls, thus "POW," "KABOOM," and many other powerful sounds reverberated around the room.

A young couple with two small boys watched from the other side. Karen called out to the parents, "Whenever you want some pool time, just signal."

"Oh no," said the dad. "My kids are enjoying the show."

Turning to me Karen said, "Sit back and relax, Mom. It will be over in thirty minutes."

The explosive sounds of four lively boys smashing, crashing into the pool continued until Dylan raised his hand, squinted his eyes close and yelled out, "Marco!"

"Polo," came the response as Dylan's strong strokes brought him to his victim.

Excited, I turned to Karen, but she was shaking her head, "Sorry, Mom. This has nothing to do with trade routes from Venice to Cathay."

"You mean they don't know about the Kublai Khan?"

"Sorry, Mom. It's just a game."

The reverberations of "Marco Polo" reached the same level of distraction as the cannon ball jumps. "Just thirty more minutes, Mom," said Karen.

"From when?" I asked, smiling, masking desperation.

Eventually, we returned to my room. The boys showered, changed, and gathered around the coffee table. Each boy devoured four big brownies and two boxes of juice in moments, seconds. Hatchet-Man then asked, "Where's the phone?"

"Why do you need the phone?" I asked confused.

"So we can call room service."

"Who will pay for it?"

"No one. It comes with the room."

"Not *this* room," I answered as Karen stopped the blond boy from slipping in between the inviting white sheets.

Shortly after, the boys began to tumble from the room accompanied by bumps, trips, hollers, and thank yous.

"Can we come again?" asked the blond sheet intruder.

"Hmm. Let's make a deal. The cup cake of your choice for a report on either Marco Polo or the Kublai Khan."

"But our school doesn't have...."

"So you say, but there is a fine library right across the street from the drug store. The librarians are kind and helpful."

A rare silence occurred as the boys thought over my proposition.

"I'm taking orders. Who wants what?"

Hatchet-Man, who said he was Ron, and his friend opted for chocolate cupcakes with coconut frosting.

"Who will you read about?"

They both chose to read about Marco Polo. I turned to the blond boy sorry that the activities of the day had moved so swiftly that there was no time for gracious introductions. I just nodded toward him.

"Are you in?"

"Oh, yeah. I'll look up the Kublai Khan."

What kind of cupcake would you like?"

Can you do a pineapple cupcake with pineapple frosting?"

"Sure can. It's a deal," I replied hitting his raised hand.

"Dylan, who will you read about, Marco Polo or Kublai Khan?

"I'm doing the Genghis Khan because he loved horses."

"Horses," the boys echoed.

"He had appaloosas."

"I'll bet your Aunt Janice got you interested in Genghis. Great! What kind of a cupcake do you want?"

"I'll have one chocolate and one pineapple."

"Naturally. You're on."

Karen marched the troops from the room, stopping at the door to say, "Let me get the kids situated and I'll be back this evening with take-out and a video. I immediately envisioned four boys energetically jumping on and off the bed, food fights, wild encounters!

When I didn't respond, she must have realized what I was thinking, so she added, "for just the two of us."

That Karen is really a whiz when it comes to crisis resolution.

I could envision it all!

La Boheme
by Esther McCune

Our last night in Paris, we walked through narrow streets to bid au revoir to Montmartre, colony of artistes. A light rain fell on cobblestones that glistened beneath the streetlights, as puddles rippled with neon rainbows.

The windows of our butcher and baker were dark, and shutters were drawn over the cheese shop and the fruit stands. But life pulsed beneath long awnings outside the cafes, where friends gathered on woven-back chairs for food, drinks, conversation.

We walked to a little park and kissed by the wall painted with je t'aime in hundreds of languages. Up ahead, roadways curved and twisted past restaurants and bistros where artists must have carted paintings hoping to trade them for food.

Whipped by sudden gusts of wind, patrons moved inside, improving the view for voyeurs. We watched entwined couples at corner tables; lonely people cruising the room; and good friends hunched over tables sharing tales of bliss or despair.

As customers left, the open doorways expelled strong whiffs of garlic, or savory scents of curry, carried on babbles of sound. Then the quiet night held only footsteps, the rain, and sounds of a solitary motorbike slowly humming over slick streets.

Our walk ended across from Moulin Rouge. We pictured the action within: lights flashing; can-can dancers screaming, rushing from the wings; an audience gone wild. But we grew still as we regarded the hill called Montmartre, the Bohemian haven for artists, writers, and lovers like you and me.

Tale of Two Cities
by Esther McCune

Then and Now!

"This does not bode well," Laura announced, as we moved down the hallway of the Regent Hotel in Zagreb, the first stop on our tour of Croatia.

"What are you talking about?" I asked, surprised by the gloomy forecast, since the hotel was elegant with dark green plush rugs and rose-tinted wallpaper.

"Look at these photographs," she said, pausing to underscore her point.

All along the walls were large black and white prints of movie stars and members of royalty as they sat in their compartments on the Orient Express. A plaque indicated that the Regent Hotel was built to provide an elegant resting place for passengers pausing a night or two before continuing on their journey to the inscrutable East.

However, I wasn't worried until I saw our room. Wide windows were dressed in damask and organza. They overlooked a beautiful park with cobbled walkways, flowers, trees, and a fountain that exploded with jets of water. The marble bathroom offered us fragrant toiletries, and loaned us each thick white robes and slippers.

"You're right," I agreed. We are in trouble. On a tour you always have to compensate at the end for luxurious digs in the beginning."

"We'll end up in some remote place with bunk beds," groaned Laura.

"Probably in a stable," I moaned.

"Sharing our food with the animals," Laura wailed, plopping on her bed.

Dramatics over, we each took a long, jetlag-adjusting shower, followed by a short nap, before joining fellow explorers for an included dinner at the hotel.

Returning to our room after dinner, Laura and I made attempts to read out books to relax; but, that night books were not required, for sleep arrived quickly and easily.

The next morning our group was led on a tour of Zagreb by a local guide. We all enjoyed her commentaries about an arched cemetery walkway that was so brilliantly conceived, it is still being fathomed by architects. The designer burned all of his papers before his death, and, to this day, his plans and methods remain a mystery.

Our guide led us along the Promenade of Gradec to view the churches, private dwellings, and businesses of Zagreb. She also pointed to tall white buildings standing in sporadic clumps at the edge of the city. These were the dwellings built for the workers during the years of Communist rule. Fashioned from simple concrete blocks, these structures were not graced with molded trim for the windows, or colored paint for the doorways. At the outskirts of the city, practicality, not artistry was the intent.

This is why we loved the main sector of Zagreb. Riding through the city on our tour bus, we thought we were in the middle of Vienna, because of the elegantly designed buildings, and the generous spaces set aside for parks along the wide boulevard.

That afternoon, tour members were offered an excursion into the countryside. But Laura and I, wanting to merge into the Austro-Hungarian Empire, opted to walk the street of Zagreb.

At Jelacic Square, we paused at an outdoor café for fresh- squeezed orange juice in a flute, and a chance to watch Croatians: tall, beautiful people with a predilection for leather jackets, coats, and boots.

As we walked along the boulevard, we periodically veered into the parks to admire the flowers and shrubs. A large bandstand graced the center of one park. "Funny," I said, "but I feel I've seen that bandstand before."

"Well, there are two possibilities," rejoined Laura, "Either you were here in another life, or you have passed such bandstands in village squares throughout New England."

"I'm going with the former life bit," I replied. "And let me introduce you to my escort," I continued, pointing to the statue of a man casually leaning against a light post.

Walking on we found a farmers' market overflowing with fresh produce and pots filled with deep-colored mums and dahlias. Adjoining the market place, young descendants of the farmers ran souvenir stands. Chatting with these young people, we found that they were quite proud of their family's retail careers.

One young man said, "My grandmother was the first businessman in our family. She had a little stand in Jelacic Square where she sold candy every day of the year. She's the one who earned enough money to buy our farm."

Moving to the broad boulevard, we passed many museums, little theaters, and concert halls, which edged the parks. The Museum of Archeology was conducting a dig where Roman ruins had been unearthed. The gate was open, and we considered slipping in and collecting a few grains of sand to slip into our ever-ready sandwich bags, but we decided to stay virtuous for the remainder of the day.

Actually, not much of the day was left. Growing weary and hungry, we headed for the underground passage beneath the park by our hotel. Tour-mates had said it was a good place to get supper.

Once there, we disagreed, as the place reeked of fried food and cigarettes. And we were perpetually jostled by people bearing parchment-wrapped; slices of thick, wet, glistening pizza.

We debated about eating at the hotel, knowing it would be expensive. Laura finally solved the problem by declaring, "If we just hand the waiter our charge cards, we won't have to face the cost until weeks from now."

Her brilliant solution furnished us with a fresh new surge of energy. We went back to our room for quick hair pinups, showers, glossy finishes, and snazzy outfits, revealing just a tease of cleavage.

We felt grand walking into the elevator, pressing 0 to reach the lobby, laughing at the strange numeration.

"Laura, did you know that nowhere is a synonym for utopia?"

"No, but let's hope that tonight we have a little utopian fun," she replied with a sly laugh.

We walked into the lounge, which held a few round tables positioned far apart. There, businessmen sat clustered around pads and papers as they drank coffee or wine. To our right, there was a scrape of chairs as three men rose to leave. The tall man in the middle with salt and pepper hair paused for a brief moment to glance at me. Startled, I stumbled catching Laura's arm to keep from falling. He put out a hand to help, but by then I was out of reach.

Laura, concerned, asked, "Are you Okay?"

"I don't remember."

"What do you mean, you don't remember?"

"I can't talk now," I whispered as we walked through the bar where couples snacked on platters of fruit and cheese."

Turning into the dining room, we were led to a table in the back beside a credenza graced with tall glass tubes holding flame-colored birds of paradise.

Pointing at the flowers, I proclaimed, "Oh, look! Utopia!"

Laura was not amused by the change of subject' and, when the wine steward asked us if we were ready to order, she said, "No. Nothing but ice water with lemon, until my friend here tells me what's going on."

"Laura, it happened decades ago. And I really don't remember."

"Remember what – a time, a place, a person?"

When I nodded, she said, "Hmm, all three. I'm waiting," and took a long sip of water.

It took me a while to decide how to begin. Hesitantly, I started with the image of the three men leaving the lounge.

"You knew one of them?" asked Laura.

"Probably not. It's just that the tall man... with salt and pepper hair... slightly resembled someone from long ago. Someone... who could... possibly have salt and pepper hair now."

"Why would you think he would be here in Zagreb?"

"Because this is where I met him."

"Here? You were here before, and you didn't remember?" questioned Laura.

"Well... let me explain. Decades ago my music-school friend, Jamie, and I did solo and ensemble work all through college. He went on to join a choral group in Stratford, Connecticut. And, just as they were about to leave on a world tour, their leading soprano was felled by bronchitis. So, Jamie arranged for me to join his group."

"And you actually came to Zagreb and didn't remember?" asked Laura more than a little skeptical.

"There was no time to look around. After performing, we traveled all night, and then checked into a hotel for a few hours of sleep before gathering for a series of rehearsals."

"When we reached each town, local conductors rehearsed the one or two pieces of new music which they planned to direct that night; then Walter, our conductor, gathered us together to perfect numbers we thought we had mastered. Each day we focused on the music. Rarely was there time for sightseeing.

"And the gentleman?" Laura asked, not giving up.

"The gentleman we passed slightly resembled... I think his name was Stephan, an accompanist."

When I settled into my chair, reached for the menu, and signaled the wine steward, Laura countered my actions with a shake of her head. "Not yet," she told the steward. "I'll tell you when we're ready." Seeming to enjoy the discourse unfolding before him, he stepped back, smiling.

Turning to me, Laura raised an eyebrow and asked, "And what did Stephan do besides play the piano?"

"Alright, there is a story, but it's not particularly sensational," I reluctantly replied.

"But there is a story?"

"Yes, and after I tell you can we eat? I'm starving."

"Hey, if you're that hungry, there's pizza dripping less than a block away."

I waved my hand, dismissing that idea and sipped a long draught of ice water, as I shifted through shades of sounds and sensations.

"We were to end our concert tour at a cathedral in Greece. But Ari, our accompanist, who had gone on ahead, called Walter in the middle of the night saying that it would be wise to cancel the concert because of political unrest."

"But how did you get to Zagreb?"

"Ari, had contacts at the Embassy in Yugoslavia and last minute negotiations were made for a concert in Zagreb to be accompanied by a local musician."

"Everyone in the chorus was worried about the capabilities of the new piano player. We had no idea that Stephan was the most sought after pianist in Europe. He and Ari had studied together in Germany."

"When we arrived in Zagreb, Stephan worked with the soloists late that morning. Jamie and I thought he was remarkable. Stephan infused new life into the Mendelssohn and Bach quartettes. Our singing pulsed with vibrant energy."

After the rehearsal, I walked over to the piano to congratulate him. Stephan rose, kissed my hand, and whispered, "You really enjoyed my performance? Then I must have more specifics. Will you join me for lunch?"

Reliving the scene, I continued with, "We quickly left the rehearsal hall and walked out to the boulevard along the park."

"You told me it looked familiar," Laura said softly.

Nodding, I shared, "We stopped by the bandstand to hear a young man play gypsy tunes in the garden. He wasn't a pick up artist, but a musician with conservatory training, which is why Stephan asked for Vilja from The Merry Widow.

"As the violinist began the introduction, Stephan led me into the bandstand to sing this haunting song about, 'a witch of the wood.'" When I finished Vilja, the violinist began to play the introduction to one of my favorite encores, a Magyar melody. Together we raced through scales, trills, and high C's.

"We thanked the young violinist with coins and currency, which encourage the small group which had gathered to do the same. Then, Laura, Stephan danced me into a twirl and said, "There is a special place for a special thank you. Come!" And we were off, running over cobblestones, crossing the main thoroughfare, darting into a side street, and boarding a funicular that raced us up to Gradec, high above Zagreb."

Although Laura was raptly interested, I had to take a break, so overwhelmed by long-locked images and feelings. The benevolent wine steward placed before us plates of crostini heaped with minced shrimp salad. This I devoured before continuing.

"Dismounting the funicular, we continued running until Stephan led me to a small, dark, holy place. The word Halva was written on every wall of this little grotto by the Stone Gate. Stephan told me the story of a great fire in 1730, which consumed all of the wood surrounding the gate. Only a painting of the Blessed Virgin and Child remained intact. Villagers called this a miracle. And to this day they go there with their thanks, expressing, 'Halva.'"

In the semidarkness of the grotto, candlelight flickered from a bank of votives on the far wall. "We must light one," I said, "and we did, dedicating the leaping flame to music."

Just beyond the grotto, we found a small restaurant where we enjoyed a hearty vegetable soup with thick slices of homemade bread. Then we sprinted back to the hotel, and it was this hotel, to rest and freshen up.

As we entered the hotel, Stephan whispered, "Room 353. Knock twice."

"Did you go?" asked Laura.

I nodded.

"What happened?"

"Just as things were about to happen, there was a knock on the door, and a plea from Walter, our conductor. He needed Stephan to join the chorus in conference room B for another run through of the Brahms."

"Stephan called out, 'ten minutes,' then held me close under the warm covers. After a long kiss, he pulled himself away, as we smothered our laughter."

"Just before he left the room he whispered, 'Wait ten minutes.' I straightened bedding, freshened up, and breezed out without looking left or right."

"What happened at the concert? Could you keep your eyes off each other?"

"That was a given. My eyes were fixed either on the conductor or the score. Professionals remain professional if they want future jobs."

"But what happened after? Did you spend the night together? How did you manage to lose the crowd?" Laura was ready to hear a colorful tale of romance and stolen hours.

After the concert, we piled into the bus and gathered in the lobby of the hotel to discuss where the parties would be held. I planned to stop by a few rooms, then slip away to join Stephan. But my plans changed when two little girls with long auburn hair ran into the foyer yelling, 'Papa, Papa!' and fell into Stephan's arms."

"I remember standing in a state of paralysis by the quartette and the dignitaries from Zagreb. Jamie, my dear friend, Jamie, put his arm around me as someone asked, 'Is Stephan actually married?'

"Oh, Yes," said one of the Yugoslav women, "happily married and has a new baby at home. But he is European. You know how you Americans say, 'He has a girl in every port?'"

"There was laughter as Jamie asked, "So Stephan has a girl by every piano?"

"Exactly," she replied as I filled with tears, feeling like such a fool. Fortunately, Jamie hugged the quartette together and called out, "'Star Fall,'" the signal to sing Nicolai's chorale, "O Morning Star How Fair and Bright." Happy to sing one more time every chorus member joined in singing Bach's rich harmonic lines.

"I know that piece" said Laura, "and Bach's arrangement is beautiful, but what did the concierge do?"

"The trick is in the timing. By the time a concierge determines that there is a disturbance, the song is over. It's perfect lobby music."

"How did you get through the evening?" Laura reached for my hand.

"Jamie took over, ushering me into an elevator, and insisting that I had to help him set up for the gathering in his room. He stuck by me all evening, leading me to a round of parties."

"So you survived."

"You could say that, I guess. But I felt like such a fool, a stupid fool!"

"But why?" asked Laura. "Don't you realize that in Zagreb, you were the girl by the piano?"

The wine steward appeared by our table, having decided that the story was over. "Champagne," I announced.

"You know I don't like champagne."

"Then you order your pinot gringo or your chardonnay. Tonight, I'm drinking a toast to the girl by the piano."

Peking Rose
by Esther McCune

Beneath a murky morning sky lit by the palest of suns, a guide leads four assorted Americans to a park in Beijing where we join a group of villagers for a round of Tai Chi.

The ladies smile their assent as we join them in "The Form." But the husband of one woman scowls disapproval from his seat on a near-by bench, remorsefully shaking his head.

To please him, and them, and us, and our "master," we lower our shoulders, loosen our wrists and fingers. then slowly raise our arms. The husband almost smiles.

As we pivot and bend, rounding arms and hands, holding balls, patting horses, spreading arms to move like cranes, the husband begins to grin, and vigorously nods his head.

Empowered, we repulse the monkey, holding bodies erect. Letting our waists move our arms, we wave hands like clouds, sidestepping, no, floating, magically floating over the grass, as the husband raises his face to dim sunlight and laughs.

At the end of the sequence, we are told to close our eyes, and inhale deeply to capture traces of fragrance (from the smog). I follow instructions, then express a surprising, "I smell a rose!" And the ladies are pleased. But my friends are shocked.

One whispers, "How could you smell a rose in this rancid air?" Another protests, "I'm gagging in this yellow fog. A rose?" But I did smell a rose, and I know exactly why.

How Jordon Inspired "The Student"
by Janice McCune

I wrote "The Student" while attending Jordon Pecile's writing workshop at Manchester Community College. I was inspired by a lesson he gave about the literary technique of "beginning in the middle of things." One begins the story "in the middle" and then uses flashbacks to bring the reader up to speed. Writing with this method lets me pounce right into a specific moment without worrying how my character arrived there. I find it keeps my writer's block at bay as once my character is in the tension of the first moments the story reveals itself to me.

The Student
by Janice McCune

I'm staring at the computer screen. My hands are on the keyboard. I'm in the local Computer Landing store, seated at a computer desk by a large glass window looking out on a congested New York City street. It's 6 p.m. I can't write. I can't write and I'm starting to panic.

My cell phone buzzes. It has been buzzing. This is the tenth time it's buzzed. I reach for it as it vibrates on the desk and flip it open.

"Hello?" I say.

"Where are you?" It's Michael, my boyfriend.

"I'm at Computer Landing, I…"

"What are you still doing there?"

Two months ago, I met Michael at a party in SoHo. He was strong. He danced like a Russian, bending his knees and kicking out one foot then the other, arms folded on his chest. He had a wide chest. Six of us played Pictionary. I was quiet at first. Then I yelled curse words when I guessed wrong. He thought I was charming. Leggy Debby wanted him too. He walked us both to the subway. She took the C train and I took the 1 train. He walked us to the C train first. We continued on without Debby. He kissed me on the cheek when we said goodnight.

"Why are you still there? I'm coming over." He says.

"Michael? Michael?" There's silence on my cell. He's coming over.

After the party, Sarah had called.

"Michael likes you, he wants your number," Sarah said.

"What do you think?" I asked.

"I think you'll like him." Sarah said.

"Okay, give him my number."

Michael called. We made small talk. In high school, he played Captain Von Trapp in the Sound of Music. It was my favorite musical. This must be fate, I thought.

I'm staring at the blank screen. My term paper is due Monday. It's Sunday night. I don't own a computer. My laptop was stolen in September. My friend Jared let me use his this afternoon. It's his moving day. He waited as long as he could. He packed everything else.

"Anna, sorry, but my Mom is ready to leave," Jared said.

I saved my paper on a thumb drive. I called Computer Landing where Tony works.

"Tony, I'm desperate, can you set me up with one of your display computers?"

"Come in at five. I should be able to get you on a computer. You'll have to leave when my shift ends." He said.

For our first date, I met Michael at a bar on the 29th floor of a Times Square hotel. The bar floor slowly spun as patrons chattered or gazed down on Manhattan through the glass windows. The cocktail napkins diagramed the view. Little arrows pointed to drawn images of the landmarks, churches, rivers, and parks. We drank and then we went to the ice rink at Rockefeller Center. We rented skates and I leaned on him as we glided about. I would have fallen, but he held me tightly.

We took a cab next. I couldn't afford cabs. We went to a fine restaurant. The entertainer Jackie Mason was eating there. I had never heard of him, but Michael knew who he was. We walked the few blocks to my apartment.

"I'd invite you in, but my roommate is home." I said, standing on my front steps.

"Come over my house." He smiled.

We took a cab. He lived downtown on Mulberry Street.

I'm staring at the blank screen. I scroll back to the beginning. Concentrate, concentrate, 'Maintaining Our Leadership in a Changing Global Economy,' the title works, but do I really have an answer? I lean over. I pull my notebook from my book bag. Flipping through the pages, I search my notes. I know the next paragraph is in here. I have a quote from Madeleine Albright in here.

"Starbucks, one tall skim no-whip mochachino!" Tony appears at my side.

Tony's got a beautiful smile. I smile back, place my notebook down and take the warm cup.

"How is it going," he asks.

Gosh, he has dreamy eyes.

"Slow, very slow. Maybe this caffeine jolt will help," I say.

Tony is in my program at NYU. He's a native New Yorker. He pays his way through school working here and at a newspaper job. I've read his sports articles, and though I have no interest in sports, he can write really well.

"I got the okay from my manager, you can stay until closing." He says.

"You're a life saver; I just hope that's enough time."

"Well, I'm off work in about an hour. Why not finish your paper at my place? You can stay as long as you need to and I can help you proofread."

I hesitate a moment. That is a nice offer. "Thanks Tony, why don't we see where I'm at in an hour."

The first time I spoke to Tony was when I needed class notes. Michael had talked me into watching the re-airing of the PBS Jazz Documentary. For ten days, I skipped morning classes and stayed with Michael. We lay stretched out on his king size futon mattress staring at the TV. I convinced myself the programs were educational - time well spent. Back in class again, I approached Tony. During class, he was always taking notes. My call was a good one. Tony took excellent notes and was generous in sharing them with me.

Finding time to study was difficult. Michael always had plans for us. The Sunday before mid-term exam week, we finished brunch and Michael was walking me home. Four blocks from my apartment, he suddenly took my arm and began leading me to the subway entrance.

"Hey, what's up?" I asked.

"A surprise." Michael said.

I let him guide me down the stairs, but as we headed to the turnstile, I balked.

"Michael, I need to get home."

"Oh, come on. It's a surprise."

"Michael, you need to tell me where we're going."

"Just trust me."

"No."

Our smiles had disappeared. Michael dropped my arm and threw his hands in the air.

"Fine. Go home. I was going to surprise you with a trip to the Cloisters Museum. Just go."

His voice was raised. People were giving us sideway looks. They were curious, but a straight stare might get them involved. I was a bit shaken. People don't yell at me. I tried to calm him by speaking softly.

"Michael, you know I need to study."

He stared hard at me a moment, turned away, swiped his subway pass, pushed through the turnstile and stormed off towards the train platform.

"Michael. Michael!" I called after him.

I was baffled. What was his problem? Taking a deep breath, I turned and headed up to the street and home to study.

The mochachino is taking affect. The caffeine buzz has me feeling hopeful. Okay, so I'm no George Will, but I can write. I can do this. Taking another chino sip, I glance out the window. A yellow cab is at the curb. The back door swings open. It's Michael. He's not smiling. He has on a long black coat. It fans out behind him like Darth Vader's cape. My stomach is queasy. Sitting still, I watch as he pulls open the store door and glances right, center, and then left – at me.

"Get your stuff together. I've got a cab waiting. We can still make the 7'o clock movie."

I've seen him like this before. He is not interested in a discussion.

"Okay. I just, I need to thank Tony and let him know I'm going."

At the mention of Tony's name, Michael's face seems to go a shade darker. Okay, I just need to get us out of here.

"Excuse me; do you know where Tony is?" I ask one of the store clerks.

"I think he had to step out," Tony's colleague answers me. I imagine the smile on his face means, 'are you crazy, you think he's showing his face when you have this angry boyfriend in here looking for you.'

"It's too late for the movie. I'm getting rid of the cab. Just be out here in a minute. I'll be waiting," Michael barks as he turns and heads out the door.

He sure is high maintenance. I gather my papers and save my document, shutting down the computer. When am I going to finish it? Well, if it's late I lose a letter grade. I could do that. Right? I glance around for Tony once more. No sign of him. I head out the door.

Michael is standing across the street. He catches my eye and starts walking. Traffic is at a standstill, so I trot across, around the front of one car, behind the back of another.

"Michael! Wait up!"

His pace doesn't slow, so I trot along until I reach him.

"I'm sorry. I know you wanted to hit a movie tonight," I say.

He doesn't slow down or speak to me. I'm tiring and I slip back from him a few paces.

"What are you doing walking back there?" He says stopping abruptly to stare at me. "Are you with me or not? Don't you want to be seen with me?"

Okay, he's lost it. I don't say a word, I just catch up to him, and as we both walk I make sure to keep pace.

The air is cold. As we turn the corner to a busier avenue, pedestrians brush against us. I begin to cry. Not hard. Not even sure why I'm crying. But, a few tears are moving down my face. They feel icy.

"What's your problem?" Michael keeps walking as he speaks.

"Nothing."

"You're crying, what's your problem?"

My tears suddenly begin to gush. I dodge pedestrians as I make my way to a lamppost, finding a spot out of the way. Michael follows me.

"What's the matter?" This time his voice is gentle.

I look up at him. He looks concerned like a parent over a sick child.

"I… I just…" I can't speak. My throat is tight, choking off any sound.

I cry harder. Michael wraps his arms around me. He pulls me against him. He's warm. My cold tears lift off my face and soak into his coat. I sob into his chest. He strokes my hair with one hand. Nobody yells at me like he does. Why am I with him? I could walk away right now. I could end this right now. He pulls me tighter.

"I'm sorry. I love you," he says, pulling back from me, he lifts my chin with his hand and smiles at me. "Let's get you washed up. We'll order Chinese and watch TV."

Through my tears, I smile back at him. He hugs me again, then, gently taking my hand, he leads me on towards his apartment.

Short Bio
by Tom Panaccione

I read Hemmingway's story *The Killers* when I was in high school –over fifty years ago. After that, I have wished I could write stories one tenth as well. In the meantime, I taught high school math for thirty-seven years and forgot about this ambition to write. Then a couple of years before my retirement I was reading the catalogue from MCC and came across Jordon Pecile's class on creative writing. He advertised the use of the Iowa method for the style of discussion in the class. I signed up.

At the time, I had no idea that many very good writers would also sign up for this class and the next and the next and this would go on for the most of a decade. Jordon's leadership turned the class into a dedicated writers group. Jordon moderated the group discussion of stories in a professional manner and kept the tone civil and well informed with his broad reach of encyclopedic reading. If anything, he taught us to read well if we wanted to write well.

Fred Blish, one of the group members provided leadership outside of the classroom by taking the group discussions to his home. Sadly, for the group, Fred passed away last year. I join my colleagues in praising Fred for his generous spirit in organizing our group. His leadership guided us to publish this book of our collection of stories.

I chose to write about some of my pastimes like fishing and travel and I wrote about child hood experiences. In the class discussions, I discovered flaws in my writing as well as how to create fiction out of the experiences.

The Good Father
by Tom Panaccione

I remained seated in the car like Pop said. He closed the squeaky door on the '39 Pontiac, then he leaned into the open window and told me "A ten year old needs to learn to be quiet." His jaw tensed just enough for him to appear grumpy. But he wasn't. He took off his hat, a black fedora that needed his inspection. It was covered with white sawdust. He brushed it with his hand and blew across it. No luck. He swatted the hat against the side of his leg. Some sawdust came off but most of it was permanent. He put the hat back over his gray head. There were some fine white lines above the hatband that marked where the sweat had been.

"I'll only be inside a minute," he said.

"Okay, Pop."

The two front doors of the tenement stood atop of a stoop that was three steps high. There was a small black mailbox to the side of each door. The doors had window panels that were decorated with white curtains. Pop climbed up and knocked at the left-hand door. No answer. I could see movement on the other side of a window further to the left. I saw the curtains move. Pop knocked again, louder than the first time.

This time the door opened, slowly at first. Then Mrs. Forte recognized Pop and swung the door open.

"Buona sera, Dom. Come in. Come." She spotted me in the car, smiled, and invited me in too. She looked at Pop for approval. Pop hesitated, and then he lost a brief argument with Mrs. Forte. I was brought inside with the promise of some Italian cookies. They were the crunchy ones that tasted like liquorice.

We followed Mrs. Forte into the front room. "Set down," she said. Her voice sounded like it was telling as much as it was asking us to sit.

She seemed old to me. Maybe it was her hair, tied back in the old-fashioned way. Or maybe it was her clothes. Her dress was black with little white flowers all over it. She wore an apron like she did the last time we were there. Maybe she seemed old because she was heavy and moved kind of slow.

"Dom, sit here. I made these biscotti and this wine is from Alfredo."

115

"Where is Alfredo?" asked Pop.

"He is at the Club." Mrs. Forte smiled. She put some cookies in front of me. "Mangia. You want some milk with these?"

I looked at Pop. He was drinking some of Alfredo's wine. With the glass, he made a signal that meant yes. Mrs. Forte recognized this and went to the refrigerator. It was new since the last time we were there.

"See my new refrigerator. But it's not really new. It's last year model. A 1950, on sale at Riley Electric."

I ate cookies and milk while Pop had biscotti and wine. They talked. I kept quiet. When Pop had finished off a half glass of wine he asked Mrs. Forte, "Did Alfredo leave any money for me? I told him I would be here tonight."

"No. He didn't say nothing to me."

"When did he go to the Club?"

"About half hour before you came."

"How is your new kitchen counter? Is it working good for you?"

"It works good. You made it good Dom." Mrs. Forte smiled showing pride in Pop's work, but she seemed a little nervous.

"And the back window? No more leak?"

"No Dom. Beautiful job. Grazie mille."

Pop put the glass down on the table. At the same time, he stood quickly. We were leaving.

"Have more wine?"

"No, we have enough. Maybe we can catch Alfredo at the Club." Pop reached over, taking the glass from my hand, put it on the table. "Let's go. Say thank you to Mrs. Forte."

The Italian Club was especially busy because it was a Friday night. Most of the mill workers passed through the Club on a Friday and gave up part of their paycheck for a couple of drinks. Some stayed longer. Some played poker or cribbage.

Pop got himself a beer and me a coke. I always liked the coke at the bar because it was loaded with ice. We sat at a table of poker players. Pop recognized some of Alfredo's friends in the game.

"Pull up a chair, Dom," said Nick Maggio, "play a hand or two. The kid can sit here too." Nick shoved me a chair.

Pop played out a hand of poker, losing two dollars on a full house. His was nine high but Stan Garalski had a queen high full house. Pop got another beer. I passed on another coke. As they dealt the next hand, Nick asked, "Does Alfredo still owe you some money?"

"Yeah," said Pop "I thought he would be here. You seen him?"

"He was here but he went to a big money game over at Pepe's bar. How much does he owe you?"

"It's only a hundred and thirty bucks. I would take five bucks a week." Pop waved off the dealer. "Deal me out."

On the way to Pepe's we had to take a narrow stretch of road along the canal. Brush grew across the shoulder of the road, hanging over onto the pavement. Drizzle had started to fall. Pop had the wipers thumping back and forth. Then up ahead the brush parted and a man lunged from the darkness. He sprawled into the road right in front of the car. Face down. Pop didn't slow down.

"Look out! Pop! Don't you see him!"

Pop hit the brakes. He hit the brakes in time to avoid disaster. Pop pushed the door open with his shoulder and jumped out of the car. Quicker than I could think about it, Pop was kneeling beside the man in the wet road. Where I got out of the car I had to wade through a puddle to get to Pop and the man. We rolled the body over into the headlights.

"Is he dead, Pop?"

"No he's not dead. He's dead drunk."

"Who is it?"

"It's George Loconta."

"What are we going to do with him?"

"Help me put him in the car. We'll take him home."

We pulled into the yard at George's house where his wife was sitting in the kitchen, waiting. Pop and I carried George to the door. Mostly, Pop carried George. When the weight shifted to me, I almost fell over. But I didn't tell Pop. We knocked on the door and George's wife was there almost instantly.

"My God. What happened? Is he alright?"

"He's okay," said Pop. "A couple too many, that's all."

"Nothing new anymore," said the wife. She was full of tears, her face hurt.

"Where's the bedroom?" Pop asked.

She pointed down the hallway past the kitchen. She ran ahead to open the door and turned on the light. I tried to help Pop with the body but I don't think I helped too much. We more or less dragged him down the hall to the bedroom, his heels dragging on the wood floor. We missed the bed on our first try. George was stunned into a half-conscious state after that. We draped George over the bed on the second try. He opened his eyes and saw me and Pop.

"D-o-o-o-m-m-m-m," he slurred out. "Where did you come from?"

"They brought you home, you ass, you bum… drunken bum," said the wife.

George seemed to have enough sense to figure out what had happened. Or maybe it happened so much that he had just grown used to it. He reached into his pocket for his billfold. He pulled out a twenty, thrusting it at Pop.

"Nah, no thanks, maybe you can help me someday. Besides, I don't need any money."

George closed his eyes.

"Let's go," said Pop. He walked out into the hallway with the wife. They whispered something.

"Hey kid," George whispered to me, "here, take the twenty, and don't tell nobody."

I looked down the hallway. I couldn't see Pop. A twenty was big bucks. I took it, stuck it in my pocket quick as I could.

"Thanks."

"Thanks to you and your old man, kid."

We pulled out of the driveway. The wipers were still clearing drizzle off the windshield. The thumping blades kept the beat going home.

"Why didn't you take the money, Pop?"

"We were helping the man. It was a favor. I don't take money for that."

"Is it wrong to take money for that?"

"Well for me it wouldn't be right."

"What about for me?"

"What are you saying?"

"If it's not right for you, is it right for me?"

"Did he give you the money? Did you take the money?"

I didn't answer Pop. He knew. He turned the car around and we pulled into George's driveway for the second time that night. This time I had to go in and apologize for taking the money. I handed it over to George with remorse.

"Your old man wouldn't let you keep it, right? Yeah, I know him."

We drove home after that.

"You want me to work for my money, right Pop?"

"That's right."

Halibut Man
by Tom Panaccione

This was one of those incredibly clear days in Alaska. The Sterling highway, swerving through Ninilchik was empty except for my car and the car in front of me that was trying to make me late. But Brad would have to wait. He needed me to pay him. As usual, the guides come up with an insane time to meet up, then if you're five minutes late they expand the five minutes into an hour and blame you if they can't put the boat into lots of fish. *Today's fish is halibut.* Sure, he could just say that you were a whole hour late and now you expect me to invent a ton of fish just for you! Then if you try to argue, I *was only five minutes late*! It becomes a shouting match and nobody wins. Which defeats everything you are here for— a good time.

Did I say it was a clear day in Alaska? The whole beach had a giant layer of fog over it. I figured the next thing he would say that we could not go out in this soup. I recognized the turn in the road he described to me over the phone. "You can't miss it." he told me. Once at the turn, I was glad as hell to bid farewell to the car in front of me. My rented Ford Taurus felt as if it bent around the curve. I was on a flow now. Almost there. I remembered the rest of Brad's directions, "Take the next right after Deep Creek Fish Packing, then down the pavement until you hit the dirt, then half a mile. I will be there, five a.m. sharp. Look for the *WhaleBone*." Then he hung up and did not even let me verify the directions or anything. Here is the dirt and as I turned into the seaside parking area there was Brad's fishing machine, the *WhaleBone*, a beauty. A twenty-eight foot custom made, plate-steel boat just made for fishing. Now, what about the fog?

"Hey Rick, you found it OK."

"Yup, I did. Any problem with this fog?"

"Nope. I have a new GPS system. Never screw up. Even in a soup like this."

"Where are the other two guys?"

"You mean Al and Frank?"

I had no idea who Al and Frank were, and I did not care either. But I was happy as hell that I was not the one who was late. Another car pulled up. It was Al and Frank.

"You're only five minutes late," Brad said.

"Ready to kick BUTT—haliBUTT?" asked one of the latecomers. Everyone chuckled over the old joke. With that said, he held out his hand to shake hands and everyone shook hands "Hi, I'm Al." said the other. "I'm Rick." I said. Now that the hello formalities were over it got very quiet in the fog. The boat was under a utility light. It lit up the rear of the boat in a circle of light where Brad was filling the bait box with bags of chopped sea clams and fish heads. He poured the bait out of two-gallon clear plastic bags. In the light, when he tilted the bags just right it magnified the slimy contents of clams and heads. I recognized the heads as salmon heads. Then he rummaged around in the back of the boat putting fishing rigs out on deck in rod tubes that were attached to the rim of the boat. Another car pulled up and parked out of the way. The driver came over and introduced himself as Pete, the mate of the vessel. He would do a lot of the grunt work- chop bait, gaff fish, toss fish into the fish well, pull anchor lines, and do what ever he could to get a big tip.

"Is the tractor on the way over?" he asked Brad.

"Should be," Brad said. "Listen, hear it?"

Fog was muffling the sound of the tractor but as it got closer, the diesel motor was much louder. Its fierce clapping suddenly took over the world of fog. The iron tractor, a sea monster, poked its nose out of the fog twenty feet from where the boat waited on its trailer to be hauled into Cooke's Inlet.

Al swaggered over to me and he spoke in a hushed voice. "Is this your first trip with Brad?"

"Sure is." I kept my voice lowered too. "Actually my first time for halibut. I'm usually trout fishing or salmon fishing with a fly rod." I tried to make sure Brad did not hear any of this.

"So, first time for halibut and the first time for Brad. Believe me; today's fishing won't be anything like fly-fishing. We've been out with him plenty of times and we always catch loads of fish. But remember, he is the boss on his boat. Sometimes things bother him that you may think are small stuff, but it might not be small stuff to him."

"Jump in." Brad commanded, raising his voice above the motor clatter.

Everybody found places on the trailer to place a foot and a place to grab onto and we pulled ourselves into the boat.

"All set!" Brad yelled to the tractor driver who had hooked the boat trailer to his tractor. And the tractor pulled us into the sea. It's a gentle slope into the water. That is one reason for launching by tractor; it is not deep enough to provide safe entry into the water by a boat ramp. Brad took this opportunity to give us instructions in safety and tell us what behavior he expected under his command. "Never forget, I am the captain of this vessel and I have the final word on everything. There can only be one person in charge and I am the one in charge here. I am also responsible for everything that happens. Now listen up while I tell you how to have a safe and enjoyable day of fishing." Brad went on to give a quick and accurate survey about the safety features of the boat. He assigned each of us a life jacket, told us how to use the radio, pointed out the first aid kit wishing we would not need it. Brad's face was intense and serious as he concluded his practiced safety lesson. It was as if he was saying grace before a meal. Then just as the boat entered deep enough water, it floated off the trailer and Brad said, "Now let's go kick some BUTT."

He started the engine and away we went to the first good spot, which he told us held fish during low tide. "When the tide begins to move, we'll move out to the deeper water where the bigger fish are." Everyone nodded, not really knowing what to think. Soon the anchor went down and Pete had our hooks baited with chopped up pieces of sea clams. It was only five minutes until Frank had a thirty-five-pounder on. His arms easily pumped the fish up from a depth of twenty feet. It went like this: pull up reel down pull up reel down, a rocking motion. Each pull with the rod fought the fish. "Let the rod do the work." Pete said. "Just pull and lift. Now reel down, bring in the line, and reel fast. Good... good. He's coming."

When the fish was in view, ready to bring into the boat, Pete gave orders to Frank. "Listen up for me to tell you to lower your rod tip taking tension off the line. Otherwise, if the hook lets go of the fish...and it happens...then it comes flying at *me* because I'll be standing over your fish in the same direction you are pulling on the line. Not only that, do you see the lead weight on the line a few feet up from the hook?" Pete pointed and waited for Frank to signal that he could see the weight. Frank nodded. I nodded too anticipating my turn at this. "This fish will come in tossing his head from side to side. Can you picture the weight jerking back and forth?"

"Listen up good," Brad said, adding a captain's authority to Pete's directions. "That weight smarts. Look at my bruise." Brad held his elbow out at an angle. Frank was holding onto his fish but took a quick look at Brad's elbow, red and swollen, surrounded by purple. "I got this three days ago when a client let go of the weight. Do not let the weight smack into my boat or equipment either. So, when Pete brings up that fish, he will hand you the weight. Hold it in your left hand and hold the rod in your right hand with the butt of the rod on the deck. Like this." Brad stood like a soldier at attention, holding a rod and a weight as he described.

Pete reached over the side and aimed a gaff at the fish's gill plate. Perfect shot. The fish was stabbed and Pete lifted the fish all in one continuous motion and had it kicking and thrashing its tail all about our feet. "Not too big, but it is a keeper," Brad said. He subdued the fish between his rubber boots. "Pick up the hatch on the fish locker," he said to Pete. Pete obeyed. Brad whacked the fish on the head with a billy club. The fish slowed down considerably. Brad looked around at the three paying clients and must have thought he needed to give a mini lesson about halibut. "See how the eyes are both on the same side of the head. When these fish are young, they are like any other fish with eyes on both sides. As they get older, one eye migrates to join the other, until they are both on the same side of the head. They swim near the bottom flatways, like an oblong doormat with the light side down and the darker side with the two eyes up. And as you can see they grow big and heavy." Pete grabbed the fish by the tail and slipped it into the locker that was under foot on the rear deck where we were standing. If we caught our share of fish, we would be filling it with about five hundred pounds or so.

"Fog's lifting nice." Brad said. "And the tide is starting to move. Pete, pull anchor. Let's move out about twelve miles to the spot we caught them a couple of days ago." Brad set his GPS navigator to the *hot spot* and throttled the diesel into high speed.

Sun bounced from every surface. It glared from the cleats that held mooring lines. It bounced from the white cabin of the boat. It glistened from the sea, mostly blue, but it was white in the foam that trailed behind the pair of boat motors. Far off, at the distant shores snow-topped mountains shown against pristine skies under the severe light of the sun. I was ready to have the motor shut down when it did. The quiet fit better today. A little more noise disturbed the view while Pete put the anchor down. I avoided the bait boxes that Brad packed with rotting salmon heads and sea clams. If the smell of rotting fish had a color, it would be green. My nose found refuge on the rear deck where a summer breeze fanned the boat.

"Look! Wow!" Al pointed to the northeast, toward one of the volcano shaped mountains. We all looked in that direction in time to see a killer whale breach, make an arc with its body, and disappear into the sea again.

"That's good luck." said Pete. "Remember last week when they were around? We caught a great catch of butt that day."

The fishing came alive, we all caught our share, the hatch that covered the fish locker opened and closed in repetition, and time seemed to stand still. Al hooked onto a big one.

"Hang on." Brad said. "That one will go over a hundred."

Al hung on and at the end of the fight with the fish, Brad ordered Al to bring the monster over to one side of the boat. He grabbed onto the fishing line and hoisted up on the fish until it was half in the water and half out of the water. Then he leaned over the side and swung the large pointed metal gaff directly into the target, behind the two eyes. No hesitation. He picked up. Now it was not easy to tell whether the fish controlled Brad or if he controlled the fish. The fish flung its head and Brad stumbled and nearly went down. Pete caught him. When Brad lifted high enough, he plied the fish against the side rail of the boat and levered it over and it flopped into the boat onto the rear deck. Before it was over, the head or tail of the heavy fish slapped everyone around. Brad finally got his chance to wallop the head of the crazed fish.

"THERE! THERE! THERE!" Brad pronounced in unison with his club making contact with the fish's head.

"He's puking up his guts." Pete said. Two fish heads burped out of the halibut's dumb mouth. One of the heads was the salmon head Al used to bait the hook. The other was half-digested. There was more stomach stuff, hard to tell what it was.

"We must have interrupted his dinner," Al said, laughing.

Al let go of the weight that was in his left hand. "It's not over yet!" Brad yelled but it was too late. The big fish arched its back and made one more heave of its body, flipping over. The lead weight followed the arch. The fishing line swung and wrapped around Al's middle finger. Wrap, wrap, wrap. Then down came the weight of the fish pulling on the line. All on board heard the loud POP.

Al's face cringed and he cried out in pain, "Yow, ow, yow!" He unwrapped the line from his finger and went into the pilot's cabin where he sat in a semi fetal position and nursed the pain with his other hand. He held his head down. Brad followed him. He persuaded Al that the main knuckle was dislocated.

After deciding that, Al agreed to let Brad pull and slide the joint back into place. But the pain persisted. Al resigned himself to the pain.

Pete slid the hatch off the fish locker and Brad shoved the big halibut with his foot took a couple of shoves and some help from Pete, but eventually the big fish was in the locker. Brad sat in the cabin, obviously surveying the situation. The fish were on the bite and everyone wanted to catch more. But now there was one client behind in his luck with his hand shoved into a towel full of ice, subduing the inevitable swelling. "Time for lunch." he said.

I had no idea when I booked Brad for the day that there would be such a lunch. He advertised on his web site that his was the *Best of the Sea*. Surely, this is only a manner of speaking I had thought. But Brad showed me different. He pulled food out of the cooler like a magician pulls colored cloths from under his sleeve. He set out the lunch one item at a time as he announced the menu.

"Here's a salmon salad...fried halibut chunks...smoked salmon. Fresh rolls, homemade HOT dill pickles...made 'em myself. Here are some moose ribs, a fresh salad, and balsamic vinaigrette dressing. And here is some caribou sausage.

Brad set everything out on a makeshift table made from a piece of plywood that he kept clean and dry inside the cabin. He handed each of us a paper plate and some napkins. Help yourself. I will be insulted if there's any food left. We sampled all the morsels. I had seconds of everything but I really liked the caramelized smokiness of the salmon, and now I was thirsty. I reached for the sack I carried on board with me and took out a soft cooler with a six-pack of beer. "OK," Brad said, "understand this right now. You get one beer for lunch and one more for the trip home. That's it. You can drink your own or take one of mine. Mine are colder. Or have a glass of this wine—red or white. I do not drink any alcohol out here. It's not in my job description." Brad popped open a cola and continued eating, making nothing more of this but he was clear as gin. *Drinking was limited.*

"How's the finger?" I asked Al.

"How do you think?" He pulled the finger out of the ice and tried flexing the joint. He winced as he made this effort.

"Should we head in? Frank asked. "Stop for the day?"

Pete was on the rear deck untangling some fouled lines, clearing chunks of fish out of the way, putting rods back in their holders, and eating a salmon salad sandwich in the other hand. He was getting ready for round two. He stopped shortly and listened for Al's answer. Pete was tossed as a wave pitched the boat. He stumbled and caught his balance.

"Not for me." said Al. "I'm OK."

Pete's face lit up. Brad's face lit up. My face lit up. Al looked around. Frank slapped Al on the back.

"What's this business about a halibut changing its eyes to one side of its head?" I asked.

Frank answered. "It's like with people. It's a matter of doing what nature demands."

"Is it doing what nature demands? Or does it just happen?" I continued with questions.

"Weather's moving in on us." Brad said. "It'll be a little rougher in round two. Say, Rick, do you like catching these fish? Not like fly-fishing is it?"

"No it's not but..."

Pete picked up something new off our stern. "Look," he said, "isn't that Bill Etteger off our backside?" He pointed to a boat anchored not more than 150 yards behind. Both boats were rolling in the increasing waves. "Why does he have to pull up so close to us every time? We always end up finding fish for him."

"Is he drinking?" asked Brad.

The answer came to all of us from the other boat. One of the clients had a fish on and we could hear a cheer go up at every move the fish made. Too much cheering going on for a sober bunch.

"Let's go fishin'." said Brad.

He started picking up the lunch goodies, leaving our desserts, which were chocolate chip cookies that we stuffed into our mouths at the last as we picked up the mess and put it into garbage bags. Pete tossed some bait over the back of the boat *chumming* the current behind us to attract more halibut to our lines. I was the first to catch a fish after lunch and proudly carried out the details of getting the fish into the boat exactly as the others had done. Then Frank caught one. Then he caught another. We were into a good bite in the afternoon. Bill Etteger's boat did well too. It sat in our wake for the next hour and a half and it pitched and rolled in the waves as we did. And the fishermen on board had the advantage of our fish finding and our chumming of the water as we saw their fishing rods bent over, catching fish.

We heard them cheer whenever they hooked or boated a fish. Brad pulled anchor and moved once to shake the boat behind us but they quickly followed, anchoring behind us once more. A huge roar went up from the Etteger boat. "Must be into a big one." Brad said. Sure enough, as the Etteger boat pitched and rolled we got glimpses of a doubled over rod. We saw the fisherman pull up and reel down, pull up, and reel down. As we caught two more fish, the Etteger fisherman was still working on the same fish. Finally, we saw a great mass lifted to the side of the boat. Bill was bent over the side when the boat rolled and pitched and tumbled him across the deck.

We heard one more roar from the Etteger boat. Then it went quiet. "They lost the fish." Pete said.

In our silence, we heard the water sloshing against the sides of the *WhaleBone*. The fish catching action stopped on both boats. The Etteger boat headed off quickly in the direction of shore. Brad was uneasy as he watched the other boat go in early. I felt a big tug. "Fish on!" I yelled. My rod wrapped down in a curve keeping tension on the line that shot out through the guides. The line hummed and the drag of the reel let go a controlled yardage of line to keep up with the fish that swam deeper and farther to get free. "Whoa! This one is headed for Dutch Harbor." I wore a satisfied fisherman's grin, gritting my teeth at the same time. In part, I felt the joy of the sport in fighting the fish and in part the thought of possessing the quarry. And I knew this was the biggest fish of the day. Possession of this one would put me on top.

"He's over a hundred!" Brad said.

I held the fish for two more big runs. At the end, the fish pulled on the line in three jerks. The reel released the line in three spurts. The rod resiliency bowed to absorb the strain of the tugs. The hook remained stuck in the jaw of the fish. The line did not break.

Finally, I brought the fish up alongside of the boat. "Pete, get the pistol," Ordered Brad. "I don't want this butt all over my boat."

Pete retrieved the gun from the console inside the cabin, hurried out, and handed it to Brad. Brad had the halibut dangling from the gaff, kicking its tail. He reached over the side and put the barrel near the head of the fish, firing a shot that passed through the brain. The fish involuntarily kicked twice, then quivered and then nothing. Brad pulled the giant over the side. It landed on the deck near the fish locker but this time there was no thrashing about.

Brad picked up the cover. Frank and Al were marveling over the size of the fish. Pete shoved the monster onto the mass of fish already in the locker but there was not room for the whole thing. The head of the fish slipped down between the other fish. When it went in, the mass of fish underneath moved and made a sucking sound and then, what was that? A hand. It was somebody's detached hand! Before I could say anything, Pete had the cover back on the hatch with most of the fish hanging out. I looked around quick as I could and took an inventory of hands. Everybody was wearing two hands, so what was that I saw? Whose hand was it?

I searched for answers in Brad's face. But if he had an answer, he did not say it. The green smell of the bait clutched me. The pitching and rolling of the boat in the waves was the feeling of green. The animation of the eye of a halibut moving from one side of its head to the other was the look *of green*. I felt a grip from the back of my throat to my stomach. "I've got to puke!" I lunged for the rail and hung over until my guts stopped wrenching. This gave me time to think. When I turn around again will anybody else know about the hand?

Brad was on his cell phone. He had dialed up the Etteger boat. He was surprised when one of the clients answered the call instead of Bill Etteger. "Yes we saw the big fish that got away. Why did you leave in such a hurry? An accident? What? A bait knife hung up on the rail? The boat pitched and sent Bill across the deck. His hand?"

I retrieved the hand from inside the half-open fish locker and held it up for Brad to see.

"We've got Bill Etteger's hand." Brad said into the phone. We had one more beer on the way in anyway.

The Italy Thing
by Tom Panaccione

Aldo barely heard Carina at this point. He was reading about the trip coming up in two weeks on September 22. He wanted to get out of the rut the baby boomers call the good life. Get away from mowing the lawn, get away from going to the same restaurants, and get away from the so-called pleasures of the retired life. The golden years are the boring years. He craved the adventure of new restaurants, new foods, new places where life is different and exciting. Carina insisted that they go to Venice, Florence, and Rome but he added Cassino to the list. Aldo's father grew up there, near Naples. Maybe he would want to buy land in Italy, find a new home, a new place to work, a new kind of work. He could make wine, farm the soil, raise sheep, and make cheese. He could do the things his father had talked about. Carina could learn to get along too. Could she be happy in a new land? Could she love Italy?

"Aldo, I'm talking to you," she said.

"Yes, I know. What did you say?"

"It's not important."

"What do you want to find on this trip?" he asked as he thumbed through one of the new books, *Drive Around Tuscany and Umbria.*

"Aldo, you *are* a dreamer. What makes you think I'm looking for anything?" She fumbled through a clothes drawer tossing a couple of garments on the bed. Aldo didn't respond. He was reading the *Drive Around* book. "We've been talking about this trip for over a year and you buy the guidebook two days before the trip. You've already got a shelf full of books on Italy... why do you need another book?"

"It's a guide for driving around."

"We wouldn't need a book on driving around if you had listened to me."

"You mean if we took a Perillo tour like you wanted? Where's the adventure..."

"Oh, you and your adventure. Why do we have to leave the country? Why can't we go to Holland, Michigan or Walla Walla, Washington?"

"How did you come up with that?"

"In *Money* magazine, there was a list. That's where the baby boomers are going. And they're going to St. Simons Island, Georgia too. Why can't we look at least?"

The Vines of Sant' Antimo
by Tom Panaccione

The sign on the door said SCONTO 50%. Carina went inside. Aldo followed.

"Buon giorno," said a woman's voice from a desk that was partially hidden behind a display of glassware.

"Buon giorno," they replied.

"Look Aldo, some of this glass is even cheaper than it was in Murano," Carina said.

"Who would have thought it would be cheaper here?" Aldo said. He picked up a small glass fish. Price: seven Euros minus 50%.

The saleswoman smiled and offered an explanation. "We go to Murano and buy very well, so we can offer a good price."

Carina waltzed a little as she moved to the clothes rack and held up a dress. She appraised it looking into a convenient full-length mirror next to the rack. The dress was red, not a bright red but darker, close to a wine color. Carina looked down and estimated how much skin would show in the open neckline. She nodded to herself in the mirror.

"It goes very nicely with you, Signora," said the saleswoman who was now standing by the desk.

"I suppose so. The white hair goes with anything," said Carina, putting the dress back on the hanger and she hooked it on the rack.

"We'll take it," Aldo said and he raised his voice.

Carina froze for a second, leaning on the rack with her arm outstretched and her hand on the hanger. She was off balance but she caught herself and returned to full control.

"I haven't decided yet," she said.

"I think he is right," said the saleswoman as she checked the price tag.

"The price is right too, only sixteen Euros with the discount."

"I'll think about it," said Carina and she moved on to a display of scarves.

She wrapped a black scarf around her neck and flipped one end over her shoulder.

Aldo changed the subject. "We have noticed lots of wine for sale in town. And the prices are all over the place. What should we look for in buying wine? We thought it would be fun to go to a winery."

"Here, in Montalcino you can buy many wines, it is true," said the saleswoman. "But the famous wine here is Brunello or 'super Tuscan' and, for that, you will pay more. The prices for wines of equal value are not different from one shop to the next and not different at the wineries on the side of the mountain either... maybe one or two Euros difference."

"I've made up my mind," said Carina. She brushed past Aldo, between him and the saleswoman, returning to the dress rack. She unhooked the red dress and slung it over her arm. Then she approached the glassware. She picked up the fish that Aldo had handled a few minutes ago. Then she looked at the other glass animals and decided on a blue-headed turtle with a green back and she also picked up a horse that was reared up, ready to run.

The saleswoman smiled.

"We'll take these," said Carina. "I'll wear the scarf."

The saleswoman packaged the articles, taking care that the glass animals would not be harmed. "You know," she said, "there is a place you could go.

If you go down the mountain on the other side, follow the signs to Sant' Antimo. After a while, the road will turn to dirt but don't worry. That road is safe. After you drive for five kilometers you will find the wine... the total is twenty-six fifty please."

They drove through the stony streets of Montalcino, then down the other side of the mountain. The autumn sky was forming grey clouds in the distance over the furthest hills. Traveling in the car, they were still warmed by the sun. Leaves, high in the trees were lit, and glowed against the darker sky. Carina settled into the autumn warmth inside the car; the small diesel clattered softly. Carina was soon asleep.

Aldo was alone in his thoughts. There you have it, he thought. The woman in the shop didn't have a suggestion until you spent some of your fixed income, pension money... or Carina spent it. Now you find yourself on this beautiful road and no tourist traffic either. There is the sign, Sant' Antimo. You could find an old farm on this country road. A place to live a quiet life, what was left of it. Would you be able to build a vineyard like the ones here? Here's the dirt road. It's not bad. Like the lady said, it's safe. Here's a place to pull off.

He drove off the road onto a shoulder that was the gateway to a vineyard. He turned the key and got out of the car.

Carina woke up. "What are you doing?" she asked.

"I want to taste the grapes."

"Why?"

"Because these grapes are famous. All over the world people know these grapes because of their wine."

Aldo walked to the nearest vine and picked several of the mature grapes.

"They're loaded with juice, ready to pick. We're lucky to be here now.

Any later and they'd be gone." He tasted one. "Delicious... want to try one?"

"No thanks. Shouldn't we get going? Look at that sky."

The dark sky was closer now. But the sun still shown on them.

"Look at the golden vineyard against the dark sky. Smell the juice of these grapes. Everything is ripe. Would you want to call this place your home?"

"I have a home. You sound like you got drunk on those grapes. I have a home."

"I could find a home here," said Aldo, as he tasted another grape. "Sweet, sweet, these grapes are going to make a great wine."

"Now you're the professor of wine. How do you know that? Come on, let's go."

"These grapes will make great wine. Take my word for it."

They drove off. Around the next turn, they came to a driveway with a sign that said vendere dirette.

"We can buy some wine here," Aldo said. He turned up the driveway that was furrowed from the last torrent of rain, but passable.

"I hope we can get out of here," said Carina.

"We'll be okay."

They pulled into the yard of the farmhouse and parked beside a low stonewall beside the house. The house was made of stones and mortar, a rustic style. To the left there was a large shed with a sign, written in English that said 'wine tasting'. Vines were lined up in all directions with the house and several sheds in the center. Grape leaves were golden among heavy clumps of grapes. Some of the vines had been picked clean. Aldo got out of the car and heard the din of a tractor in the vineyard. He looked over the wall. About seventy-five yards away a man and two women were loading crates of grapes onto a wagon that trailed behind on a hitch. Aldo went to the house and knocked at the large oak door. He got no answer.

Tractor noise stopped and the man strode toward the house, his light grey coveralls solid with muscle. He was a bald man with a mustache. His mustache was dark. His face was round but not fat and his eyes were dark.

He was ruddy from his working outside. His stride through the aisles between the vines was quick but he did not rush and he was not annoyed.

Aldo met the man as he came up to the wall and pulled himself up and over. The man extended his hand. The hand was soiled with purple and his fingers were thick and had cracked nails. Aldo took the hand and felt the leathery grip that soon let go because the man kept moving.

"Vino?" the man asked.

Aldo decided that the man would have more trouble with English than he would have with Italian. So he tried his Italian, "Si, voglio comprare del vino, per favore. Mi chiamo Aldo."

"Mi chiamo Luigi," said the man. Luigi turned and headed for the shed that had the wine tasting sign on it. Aldo followed, trying to keep up with the purposeful strides of the man.

A discussion went on in Italian. Aldo picked up some of it but it was too fast for him to follow every word. He managed to taste several wines and he bought two Brunellos, one for twenty Euros and one for fifty, less money than in Montalcino. In the discussion, Aldo asked Luigi why his grapes made superior wine. Aldo understood the words for altitude and rain and sun and climate and earth, ingredients from nature that nurtured fine grapes.

Back at the car, Carina had found Luigi's wife and eight-year-old daughter. Carina was outside the car talking with her when Aldo and Luigi returned to the car. Luigi stopped momentarily, shook hands with Carina, and then strode back to the tractor with the same businesslike pace that he had set before. He said a couple of words to the two women helpers and then started the tractor moving again.

Luigi's wife was Amanda. She held one arm around her daughter. She was calm and had some time to talk. She looked across the vineyard to the hills and the clouds. Aldo understood that the clouds and hills were part of the life here. Streaks of sunlight penetrated the clouds in a few places and lit some of the hillside. Aldo asked the woman if she could ever leave this place. Could she remove her daughter from the vineyards? Never, she said.

Carina removed the scarf from her neck and wrapped it around Amanda. "Good for you," said Carina.

"Is this scarf for me? No. You keep it." Amanda removed the scarf and returned it to Carina. She smiled so that Carina would not be rebuffed by the gesture. "The warmth of the scarf will remind you of your trip to Italy. You will remember us."

Finally, Amanda walked across into the vineyard, disappearing among the vines with her daughter in her arm.

Aldo and Carina were quiet for several kilometers as they drove away from Luigi's vineyard.

Aldo thought about the countryside of Sant' Antimo. You are very close to what you are looking for. Luigi put a face on the idea of living here and working in the vineyard. His family loves the place too. Surely, Carina must have identified with Luigi's wife. You can never be sure about her but you know you could live here.

"I could live here," said Aldo.

"Oh please, don't start that again."

"I would be able to do this."

"Stop. Stop being a pompous old fool."

Aldo stopped to think. You are a pompous old fool. You think you can do anything. You think you can be a farmer here in Tuscany. You think you know how to plant grapes. You think you know when to pick grapes. You think you know everything. You pompous old fool. But you would work at it. You would learn. You would work hard.

"Did you see how hard that man worked?" said Carina.

"What makes you think I wouldn't work hard?"

"Did you see his hands? Did you see his worn coveralls? Did you see how high he carried his chest? How strong? How young? What about our home and all of our work?"

"I could live here," Aldo asserted again.

"Fine. What about me?"

"What about you?"

"Watch where you're going."

"Don't worry. The road is safe."

Cinghiale
by Tom Panaccione

On their way back from Sant' Antimo Aldo started to make the turn onto the road to the agriturismo but Carina had another thought. "Let's eat in tonight. How about picking up something at that little market up the street?" She pointed straight ahead where the market was situated well below the towers that clustered on the hilltop of San Gimignano. Most of the towers were square on top but the two tallest ones were pointed and although primitive looking they resembled skyscrapers of modern cities.

"What do you feel like having?"

"O-o-oh, whatever you feel like making."

Sure. You do all the driving for most of the day and now you do the cooking. We could go out to eat but that would be too easy. Anyway, in spite of her demands she's giving the best conversation of the day so maybe you'd better just go along with it.

"Okay," he said and drove up to the mercato.

They went into the small modern brick building together but soon split up. Aldo went to the meat counter and Carina shopped for salad, eggs, and pasta.

Aldo met up at the meat counter with a lady dressed in hand made dark clothes. She was hunched over and Aldo guessed she was five or so years older than he. Aldo picked up a package of veal that had two culets of the right size for dinner. Not sure if he had chosen the best, he decided to ask the woman who by now had said "Buona sera." to every single person who passed her or saw her in the store.

"Questo vitello e buono?" Aldo asked and smiled to win quick affection.

Her eyes bumped up at him, surprised that this stranger had asked and the folded skin around her mouth moved gently as she smiled. She took the package from Aldo, looked at the color, poked the flesh with her finger, and then replaced the package in the cooler. She picked up several other packages and, looking and poking, put them back until finally she handed one to Aldo. "Questo e buono," she said and smiled.

Aldo tried to figure out what she was looking for and what she learned from poking the cutlets the way she had. He asked her "Perche questo e il migliore?"

She rubbed her finger and thumb together toward Aldo's face. "Al tatto," she laughed and walked off.

On the way to the deli counter, Aldo picked up a fresh loaf of crusty bread and a small bag of Italian herbs that he held to his nose and sensed the presence of basil and oregano and thyme and rosemary. He didn't need salt because he remembered seeing that the previous guests had left some sale de mare in the cupboard along with some olio di oliva and some pepe. He grabbed a couple of cloves of garlic. He loved the way the Italian market always smelled garlicky, spicy, and bready.

At the deli, Aldo ordered half a cinghiale salami and a chunk of cacciocavalo cheese. Aldo liked the looks of the mortadella that had peppercorns and olives in it so he ordered six slices, "Sei fete di mortadella, per favore."

Carina was waiting near the checkout line and moved the eggs, pasta, and lettuce from her basket into Aldo's basket. She noticed some sweet red peppers on a shelf close by so she took the time to pick one up. "Looks like everything we'll need for supper," she said. "Oh, look some wine."

"Pick up the one that says 'Vernaccia di San Gimignano'," he said, "the straw-colored one. It's a good local wine."

They left the mercato with their haul, loaded the bags into the car, and headed back to the agriturismo. By the time, they arrived at the end of the dirt road there was about an hour of sunlight remaining and most of the clouds that threatened rain earlier in the day had dissipated. The sun was angled in the sky, creating long shadows and golden light. Stones and mortar of the old farmhouse dazzled with texture in the late day sun.

"Let's walk around the place before we eat," she said, "the light is more beautiful than on our whole trip."

They put away the food and placed the wine in the refrigerator. Once outside, they decided to walk through the lower field. As they walked, the grass covered just above their ankles. They guessed the vineyard keeper kept it mowed and tidy to clear the way for the tractor to move from one vineyard to another. Ruts that the tractor dug served as a crude roadway that they walked along.

A couple of hundred yards below the house the tractor road forked. One branch went further down to the left to a small vineyard while the other branch went uphill to the right also to a small but new vineyard. They had seen the farmer up there planting new vines early in the morning.

"Let's walk up there," Carina said.

"Okay."

The first fifty yards went uphill slightly, easy walking. But then it dropped down to a gully not visible from where they had started. At the bottom, they faced a narrow creek with a trickle of water from an irrigation pond that made soggy-going. Aldo took Carina's arm and they maneuvered across the gully. The hill steepened from there. The tractor road went straight up the steep hill for two hundred yards to a fence that marked the boundary of the new vineyard. The road went to the left and around the vineyard to a neighboring farm.

When they reached that point she said, "Can't go any further." She turned and her eyes widened, she exhaled and said, "Wow!" She gave Aldo a tug to turn him so he was facing the same direction. She put her arm around him and leaned on him, and he caressed his face across her hair and her forehead and he admired everything.

They were standing high enough on the hillside so that could look down on the red-tiled roof of the agriturismo and they could look over the vineyards and across another steep hill to the top of San Gimignano and the small skyscraper towers of the town. The hillside was a hanging fabric, a quilt. The patches of the quilt were the rectangles of vineyards laid out in golden sunlit textured rows and rows of olive trees here and there. Tuscan cypress trees spiked up around stucco and masonry houses. Utility poles formed a pattern of communication, suspending wires at a height above the rest. The fabric covered a town that went back to the turn of the first century.

They held on for a few minutes longer, sharing the view that they had climbed to see. Neither spoke. Together they walked down to the agriturismo, down the steep hill, across the creek, through more grass to the stone house and up the stairs to their apartment.

Once inside they shared the task of making a meal. Aldo pulled the wine from the fridge, and poured two glasses and sliced some of the cacciacavallo and some of the salami. "What kind of salami is this?" she asked.

"Cinghialli."

"What is that? It's good."

"Wild boar."

"E-e-w," she pushed it away. "You really know how to treat a lady, don't you."?

"What's wrong?"

"Not exactly appetizing to me."

"It's a specialty here."

"Okay, eat up."

Aldo had scrambled some eggs and ground some bread into crumbs from a loaf of stale bread they'd been lugging around since they left Venice. He set the plates side by side, and dredged the cutlets, first through the egg and then, with egg drooling, dropped the cutlets into the crumbs. After this preparation, he placed the coated cutlets into a pan of hot olive oil and seared both side until golden brown. Carina had been busy with the spaghetti. The water was boiling and the spaghetti had three minutes for al dente.

"The salad is ready but we forgot the vinegar," she said, "I'll bet Maria has a little she would give us. I'll go ask her." [Maria is the owner of the agriturismo who spends evenings there with friends, as she is this evening] Carina disappears and a few minutes later returns with a small bottle of vinegar. "This is an extra bottle she had on hand."

Aldo poured two more glasses of Vernacchia and served the veal and spaghetti. Carina stepped close to Aldo. "Thanks for the wonderful veal Milanese," she said. She pulled Aldo close and kissed him. Aldo kissed her. For a moment, they seemed to forget dinner.

"Dinner might get cold," he said.

They sat and ate slowly. They looked out the window where they could see across the small creek up the steep hill.

"Was a fabulous day."

"Yes."

"Maria said we could pick fresh figs for dessert," Carina said.

Sun had set. Maria had turned on a couple of lights under the canvas where they sat a small table. They had eaten and were sipping wine and smoking cigarettes. Aldo and Carina went down the steps and as they passed the group they simply exchanged, "Buona sera."

The evening turned cool and purple and they were returning with the figs when they heard an engine burst through the vineyard on the steep hill up to the right. A farm truck barely visible stormed around the corner of the fence, its headlights grazing the tops of the vines. Then it descended the steep hill and pitched into the soggy creek at the bottom. The engine cried as the wheels spun in the soft wet earth. The wheels caught again and the truck came out of the creek with the two front wheels off the ground.

Aldo and Carina joined Maria and her friends.

"Cosa succede?" Aldo asked Maria.

"Cinghiale. You know cinghiale? He dig in the vine. He ruin the vine. So the farmer chase him."

The truck veered and the boar snorted and ran down into one of the lower fields. The headlights circled around down there twice and then back up the hill toward the house and the boar came to a fence around the agriturismo and that forced him to turn to the right where he came close to the spectators and he headed around toward the dirt road. The headlights were close behind. In the clear space, the truck picked up the pace, and overtook the boar and ran into it.

It happened where the group couldn't see. But the boar squealed and cried. The truck stopped. Men got out. The club sounded against the flesh of the boar. Whump. Whump. The boar squealed. Whump. Whump. And it squealed again and again. Then it was quiet. Then again, whump! And a cry, and so human. Then it was quiet.

Maria was crying.

"The farmers. They do this. I don't think is good idea."

The men tossed stuff into the back of the truck. The sound of a body tossed in, grating against dry dirt in the carrier and other stuff and the sound of the club hitting inside, bouncing, and rolling. Everything gathered up the truck slowly carefully exited by the normal route down the dirt road to the main road.

Aldo was holding Maria in his arms. She was still crying and angry. "That son-a-ma-bitch!" she said in English.

Aldo and Carina retreated to their apartment. "Nothing like a good swine killing to wreak a romantic night in the hills of Tuscany after a delicious Italian dinner."

"Why do you say it's ruined?" she said. She went to him and it wasn't ruined. Not at all.

The next morning Aldo was up early, heated the water, and made cappuccino. He walked up to the dirt road and along the grass clearing, until he saw the truck wheel marks along the side of the road. He started to feel sick. Did he smell human sweat? Blood. Death. Oddly, it was sweet but rank. He saw there in the matted grass, matted with blood where the cinghiale had died from the blows of the men in the truck. Why did the smells gain in strength?

Aldo stooped to look closer at something that stood out differently. He stirred at a piece of hairy clotted blood. The hair was long, too long. This could not have been hair from the cinghiale. He recognized human hair.

You always have to be so clever. Now you've done it. You are involved. Just when things were stating to go better with Carina. You have to come up with this. But you can't ignore it, so face it; you've got a problem here.

Aldo walked over to the table by the pool where Carina sat with her cappuccino and he sat with her. "Are we going to Volterra as we planned?"

"No. We're going to the police station."

"Why?"

"Don't worry. I'll take care of it."

"What do you mean; you'll take care of it? What's going on?"

"Because of last night."

"You mean you're going to the police because a farmer killed a pig."

"A boar."

"Okay, a boar. Let's not get involved in that."

Aldo drove toward town and went into the mercato because it was easier than driving the narrow way into the center. He went inside and inquired about the polizia. He returned to the car with the news, "Looks like we'll travel to Volterra today after all. That's the nearest police station from here."

"Explain what we're doing," she demanded.

Aldo buckled up and turned to her, "This morning I took a walk to the spot where the boar was clubbed last night. There was plenty of blood in the grass and there was a miserable smell and..."

"And what?"

"In the mass of bloody grass I found what I think is human hair connected to a piece of human scalp."

Carina took a deep swallow as if to drink in this piece of information that she did not see coming, Her swallow was anything but appetizing. She stretched he mouth in disgust, then she relaxed as if she was resigned to this new twist in their itinerary. "Go to the police in Volterra. Is that the best thing we can do?"

"It's what I think we should do."

"What if we let this go? Why not leave this to Maria?"

"Maria wasn't there this morning. We don't know when she'll be back. Something this urgent needs to be reported as soon as possible."

Aldo put the car in reverse, wheeled backward, made his way toward the exit, and then drove off to Volterra.

Jordon Pecile
by Barbara Passmore

I have taken several writing classes in the past and have struggled to find my voice. It wasn't until I spent time in Jordon Pecile's classes at MCC that I discovered humor in my writing. Jordon noticed it and encouraged it. I still struggle with my voice, but Jordon's recognition of my ability to write in a humorous way has helped me better understand what that voice is.

Why I Write
By Barbara Passmore

Writing came to me quite unexpectedly after I enrolled in a writing class as part of a graduate degree I was pursuing. Write what you know, the instructor told us. What you know is what you have lived so I wrote about my life experiences. I found I loved words, the way they fit together, the way they could convey subtle meaning. For my final project, I wrote a memoir of my mother's decline into Alzheimer's Disease. She had just passed away and I was trying to make sense of this terrible disease and what it did to her.

I have ideas that I would like to take from thought to word. This is not easy and I struggle with how to do it. I tried writing short stories because I love the way short stories convey an idea with an economy of words. I have not been successful in this effort.

A year or so ago I read a novel that was written all in letters. I loved this book and realized that I love writing letters. This is done mostly on the computer via email, but still letters. This kind of writing comes naturally, the words flow through my fingers.

I have a writing project in mind. It is a memoir of my experiences researching my grandfather's hand written autobiography. It involves people I've met, places I've visited and things I have learned through the course of my travels to the places he lived. I reconnected with Jordon's Twelve because the support and encouragement of other writers is invaluable.

The piece I submitted for this book is one of a series I wrote about my experiences as Mother of the Groom.

Make-up, Who Needs It?
by Barbara Passmore

In a sudden flash of insight, I knew the young woman sitting next to me wore makeup. This was not something I would have known a few weeks ago, but when I looked at her face close up, I recognized the way my own face looked. It was very natural.

I'd gone to the Mall to get make-up to wear to my son's wedding. I needed help because I had stopped wearing make-up every day when I stopped working full time. Wearing make-up now went with dressing up. I began my quest at a cosmetics counter in a department store.

"I need makeup to wear to my son's wedding in California," I said to the makeup lady.

"What kind of makeup do you want?"

"I don't know. The ceremony will be outside, in a park," I told her, thinking this piece of information was critical to determining what makeup I would wear.

"Something to go with my dress," I added, pulling the jacket out of a shopping bag.

"Periwinkle. That will look nice on you. Are you going to do your own makeup or have it done?"

"I don't know," I said, suddenly confronted with the option of having someone do it for me.

"I guess it depends on how difficult it will be for me to do it myself."

"I can make it simple, just basic foundation. Do you want color on your eyes?"

"I don't know. If I have color I don't want it to be dark and obvious, something to match the dress," I said, again pulling the dress out of the shopping bag.

Seeing that she was getting nowhere with me, that I didn't have a clue about makeup, the makeup lady began pulling various products out of drawers. First, she had me clean my face with a cream followed by toner. I knew about creams and toners from the past, but no longer used them. I wash my face with soap, a fact I would never divulge to any makeup lady. Next, she had me apply two different creams, one around my eyes, and one on the rest of the face.

"Your skin is very dry," she announced.

What could I say? I used soap. I never used creams, until now that is. I discovered that the concealer, a nice name for shadow/wrinkle hider that she put under my eyes, went on much easier with the moisturizing cream underneath. Likewise, with the foundation, or blotch hider, which she put on with a special sponge. I was astonished at the results after she applied concealer under one eye and handed me a mirror. The eye with the makeup was no longer competing with the shadow underneath. After she applied a light base coat to the eyelid, my eye became the focal point, surrounded by light. All that light around my eyes cried out for something. That something was eyeliner.

"What kind of liner do you want?"

"What kinds are there? Should I wear brown or black?"

"Black. You will wear black," she informed me as she pulled out an automatic eye pencil with a sponge tip on the other end.

I'd used eyeliner before, confident in my ability to apply it. I couldn't watch her put it on, but when I opened my eyes, I could see that the liner was only on half of my eye, the half that went toward the outer edge. I watched as the makeup lady went over the lines with the sponge and then finished by smoothing the upper lid liner with the shadow applier.

"You only put it on half my eye," I stated the obvious.

"You don't want to line the whole eye. It should not look like a line. You want it to have a foggy effect," she informed me.

Waterproof mascara in case I cried, lip liner and lipstick over a lip smoother, blue mascara also applied on one-half of my eye and rouge completed the effect. I had to admit that my face looked very natural and my appearance was noticeably improved without looking like I was wearing a mask. The makeup lady was an artist.

"Southern women always wear makeup," she told me as she examined her work.

The makeup lady spoke as if this was a self-evident truth. It gave me a jolt and I wondered why. Were Northern women lacking in some way? I thought, as my inferior self stepped in. Maybe it's true about

Southern women and makeup. I don't know if I would have noticed that the woman sitting next to me wore makeup if she had not told me that she was from Texas, but the connection was made. Southern women always wear makeup and this woman was from the South.

"Are you wearing makeup?" I blurted out.

"I always wear makeup," she replied.

"The lady who did my makeup for the wedding told me that Southern women always wear makeup. Is that true?"

"Oh yes. I would never go out without it, but I really resent the time it takes. Then at night, I have to take it off and put on all these creams. I wish I could just go without it. Northern woman don't have to wear make-up. They are free to go natural. I envy them that," she said."

This took me by surprise. From the makeup lady's point of view, a woman without makeup was not a proper woman. Now, here was a young woman telling me she felt trapped by the makeup protocol and I'd just started wearing it again because it improved my appearance appreciably.

The train entered the tunnel as it approached the station. I'd enjoyed talking with this young woman. I'd had a conversation about makeup that I never would have been able to have a few short days ago. She wrote down the name of a new cosmetic brand that is supposed to make you look younger. I could order it on the Internet she said as she pulled out a mirror and began applying lipstick.

Jordon—Creator of Writers
by David Porteous

Jordon Pecile is much more than a writing teacher. His passion, guidance and astonishing embrace lifts the best from every student to rise to a more exacting authorial role writing and editing together to create more than what any of us alone could do, the heart of the Iowa Writing Workshop. Jordon is an inspiring leader of writers through the thickets of foggy thoughts, gross verbiage, and lost voices to hone clarity and power from our writing.

I worked with Jordon for several years in writing classes. The breadth of his erudite and pertinent comments, criticisms, suggestions, and recommended readings of other writers always astonished me. He brought me into the rich and broad heritage of the writing world. I journeyed from navel gazing writing to a more reader-oriented writer. Jordon has shown me how the hard writing process is within our capabilities if we stay alert to learning from our re-reads and the edits of our colleagues with the reader in focus.

Jordon worked as hard as any of his students, reading everything and commenting in depth. His caring made you want to listen and care, even when his feedback was unflattering. You knew he loved good writing, knew how to help you move towards it, and would be there every step of the way for you. What more can a writer ask for?

Why Do I Write?
by Dave Porteous

I must write. It is essential to breathing.
Breath, consciousness live through inhalation
Exhalation, leaving behind distractions thoughts.

Clarity and velocity, moving in a direction
Known to all who read you.
That's why I write.

Searching for sculpting out the voice
The person-in-motion
Living loving breathing suffering life
Taking it in giving back.

A perspective
A life, love of life
Our duty to articulate & share.

Writing pure diamond heartfelt life
Distilling energy, vision,
Experience naked conveyed to an Other
No matter the genre

Speaking to an Other
Nuclear language draws readers to the edge
The Black Hole
Transports energizes enraptures
Readers, other worldly

Discovering through this journey together
The writer the other
Perceptions living knowing
Flesh feeling sense known for the first time/place

Language conveying the unspoken
Reach through listening seeing feeling beyond
Offering as writer an experience, eliciting in you
Life not tasted touched kissed like this before.

Is it clear why I write?

David Porteous has published in the op-ed sections of the New York Times and the Hartford Courant.

Bulgarian Heat
by Dave Porteous

Sasha's relaxed self-assurance was evident the moment her long, lithe micro-skirted legs slipped onto the back seat of the compact Eastern European two-door sedan. She radiated a worldly confidence though she was only in her early twenties. As she settled into the seat I introduced myself and asked, "What are we keeping you from doing today?"

"Work. I can do that anytime. I am translating another book. It is best to take breaks from such concentration. And I get to meet new people. You are American?" she asked.

"Oh, yes, very much so," I replied. "Like most Americans I don't speak another language. So you have a translating job?"

"Of course," she said with a wide smile. "Why would you need to know another language in North America?" Her question struck me as well informed, knowing that English worked for North American travel, except maybe in Quebec. And she was kind, not stating the obvious fact that the monolingual limit of most Americans reflects our sense that we need not relate to the Earth's peoples who don't speak English.

"You're right about that, Sasha. It frustrates me. Since I didn't learn another language growing up, it's harder to learn one now. I learned a little Latin, and German, but only to read and write, not to speak. I studied Bulgarian before this trip, but speaking it is not easy."

"Don't worry. I will take care of you," she said with certitude and a playful smile in her eyes. I had the sense that she definitely liked being the one in charge with this American.

"Great. Thanks. Since my friend Viktor isn't here you are my eyes and ears, and my mouth," I said, looking into her intriguing brown eyes. Traveling in a land where one feels language-less because we cannot speak or understand anything is humbling. She didn't know how much I felt my life this day was like clay in a potter's hands.

Glancing out the window, I noticed that we were leaving the ancient bustling metropolis of Sofia. I paid attention to the land for the first time. The gently rolling terrain of the central Bulgarian plateau encircled us. The flatland allowed Ivan, our driver and host, to speed us along at 140+ kilometers per hour, producing a dizzying sense of the landscape where trees lined the road. Soon, undulating light green fields bordered with dark green groves appeared, behind which sinuous faraway hills lay, overlain by a cloudless blue sky. I was buoyed realizing the day's travels were in the hands of others, except for the business lunch—the purpose of this trip, and even there Sasha would help make it happen.

Highway thrills grabbed my attention when wide trucks lumbered in our direction, swaying back and forth. The road wasn't wide enough for both of us. For seconds that felt like hours life's fragility overwhelmed me. Ivan and the trucker dodged and squeezed by each other within inches and at the last possible second. Collision appeared likely many times over. I wasn't sure if I was the only one in the car shaken by these close encounters, or if the others better hid their anxieties.

I decided that conversation was preferable to anxious near misses. It was also a chance to learn about Bulgaria and my translator.

"So, Sasha, how did you get into translating?" I asked.

"Easy. I studied in an English school. I translate books too."

"Wow. I'm impressed. What kind?"

"Do you know Judith Krantz books?"

"Yes, of course, she's well known."

"I translated two of her books for a Bulgarian publisher. Viktor knows my Dad. He asked if I wanted to earn some money translating. So I am here," said Sasha.

"You speak excellent English, with a slight British accent. How did the accent happen?" I asked.

"My English teachers in earliest schools and gymnasium were British trained, so I learned what they knew."

"And you learned their accent too," I said.

"Yes, of course," she smiled. "Is it obvious?"

"No," I replied with a smile. "It's barely noticeable. I listen to accents, as there are many in the United States. Where I grew up we spoke plainly, without an accent, or so we thought."

Sasha smiled at me again. "Yes, I have heard different accents from Americans, like people from Boston and Maine and New York City. Oh, look," she said, pointing to the road.

Heading towards us was a tanned, leathery-skinned old man in a rickety wooden cart. A donkey pulled the cart and driver along the shoulder of the highway. The persistence of these donkey cart riders in our warp speed cybernetic age fascinated me. I admired their freedom from hurried lives and head-on collisions, though a hard life under a merciless sun and the absence of micro-skirt distractions didn't appeal to me.

As our route turned upwards into highlands, weathered white sandstone peaks emerged amidst shimmering green splotches on the mountainsides. Cruising narrower roads in the mountains with little traffic brought fewer opportunities for crash-and-burn scenarios, but the few encounters were memorable. When a narrow road winds along the side of a mountain, even a short, weathered mountain, and there are no guardrails or other barriers to careening off the road and plummeting hundreds of feet, the infrequent confrontations with larger vehicles can be terrifying, and they scared me to death.

And it's difficult to be reserved and friendly toward my translator when she is thrown in my direction on one swerve, and I am nearly splayed across her supple body and nearly naked legs seconds later. Discretion feels absurd when death seems so close, but I held my tongue and smiled.

A breathtaking view emerged as ridges of red and white sandstone crisscrossed the land to the horizon. Nestled on the opposite ridge was a multi-storied white walled compound with a red tiled roof.

Sasha spoke. "This is the Rozenski Monastery. We will stop to look."

"Oh, good," I exclaimed. "I need a break, and this looks interesting. How old is this monastery?"

Sasha said, "Maybe 800 to 900 years old. And it was built on the foundation of an older monastery."

"I'm impressed," I said. Ivan drove down to the entrance, stopped, and I said, "Blogodarya" (thank you) as I opened the door and leapt out. It was great to have my feet on the ground again.

We explored the monastery's treasures--an intricate carved pulpit and confessional, fine frescoes and icons. Prolific clusters of ripening grapes and wine barrels spoke of a productive vineyard at this austere site.

We climbed back into our little car for more road excitement on the way to the plateau, where the death I escaped in a head-on crash in the flatlands was a welcome alternative to plunging down a mountain. I relaxed, crawled out of my trepidation and related to my hosts. My life insurance was paid up, and Viktor would notify my family if I didn't survive.

Soon we were zipping along at 140 kph on level land and I was confident enough to initiate another conversation with Sasha.

"Did you study at the university?" I asked.

"Yes. And the only thing I know I am good at doing is translating, so I want to do more of that. Maybe I can go to the States and study more. Then I can do other work too."

"Sure. You are doing highly professional work translating for publishers and business meetings. That's very demanding. You can move on from there." I looked at Sasha and smiled. I liked to encourage people to believe in themselves, get the training or education they needed, and do it, whatever their hopes. Her voice and manner already radiated self-confidence.

"Look ahead, David. That's the border check point with Greece."

"Wow. I didn't know we would be that close. It gives me a broader sense of what Bulgaria is to be here, seeing a Mediterranean country as well as a Balkan country. You have a powerful brew of cultures here," I said, smiling.

We quickly turned left. Sasha's slim body was thrown onto mine. There were no seat belts. I smiled again at her, warmly, and said, "It feels like we are ping-pong balls in the back seat."

"Yes, that's usually the way Bulgarians drive. I'm used to bouncing all over."

It felt difficult to describe to her how I felt bouncing around in the back seat with her. She may comprehend how a married man 20 years older might feel constrained in this situation, but could she fully grasp the reserved sensibilities of a Midwestern-born American striving to be a gentleman in a saucy situation he did not control? It occurred to me that maybe she knew exactly what she was doing—that she was playing with me. I didn't see any reason for concern anyway. I knew I needed to be flexible and enjoy the adventure.

Since we turned onto this road near Melnik, mountains were on all sides, with red sandstone on the left, a contrast to the white sandstone we had seen. Another sharp left turn tossed Sasha nearly onto my lap again, her long black hair covering my face. While I felt honored to catch her beautiful body, I wanted to respond in a personal way to this unexpected intimacy, so I asked, "Is your perfume made in Bulgaria from the Rose Valley roses?"

"Yes. Do you like it?"

"Oh yes, Sasha. It's definitely a rose aroma, yet subtle."

"Have you been there?" she asked.

"No, I hope to visit it sometime when the roses are in bloom. I can't imagine how a valley full of rose blossoms smells on a warm afternoon. Is it intoxicating?"

"That's a good word for it. Yes, it is. Look ahead now. We are entering the valley. The little town of Melnik is all that is here."

The first house clung to the white sandstone valley wall. The rock foundation was constructed from conglomerate outcroppings on top of which sat the first floor framed in wooden timbers outlining white stucco walls. The red tile roof completed the rugged Mediterranean look, which epitomized many village houses.

As we followed the winding riverbed, Ivan pointed to a road up the side of the valley and said something in Bulgarian to Sasha.

Sasha interpreted, "David, that is the vineyard where Melnik wines come from."

"Oh. Viktor said they are a fine wine, one of the best in Bulgaria. I am looking forward to our lunch. Are those wine casks over there?"

"Yes. They store the wine in caves deep in the mountains. When the casks are emptied for bottling they leave them outside."

The car veered left onto a driveway, though this turn was slower so Sasha was not tossed. She turned to me, smiled, and said, "We are there. This is the café where we will have lunch."

"Oh, good. Can we take a walk?"

"Of course. Let me show you a tree over here. It's unusual."

"Please. I love trees of all types. What's special about it?" I asked.

"This plaque says its 600 years old. There are more here over 500 years old. They're called plane trees."

"Wow! It's amazing that they survived all the people who probably wanted to cut them down. I'd guess there weren't many people in this area and that's why they lasted this long. Does it have special protection now?"

"Yes, by the government. But Melnik had 20,000 people one hundred years ago. It has been a town for 2,000 years, Greek and Turkish and Bulgarian. It was an arts center and Melnik red wines were famous across Europe. Did you know Melnik wine was one of Winston Churchill's favorites?"

"No, but I don't know a lot about Bulgaria. I'm learning. The architecture and natural settings of your country are outstanding. And your history is so long and rich," I said.

"Thank you," said Sasha with a smile. "We must go back to the café now."

"OK, let's go," I replied.

Sasha turned and strode along as confidently as anyone I knew, whether attired in a tiny skirt or a business suit. We walked into the patio nestled under a canopy of grape vines supported by a latticework wooden frame. We sat down at our table with my hosts, Ivan and Demetriev, who sat in the front seat with Ivan. They had ordered the first bottles of Melnik Harsovo wine. Our drinks had been poured into classic tulip-shaped glasses for the wine to aerate.

I looked Ivan and Demetriev in the eyes, smiled broadly, swept my open palm over the glasses of wine and said, in Bulgarian, "Blagodarya." Thank you.

Ivan smiled back and said, in Bulgarian, "Nyama zashto." You're welcome.

Turning to Sasha, I inquired if she could ask Ivan and Demetriev if the wine had breathed enough for us to start with a toast. As soon as she conveyed my request, the answer was apparent in the bright smiles of our hosts. "Da. Da," said Ivan, nodding. Yes, yes. Ivan lifted two glasses by the stems, handed one to me and the other glass to Sasha. He and Demetriev then each picked up the last two glasses.

I asked Sasha to tell our hosts that I wanted to toast our beautiful day and the good business that would come from our meeting. When told, Ivan and Demetriev nodded, and said to Sasha in Bulgarian, "Yes, and we toast the beginning of a long partnership." We raised our glasses, I said "Nazdrave!" and they said, "Cheers." We all laughed at our mutual efforts to speak the language of the other.

Before we sat down, Ivan told Sasha in Bulgarian that he wanted me to know we were having only their best wines today. Once she conveyed that to me, I shook the hands of my hosts heartily, smiled broadly and said "Blagodarya." I also asked Sasha to thank them for bringing us to this beautiful place, and to request that we settle the business early so the wine and the day could be fully enjoyed. I learned to clarify details and agreements early in Bulgarian dinners, and reaffirm the agreement at the end. The large quantity of wine consumed made this imperative.

I asked what they had in mind for exporting wine to the U.S. They told me of the Western European countries that imported Bulgarian wines, verifying the quality of their wines, which were mostly reds. I agreed that the Bulgarian reds I had tasted were consistently rich, full-bodied and without a sharp after-taste. I asked if they knew of any Bulgarian wines being sold in the United States. They mentioned one that was regarded as middle tier in quality. Sasha easily and knowledgeably translated wine tasting terms for all of us.

I asked if they knew that I didn't learn of their business interests until I had arrived in Bulgaria, and therefore I could only guess at the challenges we faced. "Da," said Ivan, who often spoke for both of them. He said more and Sasha's translation informed me that they just wanted me to investigate the possibilities for U.S. sales.

"I have no experience with this product," I explained, "and wine is highly regulated. This usually means it takes a long time and is more costly to import. The U.S. market is probably controlled by distributors."

Ivan said "Da," and elaborated. Sasha told me that they knew from our mutual friend Viktor that I would be an honest, careful and competent person with whom to do business. I thanked them in Bulgarian for their trust in me.

In less than an hour, on our second bottle of wine, we had exhausted our questions. I took notes and would communicate further with them via my partner Viktor.

I asked Sasha to translate a toast to my hosts. I thanked them for their hospitality in bringing us to Melnik. Then we began our third bottle of Melnik Harsovo wine and our lunch. A huge steaming plate of shish kebab arrived with delicious chunks of lamb, tomatoes and sausage. I realized that I was eating a food whose name—shish kebab—came from this region, Turkey to be exact. Sasha said that the sausage was to add spice to the meal, and it did.

The sharp tomato juices were softened in the roasting fire, offsetting the sweetness of the tender lamb. The lusty roasted sausage taste yearned for the robust Harsovo Melnik red wine. After starting this fine red on an empty stomach, my loosened taste buds savored each bite of this intense sausage. The sausage was an assertive spicy meat mix, and with each bite, I longed for another quaff of the full-bodied red wine, a craving to which I submitted. Imbibing this fine wine in a simple feast swathed in a grapevine-filtered sun lifted me to a luscious paradise.

Business is often based on relationships as much as on products and prices, and in Bulgaria, wine was central to those relationships. The tastes, the weather, the exotic setting and the conviviality of the moment created a meal never to be forgotten.

Once business was dispensed, we loosened up with the fine wine and food in an intimate setting bathed in the bright dry heat of noontime.

On the drive back to Sofia stayed out of the mountains, making for a faster and more relaxed journey. As we reached full speed on the highway, I decided that I couldn't do anything to change the chances of an accident, so I might as well enjoy the ride.

"Why are you here?" inquired Sasha after we had climbed into the back seat.

"Good question. I like good questions. They're revealing. I'm here because my dear friend Viktor, who is arranging other meetings today, asked me to explore business possibilities," I answered.

"Do you think you will get rich in Bulgaria?" Sasha said with a serious look and a gentle touch on my arm.

"No. I don't expect to get rich here or anywhere. I'd like us to make some extra money for my family and Viktor. Viktor has lots of business ideas, but none of them are easy. We will do what we can," I replied.

"You are serious and know a lot. I wish to go to the United States to study some day. Maybe I will visit with you when I come to your country."

"Yes, of course. Here is my business card. If there is anything I can do to help you, let me know," I said, handing Sasha a card.

Sasha and I were dropped off in the vicinity of Viktor's apartment and her home, in the dark. We had become better acquainted as we discussed her desire for an American university education and my Bulgarian business goals on the way back. I felt a genuine interest on her part in my life, and I was curious about this precocious beauty from the edge of the Western world, wondering where and how her linguistic gifts might thrive.

The sun had set, but the day was not yet over. One more surprise in a day of discoveries awaited me. Once we got out of the car, I looked at Sasha and noticed how the twilight touched her high cheekbones and led my vision to her smiling eyes. Standing and looking at her in the sharp, yet subdued light I said, "Well, we've had a full day together. I can't believe how far we've gone and what we've done in your spectacular country, all in one day." It felt as if what I said was honest, yet banal in light of the bountiful sensual and intellectual experiences we had all shared.

"Yes," she answered with a beatific smile. "I enjoyed our trip together. I hope I served you well as your translator."

"Of course you did. You were excellent. We all had a fine and memorable lunch, and moved our business plans along. And," I said with a big smile, "I got to learn more about your country from you, a bright and beautiful young woman. How could this day be anything but spectacular?"

Sasha stepped close to me, looked into my eyes with a playful smile, and said, "I want to leave a lasting memory of Bulgaria with you."

I smiled back, naïvely, and started to open my mouth to speak. She stepped closer and, with firm and gentle hands, held my face, leaned in and kissed me on the lips. Feelings and thoughts swirled. This was not an option, I said to myself. Before I could speak, her lips opened and her tongue stroked my lips. On a dark street in Sofia, this bright and beautiful young woman was making a powerful pass at me.

I opened my lips, and her eager tongue darted into my expectant mouth. The tip of my tongue met hers in a dance of reversed gender roles. Her aggressiveness tempered as our tongues touched, though I was still the modest debutante in response to her uninhibited fondling of my lingua. Ecstasy is French kissing on a dark street in Sofia. The playful titillation of our tongues was an eternal moment. Sasha ended our fevered tactile riff as she had started it, tenderly and decisively.

Sasha withdrew her tongue from my mouth, kissed me once more passionately, held my face in her long strong feelingful fingers, and said cheekily, "Now you have another memory to take home to America."

She smiled an all-knowing smile that seemed out of place for someone so young. But this older sheltered guy from small-town America didn't have a basis for judging whether anyone else was experienced in the arts of love.

I took her slender face in my hands, kissed her deeply, smiled at her with amazement in my eyes, resisted the impulse to say anything, turned and walked to Viktor's apartment, smiling.

Jordon Pecile
Teacher * Mentor * Friend
by Bob Sessions

When I first took Jordon's class, Writing the Examined life, I thought it was a one shot deal. Little did I know then that it would blossom into three classes yearly for many years. But it did and I am both richer and wiser for it.

After the first class, he volunteered to read anything the class had written. Taking him at his word, I brought in several chapters I had written five years earlier.

The following week he asked me if I wanted to continue in the same vein. I said "yes" and we were off on a very long voyage. Things went well for the first few weeks. The he dropped a bombshell on me.

He said, as we walked to the parking lot, "You know, Bob, people don't really enjoy reading stories about happy families. Those stories tend to be too similar and thus boring. But if you can write about the darkness in your family life then you will be writing something interesting that people will want to read."

It probably took a full year of hearing that lesson before I got the courage to attempt it. Now I would not have it any other way.

Jordon single handedly turned those first flimsy chapters into a full-blown book, KALEIDOSCOPE: A Connecticut Boyhood 1942- 1955.

He followed that feat by convincing me to self publish. For this alone, he has my unfailing admiration. But when you add everything else he has done for me, he has earned my gratitude and undying love. Jordon, "THANK YOU!"

Why I Write
by Bob Sessions

Each of us thinks our time of growing up was the best of times. We forget that the next generations will not have any idea of how we grew and learned.

I grew up in the 1940s as World War II ravaged the globe. As a child, we played with things we found. A fallen branch could be a rifle or a bazooka or even a bomber. A discarded broom handle could be a pirate's sword or Hopalong Cassidy's horse, Tony.

Mom had to bribe us with milk and cookies just to get us to stop playing and come in for a rest. In kindergarten, snacks and a drink always signaled naptime,

World War II came to an end and industries had to find new markets to replace the war effort. Toys became more prevalent in the stores.

Then television became popular and children's programs flourished. And the advertising grew as well.

Gone are the sticks and broom handles. Hello computers. By the age of one, many kids have their first simple computers. The paper book industry is moving toward a thing of the past because people would rather read electronically.

I write because everyone should remember when a fallen branch was a kid's horse, or gun, or bomber.

Old Blue Heads
by Bob Sessions

Saturday May 20, 1944 dawned cloudy, cool, and damp, but, by after lunch the wind had shifted, the sun was out, the air was dry and warm, approaching hot.

Grace sat on the floor of Grandma's sunroom playing house with a set of ancient toy dishes that were being saved for her until she could really appreciate and care for them. The aroma of hot lard, cinnamon, nutmeg, and other spices filled the house even with the windows open.

Grace was just serving Peter Rabbit, who lived with Grandma and Grandpa. He was there in case she forgot to bring a doll. Peter was in a snit and being difficult; he wanted to host because it was his home. But Grace prevailed. In a pinch, Stubby and I were known to have played with Peter as well. We'd be hard pressed to admit it though. The dolls she brought today, Aunt Jane I and Aunt Jane II waited patiently for their slices of homemade, fresh, deep-fried cruller that Grace was carving.

The drone of voices from the four women in the room sounded like the buzz of the early summer flies. They were bouncing against the screen looking for the source of the smell. Three of the four ladies, Grandma, Aunt Grace, Grandma's sister and next-door neighbor, and another neighbor, Miss Schmitt sat at the card table sipping tea with bath towels protecting the shoulders of their housedresses. Each had taken a turn in front of the kitchen sink putting a blue rise in their graying hair. Bob and Stubby called them "old blue heads" behind their backs. Grace was waiting for just the right moment to break that bit of news

Our mother, Doris, sat at the fourth spot sipping coffee and nibbling a cruller. The cup and bread and butter plate didn't match like ours did. The other women munched away as well. There was a dinner plate full of seconds and maybe thirds sitting in the center of the table. A box of powdered sugar was there for anyone who wanted to sweeten the treat. Only Miss Schmitt used the powder. Today Grandma and Aunt Grace were on a semi-diet.

Mom was dressed to go out in a dark brown skirt with a tan blouse. Her matching hat, gloves, and purse sat on the dinning room table inside the backdoor. Grace glanced at her legs noticing how nice and straight the seams in her sheer nylons were. In contrast, Grandma's and Aunt Grace's darker and heavier hose sagged and bunched. Miss Schmitt's were rolled down to her ankles in deference to the early summer heat.

Grace went back to her duties of carving the cruller. The sudden hush that fell over the room caught her attention. She looked up from her hostess duties to see what was going on. The three older women stared, open mouthed, at Mom. Grace wanted to tell them to close their mouths because they looked like they were trying to catch flies, but didn't.

"You can't be serious, Doris," Aunt Grace exclaimed pressing the back of her hand to her forehead. "What will Victor say?"

"Oh, I suspect he'll spitter and sputter for awhile."

"You, wearing pants? I can't imagine," said Grandma.

"Well they aren't men's pants, Mom. They're fitted and go down to mid-calf.

"And leave the rest of the leg exposed? I never..." Miss Schmitt said.

"I can't believe Victor will allow you to wear them," Aunt Grace said.

"Listen, I'm a thirty nine year old woman who wants to wear pants. What's wrong with that?"

"Well the men won't like it, for one thing. It's not proper," Miss Schmitt said.

"Proper? It's proper enough for any 'Rosy the Riveter" to wear pants. They work in the factories for the war effort."

"Special occasion breeds special needs," said Grandma. "When the war is over the men will come back to the factories. Then the 'Rosies' will be gone and so will the pants."

"The men..." Aunt Grace started again.

"The 'men' is all I hear about. Why should they rule? Look how they took valuable school time from Little Bobby. Because Victor was sick with polio 'the men,' the Mayor, Governor, and head of the School

Board all decided that Little Bobby couldn't go to school. We weren't quarantined or anything, but he couldn't go to school. Was his teacher, Mrs. Aparo, a woman, asked if he should miss school? No. Was I asked? No. Was any woman asked? No. Is there even a woman on the school board that I could have appealed to? No! "

"Well you do have a point there, dear," said Grandma. "And I must say I'm still not very happy with the minister who allowed the congregation to shun us the way they did."

"I don't believe I've heard that story, Callie. Would you mind repeating it?" Miss Schmitt said.

"Well, I suppose. Although it goes against my grain to talk negative about the Church," said Grandma. "It was April 4th last year; the first Sunday Victor was in the hospital, when Seymour and I took the kids to church. The church was crowded like it has been since this awful war started. Yet no one would sit in our row or the row in front of us or behind us, but they did sit and stare. I wanted to stand up and give the minister 'what for,' but I held my peace and took the kids out at the second hymn and went back home. I cooled off during the week and felt that the Minister would handle it. The next week was the same thing. So we didn't go to church again until Victor came home in October."

"Well, we've had the vote and more for the last twenty four years. But I can't see where we have done much with it. I raise the eyebrows of my own mother and favorite Aunt just by mentioning buying a pair of pants. I can't wait to see what happens when I trade a skirt for a pair of pants."

"But, you still have to do what the men want," Aunt Grace said.

"Why? When I was in school, we were taught when women got the right to vote they would be free. Then 1920 came along and the 19th amendment was passed and we were taught we were free. Here it is twenty-four years later and I'm not free enough to wear a pair of pants.

"All I'm saying is my life would be easier to chase after three kids. And help an invalid husband wearing a pair of pants, a blouse, and flats than in a housedress, stockings and shoes. Don't you remember, Mom, what it was like chasing after those kids while I helped Victor at the hospital every day? Wouldn't it have been easier if you were dressed more comfortably?"

"Lauzey gauzey, girl. I don't know. I've never even thought of wearing pants. Even during all those years we lived on the farm, I never wore pants; I believed pants were for men," said Grandma.

Grace remained absolutely still. She was very familiar with the phrase "little pitchers have big ears." This was the first time we were listening so closely to an adult conversation. She placed her dolls face down on the floor so they wouldn't interrupt. Then picked up a slice from Peter's plate and silently chewed.

My thoughts turned away from the discussion of pants and returned to the story Grandma told about church. The three of us had talked about why we hadn't gone to church for all those months. We never come close to guessing the real reason.

That must explain why none of our friends had visited until Daddy came home. Was that why no one besides Grandma, Grandpa, Uncle Bert and Aunt Grace came to see us? Now Daddy's anger toward his family and friends was as plain as the nose on my face. And why he wanted to move away from town and the people who had shunned us.

Scary Tales Told in Broad Daylight
By Bob Sessions

Our first summer vacation, July 1945, sets the tone for many summers to come. At eight years old, I am called Little Bobby and I'm the oldest. Following closely is my sister, Grace, the family pest, who is seven. And my brother, Stubby, who is five brings up the rear.

We stay at my Aunt Hannah's cottage that is in a town on the Maine coast. It has no inside plumbing and no toilet paper. Pages from an old Sears & Roebuck's catalog are nailed to the wall in the one holer that is at the back side of her property. Her cottage has no electricity so there is no radio. But we children do not want for stories.

Every night after supper, as the darkness settles in, Aunt Hannah takes us kids out on the front porch and tells us stories about strange animals that prowl our area and beyond, and strange houses that are haunted, and strange people like witches and ghosts. But some of the strangest stories of all are told in the bright sunlight.

During our summer vacations, my family wastes countless hours tracking down old family burial sites. They use even more valuable swimming time by picking up branches, pulling weeds, and even righting some of the tumbled stones. We kids fuss our britches off, but it doesn't work.

During another very dull morning of gravesite work, the complaining becomes pretty bad. The swarms of biting black flies think we make a great lunch and don't help our patience.

Aunt Hannah suggests she take us for a walk in the woods to get us out of everyone's hair. The grown ups think this is the greatest idea since the invention of the radio, as she hustles us off. Deep in the woods, we discover another glade that holds two more tombstones, one large and one small.

Time and weather has obliterated some of the writing. What we can read on the big stone is "Martha and John Lymeburner." The smaller stone reads "Beloved son Noah."

Auntie stands staring at the stones for so long that I finally tug on her skirt to get her attention. She looks down; her face has a different look. It's almost as if she's someplace we aren't. She curtly tells us to sit down and she will tell us a story about these cousins. We're swatting black flies like crazy, but the clipped "teacher tone" of her voice makes us obey. She starts right in.

"John Lymeburner owned the only ship's chandlery in the harbor. He and his family lived in comfort in a well built, well appointed home thanks to his thriving business and carpentry skills. John and Martha's only child, Noah, was 15.

Noah wanted to become a man and find his fortune sailing on one of the ships that were home ported in the harbor. John and Martha were smart enough to realize they couldn't change his mind or stop him. The best they could do was to find him the safest situation possible.

Fortunately, John's friend, Captain Clark, was the Master of the Fair Lady and was scheduled to depart on the morning's tide. They were headed for Cuba to bring back a load of cotton, molasses, sugar and other sundries, but would be carrying other cargos on the way down.

"We should be back in about six months just before the stormy season sets in; and I'll take good care of your boy. You have my warrant on that," Captain Clark said trying to reassure his old friend, John.

Noah was the only happy one when he marched up the gangplank with his sea bag slung over his shoulder. The 'old salts" wore long faces because they were leaving family and friends. John and Marsha's faces were long because their only child was leaving them. John kept twisting his hat in his hands as Martha tugged on her bonnet strings and fussed with the loose hair at the nape of her neck.

One evening, about five months later John and Martha were snuggled in their dry warm bed as the first big storm of the season came without warning and raged around their home. The storm had struck unusually early that year.

Every few moments a thunderclap would rouse one of them enough so they rolled about restlessly before drifting deeper into sleep. An especially sharp thunderclap disturbed John, but Martha's screams brought him full awake. A lightning flash illuminated his wife who was sitting up in bed with her head back against the bedstead. Her nightcap had slipped off; her hair framed her head like a wild wreath. John fumbled with a match trying to light the bedside lamp. It took him several tries before he got a steady light.

When he next looked at his wife, he saw both eyes and mouth open as much as her skin allowed. There was no sound coming from her mouth; her eyes were seeing something John's couldn't.

"What is it Martha? What's wrong?" His voice quavered. He grasped her shoulder and shook it. Several more moments passed as lightning flashed and the thunder crashed around their home.

As the storm ebbed, Martha's open mouth started to gasp and her eyes flooded with tears.

"For heaven sakes woman, what's the matter?" His pale hands grasped at empty air.

"Noah's dead, he's dead," Martha moaned and writhed on the bed. "Noah came to me, calling for my help. He was standing in front of the living room fireplace. He waited for my help, but I couldn't move. After a few moments, he cried out to me once more, and then he vanished. I woke up. I know he's dead."

"There. There woman. It's just a bad dream you've been having, nothing more. Our Noah will be back at the end of the voyage. That's only six weeks off. You'll see. Captain Clark promised a safe return, didn't he?"

Martha allowed herself to be lulled by her husband's voice and reluctantly got back under the covers and drifted off again into an uneasy sleep. John blew out the light but sleep didn't come easily. He tossed and turned until he noticed the eastern sky was lightening and then fell asleep.

"John. John! For God's sake come quickly," were the next sounds that he heard. His eyes opened; he stared across the bed looking for the source.

"John. John!" This time he looked at the open door and his eyes settled on Martha beckoning to him from the living room. Rising from the bed, night shirted and barefooted, he dashed from the bedroom.

"What is it woman? What is it?"

She stood there mutely pointing at the fireplace in the opposite corner. It was still dark in that corner of the room but John could see something darker on the flagstone hearth. His bony calloused hands gently lifted the chimney from the closest oil lamp and lit it. With trembling hands, he held the light in front of him as he approached the spot on the stones. He carefully put the lamp on the mantel and knees creaking, knelt on the flagstones. He dipped his quivering finger into the liquid puddled on the hearth and tasted it.

Tears formed in his eyes as he turned to his silent wife and said, "Its seawater and this lump is seaweed."

Six weeks later, when Noah's ship returned, John and Martha were at the pier to greet it. As the ship was made fast to the pilings along side the wharf, Captain Clark came out of his cabin hat in hand. He tried to look directly at them, but his eyes slid away.

Martha was inconsolable as John led her home. That was the last time she was seen in public. John was left to run the home and the business. Martha died ten months later. The Doctor said she had suffered a stroke, but the townsfolk knew she died of a broken heart.

John never remarried. Instead he built a porch on the roof of his house and spent every spare moment sitting up there, in good weather and bad, staring past the ships anchored in the cove and out to the open ocean.

The story holds us prisoners. When it ends, I'm shocked to find myself holding Pest's hand. I drop it and glance at Stubby to see if he has noticed. But he hasn't, he has his own problems. His face shows his own horror as he looks down and sees a blossoming wet spot on the front of his khaki shorts.

The next day we drive to the harbor buying penny candy in the General Store that is still called *Lymeburner & Son.* We walk several blocks to see the house our cousin built. Stubby peeks at the front of his clean, dry, dark-colored, pants to see if the dreaded spot reappears. The closer we get, the more my skin shivers while the familiar fingers of fear run freely up and down my spine.

"That story isn't real? Is it, Aunt Hannah?" I ask standing in front of the yellow-painted house.

Coming back from a dawn trip to the outhouse, Stub and I find Grandpa sitting on the front porch steps. He's drinking coffee and puffing on his corncob pipe. We sit down beside him and for the third day in a row, we watch the sunrise.

"How'd you buckaroos like to take a ride to the harbor with me?"

"Sure." Anything Grandpa wants to do is fine with us.

We park and wander through the quiet town heading for the waterfront. Grandpa pauses to take a deep breath. "Smell that sea air."

I take a deep breath. It smells like a pail of over-ripe garbage that has been in the hot sun too long. But, if Grandpa likes it, then I like it too.

My Converse All-Star sneakers are silent as we walk the deserted wharf. The late June sun warms my summer crew-cut head as I walk next to Grandpa. Stub, with his unclipped curls, walks on the other side. The wharf is deserted. Because Grandpa says any fisherman worth his salt leaves in the dark hours before dawn. The store clerks and vacationers are still eating breakfast.

We see a couple of deserted fishing trawlers with their booms sticking straight up, moored to big bollards. When we reach the end of the wharf, Grandpa shades his eyes with his left hand. He spends a few moments gazing out at the small stands of evergreens growing on very small islands that dot the harbor. He lifts his gaze to the open ocean just past the breakwater that defends the bay. Then he points to his left with his right stump.

"You boys see that worn out ship tied to that old dock?"

"Sure. The one with the tall masts?"

"Yep. She's an old fishing boat. My grandfather Jeremiah Lymeburner was a fisherman on one like it."

"Why'd you call it 'she?' " I ask.

"That's the way of the sea. Every boat or ship is a she."

"What's the difference, boat or ship?"

"Well, boy, a ship is big and a boat can be brought aboard a ship. But you can't bring a ship aboard a boat."

"You mean they had rods and reels and fished from the rail like we do at the Baggaduce River Bridge?" Stub interrupts.

"No Stubby. These men went to sea for months at a time. T'was a very dangerous and lonely job. When the ships left port, twenty or thirty small boats called dories were stacked on the deck much like the teacups in your Grandma Callie's china closet. The ships carried up to sixty fishermen plus another eight hands to work the ship. Let's sit on that bollard; I'll tell you a story about your Great, Great Grandfather."

Stub and I run across the wharf; I scuff my sneaks climbing up but I'm too anxious to hear the story to care. Grandpa crosses more slowly stuffing his pipe. He flicks the match and lights it. Blowing out the match, he sticks the stem in the corner of his mouth and clamps it with his teeth. He takes several deep puffs staring at the old ship.

"This story starts almost one-hundred years ago."

"That was so long ago," Stub chimes in. "I wasn't born then was I?"

"No, you and I wasn't born then. But I heard this story when I was about your age, Robert. I've remembered it all these years." One more puff on his pipe and he starts the story.

"Grandpa Jeremiah's last trip to the Grand Banks, off Newfoundland, started off okay. He was paired in a dory with his cousin Zeke Bowden. He thought this was good 'cause Zeke was a good worker.

The fishermen woke at 4 a.m. every day. They climbed into their dories by 4:30. They was allowed to take a bucket of water and a small bucket of food. Before they could get settled, the dory was lowered over the side into the cold ocean. Most of the room in the boat was for the cod.

They rowed several miles from the ship following the schools of fish. Sometime when the light was right, the fishermen could see the cod. Thousands of them were swimming in straight lines just below the surface. Then they all flicked their tails, exposed their silver scales, and made a turn. Flicking in unison again, they turned again moving onward.

Each dory worked a separate area so their lines wouldn't get fouled. They dropped long lines of hooks over the side and pulled them back in throwing the hooked cod into the bottom of the dory. They did it over and over again. As they fished, Jeremiah and Zeke sang Frères Jacques over and over again. It had monotony to it, as did the fishing. Each tried to outdo the other in fishing and singing.

When the dory was full, they rowed back to the ship, unloaded the fish and then rowed back out for more. At 4 o'clock every afternoon, one of the mates fired a rifle and the fishermen returned for supper and bed. The next day, they did it all over again.

One day the fish took them far, far from the ship. The breeze freshened, becoming gusts. The gusts became a gale ant the gale became a howl. The wind seemed to want to clear the ocean by blowing all the dories and ships off its surface. The swells rose and rose until they blotted out the ship and threatened to swamp the dory.

"Quick! Pull in the lines," Zeke called over the rising wind as he struggled with the oars trying to steer the dory.

"Look!" Jeremiah hollered as he pointed over Zeke's shoulder. Zeke turned and saw a wall of dreaded fog rolling towards them. Soon they were bobbing about like a cork in an inkbottle. The wind blew so hard it gave shiver to the men.

"Throw those damned fish out. We don't need the weight," Zeke shouted over the unrelenting crashing waves and roaring wind.

Jeremiah was already tossing. Zeke carefully stowed the oars in the bottom of the boat.

Soon the raging seas were breaking over their boat. They emptied the water bucket and the food pail and commenced to bail. Sometimes they had to bail quick then they would get a short rest before bailing again.

While they rested, Jeremiah prayed. "Please dear Lord, help your humble servant overcome this trial so he can continue to serve You." He repeated this constantly whether he was bailing or resting.

After hours and hours, the storm passed. The fog stayed. They had no idea where they were.

"Mayhap we're halfway to Ireland," Zeke opined. "Let's rest and watch in shifts so that we can save our strength. We'll need it no matter where we are. I'll watch first. You rest."

When it was Jeremiah's turn to stand watch, he continued to pray out loud. He kept talking to God about being his humble servant and how he wanted to do God's will.

When Zeke took over the watch he asked, "How many fellas do ya know that were in this same fix and never made it back?"

"I dunno, six, seven probably. Maybe more if I think on it. Why?"

"Cause I know some too. If ya don't mind I think I'll say a prayer or two myself."

This took Jeremiah by surprise because Zeke was known more for his taproom attendance that his church attendance.

"Sure. But remember that ya have to bargain with God and give Him something in return. It can't be all take."

The night crawled. The sea became smooth, but the men could barely see into the bottom of the boat. The top of the sky brightened and the fog split.

Zeke was dozing when Jeremiah shouted, "Look! Look!"

Zeke stumbled to his feet and stood on trembling legs. His eyes followed Jeremiah's outstretched hand. There, just a short distance away, sat their ship with wraiths of fog hanging from its bow like seaweed from a whale's snout. Zeke replaced the oars in the oarlocks and bent his back to his rowing. Jeremiah sat in the back thanking his Maker for his deliverance.

When they were hoisted aboard, the first mate came over and clapped them on their shoulders congratulating them on their safe return. Then he removed his hat and told them that several boats still hadn't returned.

The captain stumped out of his cabin, his big heavy sea boots made a terrible sound on the wooden planking. He immediately looked into the bottom of the dory and asked where the cod were. When the men told him what happened he cussed them out for throwing the fish overboard. His wind burned face grew redder when he screamed that he would cut their pay for coming back empty. Then he turned his back on them and stumped back into his cabin without another word.

When the ship returned to port Jeremiah and Zeke first collected their wages, then their gear. They walked down the gangway for the last time together. They walked through the town to the livery stable.

Jeremiah hired a buckboard to take him and his wife to his brother, Seymour's, farm. Zeke bought a horse, blanket, bridle and saddle. The he bought a pack mule. Zeke never owned a horse in his life; he'd bragged about never even riding one. Jeremiah scratched his head in wonderment, but kept his silence.

Then they went to the General Store. Zeke tied his two animals to the back of the buckboard and rode on the seat beside his cousin.

Jeremiah bought foodstuffs and farmer's clothes and boots while Zeke bought camping gear and food.

Jeremiah couldn't hold back his curiosity when Zeke bought a Bible.

"What in tarnation are you doing?"

"I'm fulfilling my part of the bargain."

"Bargain! What bargain?"

"The one I made with God that saved our sorry hides. I told God that if I every set foot on dry land again I would go to the frontier and preach His word amongst the folk who have no church."

The two men shook hands and then embraced before the parted company never to see each other or the sea again.

Stubby and I sat there with our mouths wide open.

"Is that a true story, Grandpa?" I ask.

"Swear to God!"

It must be true because Grandpa doesn't swear to God often. Here's another story to add to my collection.

I spend the rest of the day wondering what it must've been like. The open ocean, the open frontier, maybe I could get away from Father by living like that hmmm…

Hant
by Bob Sessions

My mom yawned as she slumped back against her headboard. She was watching the dust motes cavort in the early morning sunshine. The rays were filtered only by rusty screens and 1840's glass windowpanes. Over the years, the frames had been replaced and the glass carefully reinserted.

Hearing my sister, Grace, moving around downstairs Mom decided to stay in bed until Grace left for work. She had moved in with Mom unexpectedly and unwanted, according to Mom three years ago. Within a week of Dad's death, she quit her job in Washington D.C., drove up and parked herself bag and baggage in Mom's driveway until she came home.

Feelings of dread had awoken her often the previous night. This was nothing new. She both saw and sensed movements in the deeper shadows near the closet of her bedroom for years. But the dread fled when she felt the overpowering sense of being guarded and protected. Alberta did not want to see Grace this morning; or more to the point, she did not want Grace to see her. She was too tired to put on her "everything is fine" face.

Alberta felt Grace had noticed something last night because her eyes darted around the room instead of staying focused on the television. The two women followed their nightly ritual. Mom tried to watch TV as Grace knitted, but the story was hard to follow because of the clacking needles. Mom inched the volume louder and Grace reciprocated.

Just like two old cartoon characters, living alone in a mausoleum, Mom thought. And she was not ready to discuss that this morning. However, Grace would be her usual direct self and insist upon full discussion. Alberta had to have the day to prepare for it.

I'll call my friend, Alice, and invite her to come across the street for coffee in a bit. I can thrash it out with her before I have to face Grace.

She felt a deep chill creep over her body and pulled the counterpane up under her chin. The feeling wasn't in response to the seventy-degree air that wafted in the open windows.

The chill passed and Alberta sat up as she heard Grace's car idle under her bedroom window. It waited its turn to enter the traffic dance that still flowed both ways on Freedom's Way.

Alberta stood and put on her dressing gown after she heard the engine rev. Then she heard a horn blare. She held her breath, but released it only when the routine traffic noises filled her ears.

Looking into her cheval glass Alberta asked "Mirror, mirror on the wall why is my hair the messiest of all?"

She answered sotto voce, "Because you're too vain to wear a silk hairnet when you sleep. Your mother gave you that advice, years ago, stupid."

Five quick steps brought her through the "sick room" and she paused as she entered the hallway leading to the upstairs bath and the boys' bedroom.

She thought: The original garret used to be six feet by eight feet and five feet high and we turned it into poor Big's bedroom. But when we moved here, he was still called Little Bobby. And in our first house, he had to share a room with Grace and Stubby. The kids at school named him Big on his very first day.

Black cloth had hung along the sides, making the garret even narrower, but they hid the treasures the previous owners left behind against the walls. The ceiling wasn't even covered. Battings of old insulation could be seen through the laths. Big had some books, a small radio, and a table lamp on the floor next to his bed; and yet he said he was happier than a clam even with all the dark nooks and darker crevasses. There wasn't even a ceiling lamp to dispel the gloom. How I used to worry about him and checked on him every night.

I wasn't the only one who felt creepy up here. The first time I brought Mother up here; she wouldn't even go through the doorway into his room. We both felt a presence there. I never could pinpoint what it was.

At 9:30, a knock and a "hello" rolled through the old farmhouse.

"Come on in. We're in the dinning room today. I hope you brought your appetite this morning because I deep fried fresh crullers last night."

"I thought I smelled those wonderful aromas when I opened the back door. If I didn't know better I'd have thought Grandma was here," Alice said as she hooked her pocketbook over the back of a chair and sat down.

"I hope you can spend some time with me this morning because I have the deep need to discuss something with you before Grace gets home and I have to go over it with her."

Alice paused and pondered then said, "I must admit you've got my curiosity up, Alberta. Looking at that pile of doughnuts, I'd say we'll be here until the noon news. By the by, I see you're pretty nervous."

"How can you tell?"

"Because you drink your coffee black with no sugar and this morning you have cream in your black coffee and you haven't stopped spooning the sugar into it since I came in the room."

"My. You're a regular Sherlock Holmes, but that's just what I need."

"Why? What's the trouble?"

"Promise me you won't laugh or tell me I'm a silly old woman."

"Alberta, you are the most level headed person I know. I wouldn't laugh if you told me you thought there were ghosts in this house."

Alberta dropped her sugar loaded spoon dead center into her cup and the spoon thunked on the bottom and pinged against the side of the fragile china. She gasped inhaling some cruller crumbs from the piece she was holding and coughed until her face was a magenta hue.

Alice started to rise but Alberta waved her away. She caught her breath, took a deep sip, gagging on the oversweet mixture. This brought on another fit of coughing that stopped as fast as it started. Alberta took her cup to the kitchen sink and poured the vile mixture down the drain.

"What on earth made you say that?" Alberta asked pouring fresh coffee into the cup. The cup and saucer rattled as Alberta' trembling hands put them down.

"Well, my late Harry always felt a trifle uncomfortable in this house, but common decency kept our mouths shut. To be blunt about it he said he felt 'spied' upon especially in the basement. "

"You're also a mind reader, because that is just what I want to talk to you about."

"What's happened?"

"Let me start at the beginning and I'll bring you up to last night."

"Good idea," she said fixing her coffee in the mug she preferred to use. Alice didn't feel comfortable using Alberta's best china.

"Years ago, more than forty now, when we first bought this home, I was never totally comfortable here. I felt like I was always being watched."

"Did you ever feel threatened?"

"Yes, in the beginning I was petrified. But over the years, when nothing happened I felt just the opposite, I felt protected."

"But, you never mentioned it to me."

"I didn't want the kids to get wind of it. You know how they are? They listened in on everything no matter how careful I was."

"You say you were only watched?"

"Yes, mostly at night, after I'd gone to bed. I'd feel someone or something watching me. Sometimes when I woke to use the bathroom, I'd fell the presence follow me downstairs and stay with me till I was back in bed. Often I awoke from a sound sleep by sensing a stare. From time to time I'd wake Victor up on some pretext or other, or I awoke and talked with him when he used the toilet, but he never picked up on what I was trying to say."

"Yes. Victor was not good at keeping secrets or hiding his feelings, was he? So if he suspected anything you'd have known about it."

"But now the feelings are coming more and more often and from more places."

"You never told me anything like that and I'm supposed to be your best friend."

"You are; you are. The only one I talked to was Mother and only under the most secure circumstances; not even Victor knew and he was there when I was touched."

"Touched?"

"Yes. Just once. It was after Victor lost his voice to throat cancer. The house was always so silent because I wanted to hear any sign of trouble. We kept the radio off and only had the TV on if we were together. One day I was vacuuming in here facing the kitchen behind you. I thought Victor was down cellar in his workshop. As I reached the doorway to the middle room, I felt a pair of hands on my waist that moved me out of the way. I looked behind me to ask Victor what he wanted for lunch. Empty space was there. When I turned back there was Victor coming out of the kitchen with two cups of coffee. I collapsed onto a dinning room chair and gratefully accepted the coffee. Victor gave me his 'what's wrong' look. But I pretended to be absorbed with the coffee."

"Nothing like that ever happened again, right?"

"Right. I swear."

"Well what happened next?"

"Just before my Dad died, Victor and I were living here alone. Big and Stubby were in the Navy and Grace was living at school so Victor and I had the nest to our selves."

"I always had an empty nest," Alice smiled quickly and held up her hand to prevent a sympathetic comment from her friend.

Alberta continued, "One day Dad came over to borrow one of Victor's tools; he went down cellar while Victor and I watched the news and ate our lunch. After a long while, he called for us to come down. Victor stopped dead at the foot of the stairs and I couldn't see around him. When I was finally able to move him, I saw a portion of our stone foundation had been pulled aside and Dad was shinning a flashlight inside a small cave. Dad said that it was about eight feet by ten feet and about four feet high. A spring and lever mechanism operated the door. Victor and I searched for any marks inside the empty cave. Victor had Dad close him in partway so he could examine the back of the door. All we found were smoke markings on the ceiling, but no marks on the floor or walls. We asked Dad to shut it and swore him to secrecy."

"You mean to tell me that Big and Stubby never found the doorway in all those years?"

"Strange isn't it. Big figured out how to get into the safe and could unlock every lock on the property, but he never stumbled on that one. I'll bet he'll be embarrassed when he finds that out."

"You can bet the farm on that," Alice laughed. I'm sure you know that Freedom's Way was renamed during Civil War times, don't you? It was originally Miller Road after the millrace that was built on the pond," Alice said. "A local legend has Freedom's Way as part of the 'underground railway' with several stations along this street," pointing out the window at Freedom's Way.

"Yes and I know that this house predates the war too. But so does yours."

"True, but we never found anything like that. Should you have kept the cave a secret?"

"Well what's done is done. Maybe I'll call some historian about it and maybe I won't. That's not the problem. Anyway, Grace will stick her big nose in it soon," Alberta said pouring more coffee for both of them.

"Why?"

"That's what I really wanted to talk to you about. She has been coming home later than usual from school and I've seen some extra books in her bag. I haven't gotten a look at them yet, but I suspect she has been doing research at the library."

"Why do you think that?"

"Two reasons. First I see her eyes dart around the room like mine do when I get that 'watched' feeling. And second, some of the old town history books have been moved around on my book shelves."

"But why now?"

Alberta paused. She took a bite of cruller and a sip of cooling coffee before she continued.

"What ever it is is getting bolder. It or they don't confine themselves to my bedroom. When I'm sewing, or reading, or watching TV I catch sight of something out of the corner of my eye.

"About a month or two ago Grace was watching a PBS documentary about the spirits of slaves that haunted stops on the 'underground railway.' The writers made a point of saying the spirits were almost always vigilant and protective as a way of saying thanks for the help they received. The narrator went on to say that, the slave need not have died on the property to leave its psychic mark, but he, she, or they, were probably hidden there under duress for a long time.

"Grace had started watching my eyes dart around and then I noticed hers doing the same thing. I believe she sees the spirits too, but hasn't put two and two together yet."

Both women stared out the window lost in their own thoughts. Alberta noticed the diminished traffic. Only about one car every sixty seconds passed now.

"When we first moved here you could comfortably count every car that went by here in a day and you knew most of the drivers too."

"I've heard Victor say the same thing any times prior to his death," Alice replied bringing her focus back to the here and now.

"Well, what should I do?"

"You know Grace better than I, but to me she's like a dog worrying on a bone. I guess what I'm saying is just answer her questions, don't volunteer anything, and don't lie. What she wants to know she'll ask."

"That's what I'm afraid of."

Alberta wasn't hungry at lunch and could hardly follow the story line on any of her soaps.

She was almost relieved when she heard the backdoor slam and Grace call, "Mother, I'm home and I want to talk to you."

Thursday: June 1, 1995
The End
by Bob Sessions

He is glad to get under the portico and out of the penetrating mist. Wiping his head with an open palm, he feels as much scalp as hair. Pretty soon, I'll be shampooing with Simonize, he thinks.

The frosted glass doors hiss open and he steps inside the lobby. His wet New Balance walking shoes sink the proverbial inch into the multi wine colored, burgundy, claret, port and rose Oriental. He walks under a massive crystal chandelier that tries its best to keep the gloom at bay. The ivory-flocked wallpapered walls are adorned with pastoral scenes in gold leaf frames. Gilded sconces also try to brighten the atmosphere.

He knows the system. He signs in at reception. He takes a deep breath of flora-scented air. He takes two strides to a set of double doors. He yanks them open. He steps into another world.

Gone are crystals, deep rich wine tones, gilt, ivory and mahogany. This world is dominated by blue, gray, and white. The walls are covered with baby blue vinyl. The floor is slate gray vinyl tile. And the ceiling is white acoustical tile.

The first thirty feet of hallway is devoted to professional's cubicles, a staff lounge, and storerooms. Next is a round nurse's station whose staff is mandated to monitor the mobile patients and prevent them from approaching the lobby. He glances down the right and left corridors and sees more nursing stations.

As Big starts down the corridor, the floral scented air in his lungs runs out. Without hesitation, he breathes through his mouth. This is an old trick he learned early on in his Navy days. It helps minimize the stench in the air.

Some ports he's visited reek of poverty and filth. Then, after a few days, the smells become invisible.

But this is a different smell. This is the smell of old age and dying and no amount of "sweet air" can mask it. Human beings cause this stench. Some are bedridden. Some struggle with walkers. Some even roll about in their wheelchairs. But most sit silently tied in their stationary wheelchairs, drooling on their bibs, or worse. Some sit babbling and screaming. The worst are the ones who still have the spark in their eyes. They use those eyes to beg for attention please, any attention.

Big feels for them, but he isn't there to give them attention. He strides deeper into the complex, careful to stick to the center of the corridor, keeping his eyes focused on the distant wall.

Forever is a long-long time so when Big finally arrives at room number A509 he thanks God for his safe trip past those eyes. He pauses a minute to release the self-protective cocoon he has enveloped himself in.

He pushes the door open and calls out a cheerful, "Hi, Mom."

"She's sleeping," his younger brother, Stub, says. He rises from the bedside chair and embraces Big.

Aging has been kind to Big's brother, the baby of the family. His hair, now silver, is thick and shiny. His complexion reflects the hours of lake fishing he enjoys when he can get away. After a long moment, they part.

Big's younger sister, Grace, works her bulk off the small corner settee. Grace, aka The Grace or The Pest, gives her older brother a brief hug and shuffles to the door.

"Well, well, the last family member is finally here. Is twenty-five miles of traffic too much for you to maneuver these days? Or are you too busy at that bowling alley of yours, Big? We see less and less of you. I'm leaving. I've got a ton of homework to correct. Are you coming, Stub?"

"Hold on a minute, Grace. Big just got here, the least we can do is to fill him in."

"On what? She has been here for months now and a nursing home before that. The DNR sign follows her around like a ghost. The doctor said she could live another week, or another month, or go tomorrow. Or, are you expecting a miracle? There's nothing we can do about it either way. What more is there to say?"

"I see Miss Cynic is still her same caustic self. And I've wasted valuable time fearing you might mellow with age, Grace. I guess I worried por nada."

"She's right though. Mom may pass tomorrow or next month," Stub says embracing Big again.

Big feels Stub's frame shake a couple of times and squeezes him tighter before he lets go.

Stub swipes at his eyes with his rough knuckles, "I'd better go too. It's a long drive home and I have a church board meeting at 7:30. We'll have to get together real soon."

"Sure, we will," Big lies. He knows how busy they all are with immediate plans. Time is too valuable to squander on a mere brother or sister. There will be time enough for that, later.

"Well, at least she had twenty-eight more years after Dad died. And we tried to make them good ones too," Stub says.

"Here we go again, down memory lane," The Grace slumps against the door. "We'll never get out of here now."

"Well, they did have good years together too, after Dad sobered up. I hate to admit this, but I was jealous of how he treated our kids. Remember when he built the cart to tow them around behind his mower? How the kids loved that. And how they screamed for him to go faster and over more bumps? And the stories he used to tell them? And the trips to DQ for softies?"

"Yah. Where was that affection when we were growing up?" Stub asks.

"In his Seagram's bottle," Grace snips. "Now can we get out of here? I don't want to walk down that corridor alone."

"In a minute. I've got to tell Big something first. I don't now why I never said this before. Thanks for taking all the bullshit Dad handed out. You fought back, not giving in, sticking to your guns. You were my 'big brother' hero then. The way you are today, in spite of him, makes you my hero today too. Thank you."

"Oh, for God's sakes, Stub. Big isn't the Second Coming," Grace whispers.

Stub again sweeps Big into his arms.

"Oh for Pete's sake, let's cut this maudlin crap and get the hell out of here, while she's still alive," Grace straightens up opening the door.

Big and Stub shake hands as The Grace snaps a quick, "See ya," stepping out the door.

Looking around for some kind of diversion, Big notices the TV and family pictures are gone. Then he remembers someone telling him that Mom didn't want them anymore because any lucid time she had, she spent reading her Bible.

There is a print of a bright red male cardinal, sitting on a white birch branch, during a snowstorm, on the wall at the foot of the bed. Maybe the bird has replaced the family. Nobody knows what's in her mind anymore.

Along with the audible silence of the room comes the faintest beep Big has ever heard. It barely intrudes. He tracks it to a small camera assembly focused on the bed and mounted over the door. A thin wire leads from the unit along the wall and over to her chest. I don't remember seeing that before. I'll ask at the nurse's station.

He bends over to examine the wire and it draws his eyes to the faint thin scar on her cheek. His fingertip traces the line from her ear to her jaw. I wonder…

He also notices her thinning gray hair that is neatly combed on the front and sides. But the back is flattened and matted.

Camp Wigwam director, Mr. Quint, taught a sermon about a man who only polished the toes of his shoes. The man felt that was all that was necessary because that was all he could see. Mom would be mortified if she could see the back of her hair now because she felt the same as Director Quint.

Anxious for any diversion, Big glances around the room for her Bible spotting it tucked into the cushion of the settee. He pulls it out and carries it to the chair next to the bed. Sitting he sees the edge of a card in the center of the book. He pulls it out and drops it like a chunk of dry ice.

A bright red-suited Santa stares back at him from the white bedspread. *Why did she keep that Christmas card I sent her way back in1959?*

It was a fifteen-day trip from San Diego to Japan for the seaplane tender, USS Currituck AV7, during October 1958. I worked in an alcohol fog for the first week as we crawled along.

Proper prior planning postponed my predictable sobriety. My personal locker was filled with bottles of Vitalis and Aqua Velva. Most of my clothes were stored in my sea-bag, against regulations, to create more locker space. In reality, the bottles were vodka tinted with food coloring. Thank God, boot camp locker inspections are a thing of the past.

The day after I threw the last empty overboard, I taped a note inside my locker door. It reminded me to mail a Christmas card to Mom and Father. I knew I'd need this visual reminder or I'd forget. My parents, especially my father, were very-very low on my personal totem pole.

Eight days later, I was introduced to the Black Cat Club, military script, Oriental b-girls, Sun Tory whiskey the cheapest rotgut available, and Yokosuka, Japan.

Father slid further down the pole. However, I kept the pump primed by sending them matching silk kimonos before the Currituck sailed to its new homeport, White Beach, Okinawa.

A very-very short six and a half months later, I found myself standing in front of a payphone. It was outside the men's room in the back of the Cactus Club, on Broadway, in downtown San Diego. I'd spent the last three days, and the last of my money, renewing friendships with bartender pals and street women. I found my old flame had guttered out and left Strippers Palace for fires unknown. She left no forwarding address to help rekindle the spark. And it was still ten days till the Eagle shit or payday as the landlubbers and civvies called it. Now the call was urgent.

The operator asked, "Will you accept a collect call from a Big in San Diego, California?" Then a moment later I heard, "Go ahead, sir. Your party is on the line."

"Hi, Mom. How are you two doing?"

"Fine," Mom snapped. "It certainly took you long enough to call. Have you been back in the states for three days now or is it four?"

"How... How do you know?"

"Have you forgotten our new neighbors, Frank and Alice? They do have a favorite nephew, you know. He's an Admiral who serves at the Boston Naval Yard. I've written to you about all of them before. Don't you read my letters? I certainly read the very few you manage to send," her voice dripped.

"Aw, Mom. I've been..."

"I know. You've sung the same tune since your father sent you away to school seven years ago. As I was saying, The Admiral keeps Frank and Alice posted on your whereabouts. Let me guess, you must be broke again or you wouldn't call."

"Yah, I'm broke," I murmured. "But a check from you can cure that," I chuckled, trying to salvage a deteriorating situation.

"Broke? How can you be broke? You've been out of the country for seven months."

"I don't know. It just seems to go."

"I guess I can mail you a check tomorrow."

"Send it airmail, please."

"How about if we send you a plane ticket too? Then you can come home for a visit."

"I'll have to accumulate some leave first. I took a little over there."

"Well I'm sure I don't want to hear those lies. What I do want to know is where is our Christmas card? Were you too drunk or too busy on leave to send it?"

"What? You didn't get the Christmas card? I can't believe it. I remember giving it to my buddy, Ski, to mail 'cause I was working so very hard. He must have put it in the local mailbox instead of the FPO mailbox. That dumb shit. I'll kick his ass."

"Now Big, don't use that language with me. I'm your mother not one of your hoodlum friends or Navy buddies."

"Sorry, Mom. Remember that check? Could you make it out for at least...?"

A very long seven years later, I found myself on the phone. "Hi Mom, how are you and Father?"

"Just fine, Big. How are my delightful Grandchildren?"

190

"They're great. As a matter of fact, that's why I'm calling. May I bring some of their Christmas presents over there? They have a way of finding what's hidden around here."

"I guess snooping runs in the family," she chuckled. "I remember when you... never mind. Sure you can. I'll even help you wrap if you want?"

"No thanks. Keeping them will be plenty. I'll see you later."

"Oh, before you go. Your father and I were just talking about the Christmas card we never got..."

"Listen Ma, if I've told you once I've told you a thousand times..."

"I know, I know, you sent the card. I'll see you in a little while."

A very-very long five years later Big found himself answering the phone.

"Hello?"

"Hi, son. How are you?"

"Fine, Mom. We're all fine. What can I do for you?"

"Nothing. I called to thank you for the extra Christmas card

you sent me this year."

"Extra card? You got two cards? I'll bet one of them must be the one I sent you from Okinawa. I read a news story about..."

"No, Big. You signed one card and put your old Navy FPO return address on it. You even found an old postage stamp and blurred the cancellation mark. Your wife signed the other one. Your late father would have given you high marks for pulling that old college cheating scam out and trying it again."

"I don't know what you're talking about," I whispered into the phone.

"Sure you do. I'm sure you remember how you passed your first history final in college. Somehow, you managed to get three blue answer books. In the first book, you copied the test. Then you stuck that one and a blank one in your briefcase. In the third book, you wrote to us, your poor old folks. You were flowery in your praise of the college, the course and the professor. When the test time was up, you handed that book in as your test answers. Then you went back to the dorm, looked up enough answers to pass the course, and mailed that blue book home to us. When the Dean called, we read him the answers and you passed. Does any of this sound familiar?"

"Yes Mom," I continued to whisper. "Why didn't you turn me in?"

"Because you quit school and joined the Navy before we figured it out. Nice try with the extra card. Now, you really didn't send us a card in 1958, did you? What made you send it now?"

"I certainly did. I remember…" I murmured, chagrined.

Why did I pull that old chestnut out? Oh yah, I remembered that trick when I was having a couple off brews and watching a stupid TV show about college kids. That whole idea fell right into my lap between slugs. I was positive it would fool an old woman. It worked once. Oh well, I'll have to think of something better next time. Maybe I should just come clean.

No way, Jose.

I find my cheeks wet and my head resting on Mom's wasted body. My tears have soaked the thin blanket covering her. I feel smothered by the total silence.

Where is that infernal beep? My mind screams. I can feel and hear the beating of my own heart in my ears. When I can no longer stand all the pressure, I say, "You were right all along, Mama. I never sent that Christmas card. I was too drunk. Please-please give me a sign that you forgive me for lying to you all these many years?"

Something grazes my shoulder. My heart surges. My head spins. My body tingles as if thousands of volts carouse through it.

"You'll have to step out now, sir," a nurse says. She gently takes her hand off my shoulder and slowly pulls the sheet up over Mom's face. "The monitors show that your mother passed about 20 minutes ago. The orderlies are waiting in the hall. We don't want to interrupt your time with her before we have to. Or, do you still need a few more minutes with her?"

"I need another lifetime…" I stand.

Vacation
by Bob Sessions

I have always loved listening more than talking. I didn't just listen so I'd know when it was my turn to talk as so many others do.

For over twenty-two years now, I have known how lucky I am to have Patty Ann as my wife. This truism was driven home as I tuned in to a spate of vacation conversations recently.

This snippet was overheard in the grocery checkout.

Two new mothers were working in tandem trying to get the items away from their toddlers and on to the belt.

"…how was your vacation?"

"Well the beach was fine, but little Mikey got so sunburned on the first day. We couldn't even go back to the beach for four days."

"What did big Mikey do? Help you out?"

"Ha. He played golf all day, every day, with some new found buds."

The next snippet came the church parking lot on a warm Sunday morning.

I caught up with my friend just after he and his spouse returned from vacation.

"Hey Ralph, how was everything in the Bahamas?"

"Well you know. I wanted to swim with the dolphins and take some tours. See the sights and stuff."

"Sounds great."

"Yeah, but Cindy wanted to shop."

"Oh, so you must have done a lot of shopping."

"You got that right."

I eavesdropped on another vacation conversation in the gym locker room. An older man was bragging to his friend in an overloud voice.

"On our last day at sea the Captain announced on the loudspeaker that this was the first cruise in six months that never saw a drop of rain."

"Boy, you lucky duck. Bet you and Peg had a ball."

194

"Sure did!"

On that happy note, as I was slugging out my two miles on the treadmill I decided to tell my vacation story.

Just one of the reasons I'm so lucky to be married to Patty Ann is we have never had a bad vacation. Sure, I'll admit that some were better than others. But a bad one? Never.

The reason for that: we are each other's diversion. Being the central element in each other's life, we ensure that each one of us is happy.

We don't grouse about not using the pool on a rainy day, we grab our books and find a nice quiet spot to sit and read. After we're done, we find a quiet bar and talk about what we read. Or we play a competitive game of scrabble. You guessed it, the looser buys. We've even been known to enjoy an afternoon "nap" where we both win!

What we do best is relish each other's company and that doesn't leave any room for negativity.

And that is just one small facet of the lovely jewel that I married those very short years ago.

Grandpa Learns
by Bob Sessions

My youngest daughter, Dee, now a working mom, was spending a quality evening with my newest Granddaughter, Madilyn Lily.

Madilyn speaks well for a two and half year old, but still inserts her own special vocabulary into conversations.

The evening was supposed to end at bath time, but Maddy had other ideas. She sat on the floor arms akimbo and chin resting on her chest.

"Draw muffin, Mommy. Draw muffin," she chanted keeping the beat with her little feet.

"Ok, honey. One muffin and then it's into the tub." She picked up a crayon and glanced at the clock.

"Ok, Mommy, into the tub," she said as she glanced at the clock too.

Maddy peered at the paper as the muffin was created. Dee added a face to the muffin top. There were eyes, a mouth, and a nose made with small red and pink hearts.

"That's so bouful, bouful, Mommy!" Madilyn gushed.

"There now that's done. Now help me pick up your toys before you get in the tub."

"Not done," Maddy intoned as her head hit her chest. "It's not fair neither." Her arms and legs flailed independently as her head whipped back and forth in the classic 'no' motion.

"What's not done?" Dee said in a smooth calm voice.

"Didn't draw xyzg," Maddy said as she sat motionless. Her stare flicked back and forth between the picture and a bewildered mom.

"What?"

"Draw xyzg," Maddy insisted

"Do you mean tag?" Mom guessed.

"No tag. Not it, neither," she yanked her closest arm away from her mother. "Draw xyzg, pleeze!" Maddy now sat stone still, her lips sealed in a hardened straight line.

After playing an educated twenty questions concentrating on an ending "g" Dee tried, "Bag?"

Madilyn jumped up with her little face beaming.

"Yes Mommy, draw it like the one Grandpa brings muffins in."

196

It looks like Bad Grandpa will be bringing a healthier treat, maybe apples or grapes, from now on. No bag, neither.

Jordon Pecile
by Joan Sonnanburg

Jordon's love of reading and ability to recall specifics from a myriad of novels and short stories was always a source of inspiration and informed his unique ability to guide his students. His always astute comments and encouraging words improved our writing and blessed our lives.

Joan Sonnanburg
Bio

As a college English major, I fantasized about writing fiction. About ten years ago, life handed me a perfectly formed short story, so I wrote it. Since then, I've enjoyed participating in writing workshops. Writing and sharing stories is a short-cut connection to other people that gets right down to the interesting stuff.

A Taste for Vanilla
by Joan Sonnanburg

Periodically, Jean got the urge to consolidate their possessions. A cardboard box labeled Memorabilia lay open on the cocktail table in front of them. She had asked Mark to help her decide what to get rid of. Her hair brushed his cheek as she reached over and pulled out a book. She ran her fingers over the embossed gold letters that spelled Morris High School and began leafing through Mark's yearbook. When she came to a two-page spread of the Class of 1938, she stopped and searched the faces.

"Oh, Mark, there you are," she said pointing to a tall, slender boy in the back row wearing a cardigan.

Mark smiled.

"Oh and look. There I am!" Jean pointed to the girl standing next to Mark, her head tilted slightly, looking up at him.

Mark's smile dissolved. The girl was not Jean. Jean was tiny and had always worn her hair short. The girl in the picture was close to his height and had long, unruly hair.

"That's not you," Mark said.

"Yes it is," Jean replied. "Look at how I'm looking at you. I thought you were so handsome."

"No, sweetheart. We hadn't met yet."

"Of course we'd met," Jean said. "I remember that day clearly. It was fall. The sky was blue and the sun was shining, but there was a chill in the air. You took off your sweater and put it around my shoulders. I thought that was so sweet. Then you asked me to go on a hayride."

"No, Jean. We didn't have hayrides in the Bronx."

Jean stared at him, then shook her head, laughing. "What was I thinking? I didn't go to your high school. I was still living in Nebraska then."

Mark squeezed her hand. He didn't like to think that she was confused more often these days. He was glad she'd caught herself, happy she could still remember with a little prompting.

He looked at the photo again. He knew who the girl was. It was Madeleine.

Madeleine had been in his homeroom freshman year. He noticed her the first day of school. Her last name was Strong and his was Stroup. Since homeroom seating was alphabetical, she sat directly in front of him. His first impression was of the back of her head with its wild, titian hair. Then she turned around and asked to borrow a pencil. He was transfixed by her azure eyes and "bee-stung lips." When she faced the front of the room again, he'd had a strong desire to touch her hair.

Jean patted his arm as the sweet-cinnamon scent of baking apple pie wafted into the family room.

"I'd better check on that pie."

She handed him the yearbook, rose slowly, and steadied herself. He looked up at her. She still had the pink cheeks and green eyes of the lovely mid-Western girl who'd danced into his life at a YMCA party after the war. He'd liked her smile and asked her to dance. She used to tell their friends that she'd come to New York to find her destiny and found him. After they'd married, she'd worked as a secretary so he could finish his degree. She'd stood by him when he tried his hand at advertising and supported his decision to quit and become a high school teacher instead. They'd raised a son and daughter together and had been blessed with four grandchildren. His eyes followed her as she walked out of the room.

When she was gone, he flipped through the pages of the yearbook until he came to the picture of the newspaper staff. There was their advisor. What was her name? She'd been something of a martinet, but he'd liked her anyway. To her left, his old friend Art and Art's friend Nate sat at a big oak table. And, there, between them, was Madeleine -- Nate's girl.

At the beginning of his junior year, when Mark joined the paper's staff, he'd smiled at her. She'd smiled back, but he couldn't tell if she knew who he was. While he'd noticed her when they were freshmen, he was pretty sure she hadn't noticed him. He wasn't the kind of freshman an attractive girl would notice -- or any girl for that matter. He'd been 5' 3" and hadn't yet thinned out.

By sophomore year, he'd grown some; but by then, Madeleine had acquired friends and admirers. She didn't need to borrow his pencil. By junior year, he was 5'11" and was lifting weights. Other girls noticed him; but to Madeleine, he was a classroom fixture, like a desk. The night Nate suggested they all go for a soda, something changed. It had been a long day. They'd brought sandwiches and stayed at school late getting the paper out. At first, Madeleine said she had to go straight home. But Nate put his arm around her and whispered something in her ear. She giggled and came with them.

Six of them squeezed into a booth, Nate on one side of Madeleine, Mark on the other. He could feel her thigh pressed against his.

"I can't decide what I want," Madeleine said.

"Let's get a chocolate malt," Nate said.

"I don't know. Maybe I want vanilla," she mused.

"I'm getting vanilla," Mark said, even though he never got vanilla. "You can have some of mine." Madeleine smiled at him.

"You're in my homeroom, aren't you?" she said.

"Yes," he replied. She never talked to him. Not since the pencil.

She turned back to Nate. They snuggled and talked to each other until their sodas arrived.

The waitress gave Nate and Madeleine two straws and one extra-large glass. Mark got only one straw.

Madeleine took a long sip of chocolate malt, then turned to Mark. "Can I have my taste now?"

Mark pushed his glass toward her. She put her lips around his straw and sucked. When she finished and gave the malt back to him, his straw had a ruby red ring from her lipstick. He brought it to his lips, barely able to believe he was putting his mouth around the same straw that had just been in Madeleine's.

After that night, she began saying hello to him in homeroom. One day, before Mr. G. took attendance, she started a conversation with him. Mark was talking to Natalie Styron, who always sat behind him. Art thought she was pretty. She'd never struck Mark that way. But, that day, her head was thrown back and she was laughing. She had been trying to touch her tongue to her nose. Her light brown curls were bouncing and Mark thought she was kind of pretty. Then he felt someone tug at his sleeve. It was Madeleine.

"What's so funny?" she asked.

Mark told her what Natalie was trying to do. Madeleine tried it too. She had a long tongue. It looked like she might make it. Then Mr. G. said, "May I have your attention, please," and she turned around.

Next morning, Madeleine started talking to Mark before Natalie got to class. Soon after, Natalie stopped talking to him.

By senior year, he and Madeleine were friends; but Mark was all too aware that she was Nate's girl, until one unseasonably warm day in March. The Class of '38 was called down during homeroom to have their picture taken. They lined up in alphabetical order outside the school and the photographer arranged them on the front steps. Madeleine, of course, was next to Mark. She looked up at him and asked if he'd like to go for a walk after school. She said that Nate would be at basketball practice. The photographer snapped the picture before Mark could answer. She told him to meet her at the entrance to the park, by the wrought iron gate.

The rest of the day went by in slow motion. As he was leaving school, he saw Art walking toward him. He pretended not to see him and walked faster.

"Mark, wait up."

"Oh, hi, Art."

"How about a game of handball?"

"No, not today," he'd answered.

The sound of the toilet flushing and water running in the sink brought Mark out of his reverie. It always annoyed him how long Jean left the water running when she washed her hands. It would still be running while she dried them. She took long showers too. She'd started doing it when the kids were little and she needed time for herself. But, the kids were long gone. Finally, the water stopped and he could hear her walking down the hall. She peeked into the family room and smiled at him.

"The pie's almost done. I'm going to set the table."

Mark smiled back. He loved her apple pie. "Can't wait."

Just like he couldn't wait that day in the picture. He'd started out walking quickly toward the park, then sprinted the last few blocks. As he turned the corner, and saw the entrance, he slowed down. Madeleine was bent over, getting something out of her shoe. He caught a glimpse of her thigh. When she stood up, she saw him and smiled. She was wearing a pink dress with a white belt cinched at her waist. It was so warm; she'd left her coat at school.

"Hello, Mark" she said.

"Hello," he answered. They turned and walked through the gate. He had no recollection of what they talked about. He hoped he'd made sense. Conversation was difficult when all he wanted to do was touch her. At one point, as the sun started to dip, she said that she was cold. He took off his sweater and handed it to her. As she took it from him, her fingers grazed his.

Near the entrance gate, Madeleine stooped to admire a crocus. When she stood up, they were very close and she kissed him. If there'd been any doubt before, he knew he was in love then.

In April, baseball practice started and Nate was busy again. Madeleine and Mark took more walks. They would meet further away from school, where there was less danger of running into someone they knew. Gradually, they'd started holding hands. From time to time, they'd stop and kiss. Long, slow kisses. It got harder and harder for Mark to remember not to touch her in school where someone might see. He thought Art was getting suspicious.

Then, one day Art said, "I saw you."

"What do you mean?" Mark asked.

"I saw you and Madeleine."

Mark was supposed to meet Madeleine after school that day. When he passed her in the hall, he said "See you later."

"No, I can't," she said.

"What do you mean you can't?"

"Art knows. He's going to tell Nate if we don't stop," she said.

"I don't care," Mark said.

"I do," she answered.

After that, there were no more secret meetings. She wouldn't even turn around to talk to him in homeroom. May turned to June and they graduated. And that was that. Almost.

From time to time, over the years, especially when Jean irritated him, he wondered: what if? What if Art hadn't found out? What if Madeleine had said she didn't care either? What if he'd married Madeleine instead of Jean?

"The pie's ready!" Jean called from the kitchen. "Come help me carry it to the table."

Mark closed the book and put it down. He walked into the kitchen. The oven door was open revealing an apple pie with a golden crust. Jean was bent over sliding the wire rack out with a potholder. She couldn't hear him walk up behind her. He touched her lightly on the shoulder and she stood up. She was wearing a lacy white apron. It was pretty over the lavender sweater he'd given her for her last birthday. He had to admit, in this day and age of sweatpants and sweatshirts, Jean always looked nice.

"Let me get that, dear," he said, getting another potholder and taking hers. He grasped the edges of the pie tin and put the pie on top of the stove.

"Shall we top it off with ice cream?" Jean asked, with a naughty grin.

"Of course," he replied, opening the freezer. He reached for vanilla. Jean put a hot plate on the dining-room table. He followed her out with the pie. She went back into the kitchen for the ice cream.

Jean cut the pie and handed him the larger of the two slices. He gave them each a scoop of ice cream and got up to put the rest away. As he walked toward the kitchen, he thought about the photo in his yearbook. Jean had remembered herself into it and she'd been right. It was a picture of the girl he loved.

Dedication to Jordon
by Stacey Stone

Several years ago, I signed up for my very first class at Manchester Community College. It was a writing class, under the direction of Jordon Pecile. And right from the start, I was challenged. Challenged to explore new books, challenged to write from the heart, challenged to look at my work with a critical eye, as well as that of my fellow classmates. Jordon suggested we read Stephen King's On Writing, and from that sparked a desire to develop a routine. I began writing every day, in the wee hours of the morning, before the sun had yet to grace the horizon. I always enjoyed writing, but Jordon's tutelage helped turn that joy into a passion. With his guidance, I was able to create stories that would have otherwise remained buried in the subconscious. His dedication to our class, and to every last word that we wrote, is a testament to his own passion for writing and for literature. Thank you, Jordon, for sharing yourself with us. And thank you for connecting me with this amazing group of individuals. --Stacey Stone

Bio
by Stacey Stone

I thoroughly enjoy writing (and have been trying to do more) when not taking on my full-time job as mother-of-five! Keeping up with the schedules of two fourth graders, two second graders and a first grader keeps me busy around the clock. In addition, I work as a part-time math tutor in one of the area elementary schools. I have earned a Bachelor's Degree from Dartmouth College and a Master of Education Degree from Harvard University. Since I was very young, I have enjoyed writing stories. One day I hope to pass on to my children a passion to write, and to create tales of imagined people and places that their readers can get lost in.

Muscongus
by Stacey Stone

A gull swooped downward and landed softly on a nearby lamppost. Clara pulled her hood forward, then tightened the strings so that only a small circular portion of her face remained exposed. It was early. Service at the church was still an hour off. Only a few folks scurried about, dodging the raindrops. Absent the hum of the motored lobster boats offshore, the day was quiet. The cold drizzle forced Clara to bury her hands deep into the pockets of her slicker. She wanted to enjoy this special part of the day, yet the discovery that she was pregnant infused Clara with conflicting thoughts. Her future was now uncertain, and she could think of little else.

Turning off Main Street, she headed toward the diner. The road narrowed, no longer paved but graveled, and laden with deepening pools of rainwater. Her destination was only yards away, but beyond, the road sloped toward a tiny harbor, the boats parked by their moorings. Except for the rain cascading down, activity was slow, the day calm.

This was typically Clara's favorite part of the day. She enjoyed being alone for a few brief moments, an observer of life unfolding around her. There was Jasper at the General Store setting his "specials" signage on the sidewalk, and Bryan walking out of the bait shop with his box of worms and seaweed. There were gulls diving, waves rippling, and the occasional buoy bobbing. Six days out of seven, there was the hum of diesel-driven lobster boats hypnotically pulling her eyes seaward. Today, Clara's mind was on the pregnancy. Fran knew. Others would find out before long. Clara's new friends, in this new town, they had gone out of their way to embrace her. But, how would they feel about her now? Now that her awful past had caught up to her?

A hypnotic buzz, like that of a downed electrical line, greeted Clara as she left the damp, dark day behind and entered Fran's diner. The shop was unusually chaotic. Almost every seat occupied. Clara shook the rain from her shoulders and wiped her boots on the mat.

"Hiya, sunshine!" Fran sashayed to the door and embraced her young friend, cradling Clara against the side of a pillowy bosom. "You're it, today."

"What's that?" Clara asked.

"You're our sunshine. Weather's only gettin' worse." Fran led Clara to an empty stool at the end of the counter, several patrons calling out greetings as she passed. Fran flipped a mug and poured in steaming coffee. Clara noticed that she poured from the orange-rimmed pot this particular day.

"How bad are they saying?"

"Well, winter 'parently ain't over yet! Can you believe this is April?"

"A snowstorm? Really?"

"Ayuh. Might be calm now, but it's already beginnin' to switch over. See?" The two women glanced out the front window. The precipitation was still mostly rain, but large snowflakes dropped, dancing in between. "It's not stickin' yet, but it will. All those wet roads, they'll get icy. Gonna be a mess. Now, back to you, hon. How ya feelin'?"

"Just fine."

"Well, allrighty then." Fran's tone changed to that of a whisper. "And what will the wee one be eatin' this mornin'?"

Clara patted her midsection discreetly, but her eyes shot to the floor. Only the day before, she'd been outed by Fran. Where her generous friend saw reason to celebrate, Clara bore only the tragedy of an unwelcome situation. "Umm… Maybe an omelet?"

"With…"

"Cheese and bacon? And some home fries?"

"You bet. Comin' right up!" Fran walked briskly to the grill, put Clara's order in, then picked up the coffee pots and circled the diner to offer refills.

Clara took a moment to look out at the rain. The gloom caused her to shiver imperceptibly. She hugged her midsection, the small protrusion well hidden by folds of an overlarge fisherman's sweater. Clara was still preoccupied with thoughts of this new life inside her. She'd run to Muscongus from a town that had held her all of her twenty-six years. From a house that had sheltered her. From a family that had nourished her. But in just one night, Clara's world shattered. She'd run from a horrible ugliness, and from a family, a house, and a town that were the only ones she'd ever known. She'd run without looking back and landed in Muscongus. Now, there was a new being inside her, a part of her past that couldn't be ignored. Growing, not out of a love like she'd always imagined, but out of an excruciating pain and emptiness.

And of the home she thought she'd created here in Muscongus? What would become of it? What would become of her? Clara swallowed and lifted her eyes. The front window was beginning to fog. Her eyes wandered around the warm diner. A yellow Formica counter ran the length of the shop, a half dozen booths running along the shop's perimeter. Four tables floated in the center like islands. Every spot was littered with food-laden plates, steaming cups of coffee, and stainless flatware, all atop burgundy paper place mats. A large, chrome-rimmed clock hung lopsided above the door, the minute hand running five minutes too fast. Photographs of townsfolk and their lobster boats framed the windows. Home. Clara had made this her home, or tried to, with a little effort and a great deal of help from Fran.

Several patrons finished up, yet no sooner had they risen and the seats were filled once more. Clara's newest acquaintance, Cecil, waved brusquely from the far end of the counter, and Clara waved in return. Henry was in his customary spot, his back to everyone else. And for a brief moment, it bothered Clara that he would occupy an entire booth himself, eliminating valuable space for Fran's other paying customers. But a voice chirped behind her, interrupting her reverie.

"Look who's here, June! It's Clara-belle!"

"Hi, ladies."

"Well, aren't you a bright spot on this dark day!" said June.

"Here, sit." Clara got up from her stool at the counter, motioning for the town's two librarians to sit.

"Oh, no!" cried Annie. "We couldn't possibly take your place!"

"Please. I insist," Clara urged.

"No, no. Sit back down, Clara dear. We don't mind waiting for another table to clear."

"Really. Sit. There was nobody next to me."

"Well..." began Annie, as she looked around curiously. " I suppose... If you do have something else in mind..."

"I do. Annie, June, please sit. Enjoy. I'll just go grab an extra chair." As soon as she said it, space suddenly cleared nearby. In a blink, Fran bustled over, cleared the used dishes, and reset the table.

"Looky here, June... It's our lucky day!" Annie sat quickly in a vacated chair.

Clara sat back at the counter and Fran brought over her breakfast. The golden omelet steamed, cheese oozing from its egg blanket, bits of bacon spilling onto the plate. "Thanks, Fran. This looks fantastic." Her stomach grumbled in anticipation.

"If it tastes as good as it looks, then Gus is the one to get the credit." Fran nodded in the direction of the grill, and the burly behemoth donning the grease-stained apron.

"Sure thing."

"That certainly does look good," said another voice from behind Fran's buxom frame.

Stepping back, Fran greeted Max warmly. Clara, however, felt her chest constrict. Her breath caught. She focused on the omelet and busied her hand with a fork.

"Can I get my usual?" he asked, his broad shoulder brushing against Clara's own petite frame as he sat beside her.

"Of course, darlin'," replied Fran. The crash of a plate hitting the floor rang through the small space, and the ensuing chaos added to the din in her shop. "Damn. Lemme take care of that. I'll get you some coffee. Just gimme a minute, hon."

"No problem, Fran. Take your time." Max paused, turning his eyes on Clara. "So we finally get a date."

"Hmmm?" Clara feigned misunderstanding.

"Well, it's so crowded in here today. I've nowhere else to sit. You don't mind, do you?"

"It's fine," Clara murmured.

"See? Then it's a date. The two of us. Here. Eating. Enjoying one another's company. You know, you've been putting me off, making excuses for weeks now, ever since you came into town."

"I haven't," Clara attempted to defend herself.

"Well, it sure seems that way. How's the omelet?"

"Very good."

"Looks good."

Clara hurried to put a delectable morsel in her mouth, a feeble attempt to avoid conversation. She was flustered, uncomfortable by Max's persistent attention. Especially now, in the wake of her recent revelation.

"We're going to get hit bad today," Max commented.

"That's what Fran is saying."

"The storm has already started, and it's going to get worse before it gets better." Max and Clara simultaneously turned toward the window. The precipitation was heavier, the rain disappearing beneath the press of snow and falling temperatures. "The roads are already slick in spots."

"I thought everyone only ever walked to get where they're going. You drove here?" Clara asked, her eyes finally lifting.

"Ayuh. Already been down to Portland and back." Max paused before continuing, "You know, my mom and sister are supposed to be getting into town today." His faraway visage gave the impression he spoke more to himself, and was considering the threat the storm had on their impending arrival.

The lights flickered then, signaling their fallibility. The fluorescent bulbs buzzed, and there was a momentary lapse in the diner's distinguishable conversations. When the lights hummed back to life, the chattering in the shop resumed with heartfelt abandon.

"Throw on that weather radio, Gus!" shouted Cecil.

"It's on, it's on," muttered Gus, busy at the grill.

"Well, turn it on up!"

Fran walked over and set a plate in front of Max. She glanced at Clara's, which was just about empty. "Are ya done, sweetie?"

"Almost," Clara answered.

"Don't mean to rush ya, but folks are saying it's best to get on home and hunker down. As you can see, we're beginnin' to clear out."

Clara and Max glanced around the diner, noticing several vinyl upholstered chairs were now vacant. The buzz of electricity that had permeated earlier was noticeably dimmer, the noise replaced by gusting winds. Outside the front door, Fran's sign crashed against the building, its chains tugging at their base in an attempt to resist the wind's fury.

"Fran, let me help you with the dishes. I can clear the tables," Clara offered.

"No, no. You sit. Enjoy." Fran bobbed her head in Max's direction and winked.

"I insist. Really," said Clara.

"Nope. Stay here and keep Max company. His plate's on its way over."

"Fran, please. With everything you've done for me, it's the least I can do. Tell me what you need done."

"Okay, hon. Maybe when you're done here, and only when you're done here, you could collect some dishes from around the place. There's a bucket there, under the counter. But, only after you've finished. And, nothin' heavy, mind ya!" Fran winked again, then hurried off.

Clara made a move to get up, but Max quickly placed a hand on hers. "Leaving so soon? You seem to do just about anything to avoid me. And, just when I was starting think we were having a pleasant conversation."

"It's not like that," Clara offered weakly. "I'm just anxious to help."

"Sure. But if you're anxious to get back home, don't worry. I can get you and Fran both back safely."

"That's not necessary."

"I'm just anxious to help." Max smiled.

"I don't want you to have to wait, on our account."

"I'm only just starting my breakfast here. Go on. Help Fran. I'll check back in with you."

"Okay. And… Thank you…" Clara stood.

Max smiled, his blue eyes shining. He stuffed a forkful of scrambled eggs in his mouth. Clara collected her dishes from the counter and walked behind to grab the bucket. Annie and June, still in the diner and watching much of the previous interchange, signaled for Clara to join them.

"That Max sure is a doll," whispered Annie.

"He's nice enough," Clara responded. He had, in fact, never been anything but nice to her.

"Oh, he's more than…" started June.

"Nice!" Annie interrupted, clapping her hands excitedly.

"No, you're right," Clara agreed quietly. "Max has been very kind."

"And I think he likes you," Annie said.

"Don't be silly."

"Oh, yes! We see how he flirts with you!"

"Annie, leave the girl alone," said June. "Can't you see she's working?"

"Just helping out," Clara explained unnecessarily. "It's been a busy morning. Busiest I've seen."

"It's the storm," suggested June. "Makes folks jittery, itching to get out before they're stuck at home. They say it has something to do with the…"

"Barometric pressure," Annie finished. "Sure! But when it all blows over, come on by the library again. Will you, Clara?"

"Of course, ladies. Now, if you'll excuse me…"

Clara continued to gather dishes from the spaces that had emptied, walking them into the back. She made a second round, and then a third. She stopped, to begin cleaning the piles she'd carefully stacked. She was familiar with restaurant grade dishwashers from her summers back in Southbury, working at the local pizza restaurant. She'd also been helping Fran in the diner as a means to repay the kindness and generosity her benefactor bestowed on her. Fran had all but adopted Clara since her arrival in Muscongus a few months back. She rinsed a few of the plates and gathered everything on a large gray plastic tray. She slid it into the hold, then lowered the enormous stainless hood. It took only a moment to locate the cycle start button. She pressed it firmly, then listened to the roar of water and the hiss of steam escaping out the bottom. Clara stepped back and waited.

A few clean glasses and plates sat to her left, drying. Clara gathered these and carried them back to the front, stacking them neatly on the shelves below the counter. By the time she returned to the back room, the wash cycle was complete. Clara slid the clean dinnerware to her left and placed a new tray in the hold, closing the hood and beginning the cycle again. The monotony worked to calm her restless heart. She repeated her task several times over before Fran finally tapped her on the shoulder.

"Slow down there, girl! Breathe!"

"How are we doing?"

"Well, come and take a look for yourself."

Clara followed Fran into the main dining room. The two women stood behind the counter and surveyed the diner. They were alone, with the exception of Gus, who stood slightly behind, scraping remnants of breakfast from the grill.

"Where did everybody go?" Clara noticed that even Max had disappeared and was struck again with that familiar constriction in her chest.

"Most have gone home by now," Fran answered. "Some might be finishin' at the General, stockin' up on supplies."

"I can't believe it could be so busy one moment, then this!" Clara waved her arm to indicate the patronless tables.

"Look outside," urged Fran.

Clara walked around the counter to the door. Her palms stretched forward to touch the glass and she was surprised by its icy glaze. As she pressed her face closer, her small breaths condensed on the windowpane in a circle. Expanding, then shrinking. Looking beyond the diner's cozy interior, Clara's vision revealed a snowy oasis. The sidewalk, the road, the street signs, the houses, all were dressed with a vanilla creme frosting that drifted with the prevailing winds. "It's beautiful," Clara whispered.

"If you're not out in the wind or stuck somewhere, then sure. Listen sweetie," Fran came to stand beside Clara and put an arm affectionately around her young friend's shoulders. "Ya feelin' stuck these days? I'm sensin' it might be somethin' like that." With silent reflection, Clara continued to look beyond the glass. The two admired the winter wonderland from the shop's dry, cozy interior. "Folks in here decided to skedaddle, and I think we should do the same. You know everything's gonna be all right. Wouldn't say it if I didn't believe it. And I also wouldn't be pushin' Max on you if I didn't already know he's one of the good guys. He could be good for you."

215

"Perhaps. But Fran…"

"Yes, sweetie?"

"I just can't right now. It's too much."

"I know it is. Just don't shut him out, is all I'm askin'. Certain folks, they can be healers."

"But, that's you," Clara whispered.

"Hush now. Don't give me any more credit than I deserve. I'm your friend, honey. And havin' you around? Well, you're the one that's healin' me. Now, let's get on outta here before we're really stuck."

Gus, Fran and Clara donned their coats and flicked off the lights. Fran flipped the sign on the door to read CLOSED. Digging through her large purse, she found a key and held it in her gloved hand as the three walked out into the snow. They huddled together, sheltering Fran as she turned to lock the door.

"Can I walk you ladies home?" Gus asked.

"That's very generous of you, hon," said Fran. "But I think we'll be okay. It's only a couple of blocks. Besides, you're practically across the street."

"And I'm going their way, anyhow," came another voice, muffled slightly by the dense snowfall, insulated landscape and increasing winds.

Clara and Fran turned to see Max approaching quickly, his stride long and purposeful. Clara swallowed deeply and worked to steady her gaze, keeping her eyes lifted.

"Why, Max!" gushed Fran. "See, Gus? We're just fine. You get on home, before Sally worries herself to death."

"Yes'm. See you, then."

"'Bye, Gus," Clara called out against his retreating form. Slowly, she turned back to Max. "We thought you'd left," she said quietly.

"I took the truck to the house, but walked back. I did tell you I'd get you home, did I not?"

"Well, aren't you a sweetie. Now, give an old lady an arm!" Fran smiled.

The three stumbled off into the storm, their footprints quickly buried by new flakes. The snow was falling fast now. They arrived at Fran's house, Fran hurrying inside and leaving the young couple on the porch.

"This is very kind of you, Max. Thank you."

"My pleasure, entirely." Max smiled. He reached out and squeezed Clara's hand gently.

They stood together, surrounded by a chorus of banging shutters and clanging wind chimes. The snow fell, driven horizontally by an icy wind. Despite the angry storm, Muscongus' marshmallow landscape was breathtaking. It gave the illusion that one could fall, and find a soft landing. That one could simply let go, and be cushioned from pain. However, Clara understood it was only that... an illusion. How could Clara erase the past when she now carried it inside her? So close. She'd come so close to building a new life. Fran was her family. This weather-beaten farmhouse, her home.

She turned from Max, and from the wintry mess rapidly accumulating. Clara opened the front door, looking to follow Fran into the house. She paused on the threshold, however, and turned around. She looked at Max's retreating form.

"Thank you, again," Clara called out.

Turning, Max gave a short wave and replied, "You ladies give me a shout should you need anything."

Clara allowed a small smile to grace her lips, then turned to walk inside, leaving the raging storm behind.

CPSIA information can be obtained at www.ICGtesting.com
Printed in the USA
BVOW012113171211

278625BV00002B/6/P